# Jail Coach

## Books by Hillary Bell Locke

The Cynthia Jakubek Legal Thrillers
*But Remember Their Names*

The Jay Davidovich Mysteries
*Jail Coach*

# Jail Coach

A Jay Davidovich Mystery

## Hillary Bell Locke

Poisoned Pen Press

Copyright © 2012 by Hillary Bell Locke

First Edition 2012

10 9 8 7 6 5 4 3 2 1

Library of Congress Catalog Card Number: 2012910475

ISBN: 9781464200243    Hardcover
      9781464200267    Trade Paperback

Poisoned Pen Press
6962 E. First Ave., Ste. 103
Scottsdale, AZ 85251
www.poisonedpenpress.com
info@poisonedpenpress.com

Printed in the United States of America

# Dedication

*For Amanda Morris, who knows that Nero Wolf
never forgave Jane Austen for proving that
a woman could write a great novel, but gives
him a pass because he was a Yankees fan.*

*Jail Coach* is a work of fiction. The characters depicted do not exist and the events described did not take place. I made them up. So unless you're George W. Bush, don't kid yourself: you're not in here.

# Chapter One

Two things I can't stand: fake smoking and saying "fricking" instead of "fucking," as if you were editing your life to move from HBO to Turner. The first time I saw Carrie Deshane live, she was doing both.

"Seven takes, Gordie. Seven fricking takes, wrestling in my underwear in cold, sloppy mud—and you can't find twenty seconds for it."

The schlub she was bitching at just stood there and took it. The cigarette in her left hand looked long enough for a full season of *Mad Men*, but she just posed with the thing without taking a real hit on it, as if she were doing Pissed Off Debutante in acting class.

The eight-figure insurance bet I cared about was riding on her costar, Kent Trowbridge. Two nights before Trowbridge had played bumper car in his Ferrari with a median and several palm trees in San Gabriel, California. Apparently he was over the legal limit. Really? You think? The press reports also said something about marijuana and cocaine. So I didn't give Deshane all that much thought.

Proxy Shifcos and I followed our escort across a vast expanse of concrete floor swarming with the kind of people who get invited to a wrap party. We walked past steam tables, bar stations, and attitudes to a small, white elevator. Our escort flashed a key card at a blinking red light on the elegantly rounded door, which opened with a smooth, hydraulic purr. We stepped inside. As soon as the door closed, the hubbub outside disappeared. I mean *gone*.

Two floors up the door opened on what was either a huge office or a modest conference room. Let's go with office. Twelve feet in front of me I saw a massive slab the size and height of a Pentagon war-gaming table. With its surface polished to satin-black gloss, it looked like it weighed two tons.

Four people stood around one end of the table. I recognized Mark Korvette from Proxy's briefing book. She had explained to me on the way in from the airport that Korvette hates chairs at meetings because things slow down when people get comfortable. He was the managing partner in the partnership that was the controlling member of the limited liability company that owned New Paradigm Studios, Inc. Or something like that. My eyes had glazed over somewhere around the second holding company. Point is, that's why there weren't any chairs.

Korvette wore a desert-brown cashmere blazer that cost four-thousand dollars if it cost a cent; a yellow, open-necked dress shirt; and earth-tone slacks. He was shorter than I am, but then most people are. He had almost half-a-foot on Proxy, so I put him at five-eleven or so. Perfect teeth in a face that was a little too fleshy and a little too square, all under casually-combed brown hair.

To his right stood a guy that Proxy could have posted up on under the basket. His wig must have cost twice what Korvette's blazer did, and I still spotted it for a rug from eight feet away. Nothing particularly wrong with his face. If he'd had any work done, he'd gotten his money's worth. He figured to be Kent Trowbridge's agent, which would make him—I mentally rifled the briefing book—Saul Levitt.

A man and a woman on Korvette's left completed our welcoming committee. Him midforties, her late thirties. I don't remember anything else about them except they looked like they wanted to sit down. Proxy strode ahead of me across a rug that four Persians had spent a year on and stuck out her right hand.

"Good evening, Mr. Korvette. I'm Proxeine Shifcos from Trans/Oxana. This is my colleague, Jay Davidovich."

She got Korvette's attention. Also Levitt's. Also the other guy's. Proxeine Violet Shifcos is a dish. Jet black hair in a sassy helmet cut, alert brown eyes, and that peaches-and-cream complexion that WASPs pass on in their wills. Top of her class at University Lab High School in Dover and *magna cum laude* BSBA from the University of Delaware. Came to Trans/Oxana in the fall of 2006 to put in her obligatory two years in the real world before going to Wharton or someplace for her MBA. Had her boards taken when the Great Recession hit and she noticed that the insurance industry offered something lacking in more glamorous fields like venture capital start-ups: employment. So, at least for now, she pulls down ninety-eight thou a year working with Trans/Oxana's cowboys—me, for example.

All in all, she isn't bad. I'd give you eight to one that she's never had a taste of tobacco or a whiff of cannabis. And her idea of a mixed drink is a lime twist in designer water. But she can spend a week in Vegas at a sales convention without being a killjoy. Just don't call her "Foxy Proxy."

"Good evening, Ms. Shifcos." Korvette shook her hand. "I think you know Saul. Our other guests are Aaron Epstein and Erin Price of Epstein and Price."

*Popularly known as Aaron & Erin.* I hadn't recognized them, but I knew the names—and not from Proxy's briefing book. One of the top criminal law boutiques in California. In other words, *Oh, shit.*

Epstein said something polite while he and Price traded business cards with Proxy. Epstein glanced at her card without completely taking his eyes off me.

"'Assistant Director/Risk Management/U.S.'" he read from the card. "And what is Mr. Davidovich's function?"

I was about to say "apparatchik" when Proxy jumped in with, "Loss Prevention Specialist." That was the title on my business cards, but I didn't feel like digging one out for a lawyer.

"'Loss Prevention Specialist.'" Korvette rolled the words on his tongue like a mediocre wine he was thinking of sending back. "Well, you've come to the right place. We've got our cocks on the block. And by 'we' I mean 'you.'"

He had a point, sort of. We had insured Kent Trowbridge's Major Performing Artist contract for thirty-six million dollars. In the Trans/Oxana universe, that's more like a pinkie. But times are hard, and pinkies count.

# Chapter Two

"How bad is it?" Proxy asked the question.

"You're on," Korvette said, nodding at Aaron & Erin.

"Pretty damn bad." This from the shyster, not the shysterette. "San Gabriel County and LA County might as well be two different countries. Trowbridge is a repeat offender in SGC. Plus, this DUI violated the terms of the probation he got after the first one down there. That pisses judges off."

"'DUI?'" I tried to keep the this-is-chickenshit tone out of my voice, but I'm not very good at that. "What about the coke and the grass?"

"We'll get the coke suppressed because they've already screwed up the chain of custody." Shysterette's turn. "And he has a prescription for the grass. But the judge will know about both of them, and second offense DUI isn't 'boys will be boys' in San Gabriel County anyway. With a blood-alcohol content twice the legal limit, if Trowbridge is convicted, he could be looking at nine months."

"Which in SGC," Epstein said, "does *not* mean a-day-and-a-half with the rest off for good behavior, like Paris Hilton doing 'let's play jail' in LA."

Levitt turned paler than Minnesota *goyim* in January. When Korvette spoke, though, his voice had a no-big-deal shrug to it.

"Simple answer then: keep him from being convicted."

"Not a slam-dunk." Epstein shook his head grimly. "Not a layup. Not even a ten-foot jump shot with a good look at the basket. More like a three-pointer with a tall guy's hand in our face. You're paying us fifty-thousand bucks to hit it, but sometimes we miss those."

"Fifty thousand?" Korvette did an eyes-left at Proxy to make sure she was paying attention. "Is that what we're paying you to handle this case?"

"Yep."

"How about we make it two hundred fifty and you guarantee an acquittal?"

"How about if we leave it at fifty and guarantee you our best shot?"

Give Epstein credit. Korvette had just proposed that we bribe a judge or a prosecutor with Trans/Oxana chipping in. Epstein saved Proxy the trouble of saying no—which was too bad, because I wasn't sure she would have.

Korvette turned his attention to me.

"How much do you know about movies?"

"*The Pony Soldiers* is the only war movie John Wayne made where he fights non-Hispanic whites. That's about it."

"In other words, nothing. So let me explain *Prescott Trail* to you."

"That's the western you're about to roll out?"

"Retro-western." Korvette paused for two seconds, daring me to ask him what a 'retro-western' was. When I didn't bite, he went on. "Made the way they made them in the 'forties and 'fifties. Good guys and bad guys without shades of gray, virtuous womenfolk, blazing six-shooters, stampedes, cavalry charges, glorious scenery, and whores with hearts of gold. That gets old farts into the theater."

"Okay."

"But woven in with all that retro stuff we have a whole different movie going on. Hip jokes, winks and nudges, allusions to rap music and pot and kinky sex. All of that goes right over the fossils' heads, but the sixteen-to-twenty-fives totally get it and the twenty-six-to-forty-fours pretend to get it because if they don't that means they're not hip anymore."

"An affectionate sendup but not quite a spoof," Proxy said. "Like *True Grit* arm-wrestles *Blazing Saddles* and barely wins."

"That wasn't the pitch line for *Prescott Trail*, but it should have been." Korvette smiled at his own clever line. "In television, eyeballs don't really count unless they're under thirty. In movies, a fanny in a seat is a fanny in a seat."

The fingers on Korvette's right hand started dancing nimbly on what must have been a control panel flush with the table's surface. The lights in the room dimmed, and a section in the middle of what I'd thought was a solid granite table top opened up to reveal an enormous flat screen. NEW PARADIGM PROJECT DELTA appeared on it.

As this title slide dissolved we saw Carrie Deshane and Kent Trowbridge at a table in an elegantly wainscoted contemporary room. Her standing, him sitting. Trowbridge in white dinner jacket and black bow tie, with Deshane sporting a Lincoln-green formal gown showing enough rack to qualify for *Jersey Shore*. She poured wine from a cut glass decanter into a crystal goblet, delicately picked the goblet up, and offered it to Trowbridge. He took it, undressed her with his eyes, sipped wine, then set the goblet down:

CARRIE:   "What do you think?"
KENT:     "Beauty there is that delights the eye, beauty that exalts the soul, and beauty that excites desire. And I am looking at all three."
CARRIE:   "I meant about the wine."
KENT:     "I was talking about the wine."

"Retro-spy flick." Proxy made this comment. "I get it."

"Bingo." Korvette looked at each of us as he killed the tease and brought the lights back up. "After retro-spy flick comes retro-caper flick, retro-flag-waver, retro-*noir* private eye movie."

"You're talking about a franchise."

"Kentucky Fried Chicken is a franchise. I'm talking about a business model: scalable, repeatable, reliable, durable."

"Look, Mr. Korvette, I know your time is valuable, so I don't want to waste it. Trans/Oxana insured fulfillment of Kent Trowbridge's obligations under an MPA contract. It's a three-picture deal, so we're not off the hook just because you've got the first film almost ready for distribution. We get it. We're on the risk."

"You are goddamn right you're on the risk." Korvette said this quietly and smoothly instead of screaming it, like a Hollywood exec on *Entourage* would have. "If that pretty boy pulls a Lindsay Lohan on me before the third film is in the can, you are writing one hell of a big check."

"It wouldn't be the first one we've ever written." Proxy smiled sweetly. Korvette's attitude pivoted on a dime.

"I love meetings where everyone in the room has balls. We understand each other. Good. Bottom line: Kent Trowbidge can't handle three months of hard time, much less nine. It doesn't do me a damn bit of good for him to get sprung in time for principal photography on phase two if America has an indelible image of him curled up in a fetal position sobbing and sucking his thumb."

Proxy didn't quite sigh. I could tell she wanted to, but she's a pro.

"That's why my tall colleague is here," she said.

"Who are you again?" Korvette asked, turning toward me.

"J.M. Davidovich. Call me Jay."

"What does 'J' stand for?"

"Jay."

"'Davidovich' is Russian, I'm guessing."

"Ukrainian. Not the same thing. The Russians made the same mistake for awhile. Nixon was still President when mom and dad hit Connecticut. They were eleven and thirteen."

"The *détente* exodus in the early 'seventies? I thought that was all Jews."

"It was." Korvette did a double take, so I kept talking. "No sweat, I get that a lot. Blond hair, blue eyes, can't do compound interest in my head, and I don't even know Sandy Koufax's life-time ERA. Not exactly typecast for *Fiddler on the Roof*."

"It's a scandal to the *goyim*." Levitt said this in an exagger-ated borscht belt accent. It broke the tension long enough for Korvette to get his swagger back.

"And you think you can nursemaid Trowbridge through an eight-city pre publicity tour while the shysters do their magic?"

"What in the hell is 'pre publicity'?"

"Buzz-generation," Levitt explained. "Build excitement and anticipation while they finish post production. Hit some local talk shows, a few sit-downs with scribblers in flyover country, photo-op or two at charity events that *TZ* will eat up, give fanny-pats to guys who run regional chains. When the movie is released in two months, all Kent and Carrie have to do is show a clip on Leno and Letterman and we're on top after opening weekend."

"When does the tour start?"

"Monday."

"Shit."

"Okay." Proxy exhaled in an only-grown-up-in-the-room sort of way. She'll do some calculated swearing from time to time, just for shock value, but I've never heard a spontaneous cuss word out of her. "Next step is to talk to Mr. Trowbridge."

Levitt unholstered a palm-sized thing and started touching screens on it.

"I'll check his schedule. He may have an avail sometime tomorrow."

"'Avail'?" I asked Proxy.

"Availability."

"Bullshit." I meant that to get attention and it did. "He signed a contract, so his availability is now. Get his ass up here."

Talk about shock. Korvette, shyster, and shysterette all gaped at me like I'd given Superman a wedgie. Korvette had made billions of dollars playing with other people's money in the currency-arbitrage racket and then used a sliver of it to buy New Paradigm Studios—but Saul Levitt was the most powerful person in the room. In the building, for that matter, and probably in Century City. The others couldn't believe I didn't know that.

"What did you say?" Levitt demanded.

"You heard me. Trowbridge made the mess, so he gets to help clean it up. Call him and tell him to take twenty minutes off from banging whatever starlet got the short straw tonight so that he can join the party."

Purple-faced and pumping himself up like a bantam cock, Levitt whipped every one of his sixty-four inches around Proxy and stalked up to me.

"Now you listen to me, you two-bit thug. Kent Trowbridge is a *star*. He is Hollywood *royalty*. He doesn't—"

"Kent Trowbridge is a star, but Trans/Oxana is an insurance company. When insurance companies decide that stars aren't bondable, they aren't stars anymore."

It would have been interesting to see where Levitt went with that one, but the elevator opened and in came a female version of the escort who had accompanied Proxy and me. She was breathless. When her dove-gray blazer flew open I noticed that she was also something else: armed.

"We have a situation in the parking area," she panted. "With Mr. Trowbridge."

# Chapter Three

"So, is this like def-con five?" Proxy did *not* pant as she asked this question about three minutes later, even though we'd hustled to the scene at a pretty good clip.

"My last time on def-con-five people were shooting at me. A bloody nose and bruised knuckles is just Saturday night in a Ukrainian bar."

Trowbridge had the bruised knuckles. The mangled nose belonged to a fresh-faced twenty-something guy with a parking valet gig in New Paradigm's VIP lot. In Trowbridge's general vicinity stood two beefy guys and two non-beefy girls, and I use "girls" literally. If 17 was the over/under, I'd have taken under for a thou. A bright yellow Lexus SUV, picking up highlights from the late-June sun, provided a nice backdrop.

"It's *my* car and I want my fob *right now*," Trowbridge was slurring.

That fit with scraps of explanation I'd overheard the escort give Korvette and Levitt on the way down. Something about Trowbridge demanding his car and the valet trying to stall him because he wasn't fit to drive off the parking lot, much less navigate his way to Malibu.

"I want that car jockey fired," Levitt had told Korvette as they exited the elevator.

"He had express orders: if Trowbridge showed up drunk or high, he was to hold him up until someone could get down there and talk some sense into him."

"Then I want whoever gave those instructions fired."

"You got it. I'll submit my own resignation to myself and then refuse it. If I were you I'd start thinking about how to make the valet happy. If he calls the cops, your boy is on his own."

That's about where things stood when we reached the scene. Delivering the want-my-fob line was apparently an intense experience for Trowbridge, because he followed it up by bending over and vomiting. The beefy guys screened him while he blew supper, in case any paparazzi were around. One of the girls held his hair.

With Proxy and me right behind, Levitt approached the valet. He put his hand on the shoulder of the guy he'd told Korvette to fire thirty seconds before. Wrapping a benjamin around one of his cards, he slipped it into the valet's pocket.

"Saul Levitt, kid. I put a word in for you with your boss and you're okay. No one is blaming you. You did the right thing. And when that screenplay you have on your computer at home is ready, give me a ring."

I thought *I* was about to puke. Instead I glanced at Proxy, who was pecking away with grim determination at her iPhone.

"Who are you calling?"

"Dial a Designated Driver."

"Never heard of it."

"LA is the only city I know of that has it. Get the fob."

I sidled up to Levitt as if we were best buddies and congratulated him on a class move. It probably came off as a little sarcastic. Then I turned my attention to the valet and caught his eyes.

"I'm Jay Davidovich." I handed him one of my cards. "I'm from the insurance company. Nice work. Looks like your nose did more damage to his hand than the other way around."

"Thanks." He grinned. An ironic grin, but a grin.

"What's your name?"

"Dex White."

"Dex, we can save your report for later, but right now I'd like the fob."

He handed it over faster than a process server delivering a writ in a mobster's divorce. I pocketed the thing and strolled back in Proxy's direction while Levitt marched over to Korvette. I figured I'd be the subject of that conversation but I didn't pay much attention because I expected to have more pressing concerns in the next five seconds or so.

I did. Beefy guy number one—ex-defensive tackle build, scar between his eyebrows, curly red hair that he hadn't combed recently—sidled toward me. He was about three feet away and already had his hand extended, palm upward, when I spoke up.

"Close enough, bro."

He took one more step before he stopped.

"I need you to give me the fob for Mr. Trowbridge's Lexus."

"Never confuse wants with needs."

He rolled his eyes. Then he took another step. He might have lifted his arm. If he didn't, he would have. The next thing he did for sure was stop cold and sink down to his knees, hugging his midsection. He did this because I'd just buried the first two knuckles of my right fist an inch deep in his solar plexus. Brought the fist back under my right armpit, fingers up, and then rotated it in a snap-punch as I shot it straight forward. Takes about a quarter-second and hurts like a sonofabitch. Sucks the wind right out of you.

Standard protocol in the muscle trade called for him to get back up and come after me just for pride's sake. He had no excuse for existing except to shove people around, so his future couldn't look very bright from his present vantage point. I could tell he was thinking about it. Two gray-blazers saved him by scurrying over, with Korvette in their wake. Korvette instantly got in my face.

"What the hell do you think you're doing? This isn't some goddamn Ukrainian whorehouse."

"You're right about that. A self-respecting Ukrainian whorehouse wouldn't have underage girls—and Hulk Hogan here wouldn't have gotten in."

"Get the hell off my lot. And I mean now. Right fucking now."

"You got it."

I did a parade-ground about-face and started walking toward the entrance, which I guessed was maybe a quarter-mile away. Korvette thoughtfully told a gray-blazer to go along with me to make sure I didn't get lost. I waited to see if this guy would do something obnoxious, like grab my arm, but he didn't. Instead he started talking in a let's-be-friends voice that struck me as pretty real.

"Nice punch."

"Yep. Dumb-ass forgot the first rule of AWT."

"'If the enemy is in range, so are you.'"

So the gray-blazer not only knew the first rule of AWT, he knew that AWT stands for "Advanced Warrior Training." Which meant he'd served in the military and, other things being equal, probably liked me more than he did Korvette.

"Does New Paradigm have a lot of cartel money floating around, or do you guys just carry those cannons to impress the tourists?"

"I don't know much about the money side." If my question offended him he didn't show it. "The drug money and the mob cash usually show up in financing individual pictures. Not so much in the capital structure of the studios."

"No kidding?" I'd learned something new today. "How long do you think before they remember I have the fob?"

Something in his ear squeaked.

"On a wild guess, right now."

He touched the thing in his ear and barked his last name. I stopped because I figured we were going to have to retrace every step we took anyway. He nodded, touched the thing in his ear again, and looked up at me.

"I'm supposed to bring the fob back." He had the grace to look sheepish.

"Let's go."

I started walking back the way we'd come. He didn't.

"They'd rather I brought it back without you."

"Ain't gonna happen."

"Yeah, I figured." He joined me in my return trek. "Just thought I'd ask."

We'd gotten almost all the way back when a miniscooter whizzed past us. I saw a woman and a little girl on the thing. The little girl was wearing a helmet, but the woman wasn't. The scooter zipped around the crowd and the Lexus, then came to a stop just behind the SUV's lift gate. Korvette was now yelling at Proxy while jabbing a finger toward me.

"I want *that* asshole *off* my account, as of *now*."

What you don't want to do with Proxy, ever, is try to shove her around. She can sometimes be finessed, but blustering guarantees you worldclass push-back.

"You don't have a vote." That would be Proxy pushing back. "As long as the policy is in force, Trans/Oxana decides who's on the account. If you want to cancel, get it to me in writing by tomorrow and we'll refund fifty percent of the premium."

"Who's your superior?"

"Harrison Balk. I'll email you his number."

"Do that. Because he's going to hear from me."

"He's working on a matter right now with one-point-two billion at risk, so he may not be immediately available. He makes a point of returning calls within one business day, though, so I'm sure he'll give your views prompt attention."

Scooter lady picked that moment to sashay up with her little one in tow. I guessed the girl was eight or nine. She had her mom's blond hair and grayish-blue eyes, although she didn't yet have the generous breasts and well-rounded buns of steel that mom's cycling leathers very imperfectly hid.

"Who called DDD?"

"I did," Proxy said.

"Who the hell are you?" Korvette demanded.

Mom put her hands over the little girl's ears and glared at Korvette.

"I'm Katrina Starr Thompson, with Dial-a-Designated-Driver." She spoke with a West Texas drawl that dared you to make a crack about it. "Who are you?"

"Mark Korvette. Until fifteen minutes ago I had the impression I was running this studio. If we need chauffeur service here—"

"It's okay." Everyone looked at Kent Trowbridge, who spoke the line with professional aplomb. He didn't seem quite as plowed as he had before retching. "The insurance drones might be right. Maybe the safest thing to do is to have Miss Thompson give me a ride home."

He stepped forward to offer her his Hollywood-royalty hand and flash the smile that could launch a million ships if American females between fifteen and fifty-five ever amass that many.

"I'm pleased to meet you, Kristina."

"Not 'Kristina.'" She shook his hand. "Katrina. Like the hurricane."

# Chapter Four

The scooter was the slickest thing I'd seen since I'd come back from Iraq. Thompson flipped a couple of handles, turned a knob, and folded the thing up into a tidy metal bundle about the size of a dismounted M-60 machine gun—and a lot lighter, judging from the almost effortless way she humped it into the SUV's cargo bay. Then she focused her eyes like two blue-gray lasers on Trowbridge.

"Would it be a huge problem if Lucinda rode up front with me?"

"I think I can handle that. The other ladies and I will ride in the back."

"Also—and the customer is always right, so if the answer is no then I totally understand; I'm just askin'—but if you all could possibly manage the trip without smoking…"

"Deal." Trowbridge smacked a comely, silk-clad rump with each palm. "The ladies were just telling me about how they were planning to go smoke free."

Trowbridge's performance fascinated me, and I'm a tough crowd. A miniature director inside his skull had hollered "Action!" and suddenly Trowbridge was ON. Someone who'd just walked up wouldn't have had the faintest idea that he was drunk. The timing of his body movements was a shade off, but he seemed steady on his feet and you really had to be listening to notice any slur in his speech.

The two palookas glanced at each other as Thompson, her little girl, Trowbridge, and his eye candy piled into the Lexus. It was pulling away before the muscle could even think about hitching a ride. The temporarily flat-nosed valet needed five minutes to come up with the rental Ford Fusion Proxy and I were using, so the Lexus was nowhere in sight by the time we pulled out of New Paradigm. We were at the mercy of the rental's GPS.

LA traffic isn't as horrible as people in places like Utah and Wisconsin think it is, but even so Proxy and I had a healthy trip in front of us. Her opening line sounded musical to me.

"In case the question ever comes up, I saw that ape getting ready to take a swing at you."

"Thanks."

"So what are the chances Aaron and Erin get Trowbridge off without a trip to the slammer?"

"Zero." I replayed the shyster-speak in my head and parsed Epstein's bet hedging. "Lawyers usually low-ball their chances so that they look good if they win and their clients can't call them on it if they lose. But talking about a well-defended three-point shot is way beyond low-balling. Aaron and Erin think they're facing longer odds than Sarah Palin for president of Mensa."

"So Trowbridge is going to do some county time. And if Korvette is right, that long a stay behind bars will leave him a broken man without a prayer of ever bringing off the debonair hero number again."

"Could be alarmist."

"Big chance to take." Proxy shook her head as rain—rain in LA!—started spattering the windshield. "Robert Mitchum did thirty days for marijuana possession in the late 'forties and came out of it okay, but he had a genuine toughness about him that I don't see in Trowbridge. Besides, thirty days is one month, not nine. Nine months is ten years in movie-star time."

"So it won't exactly break your heart if Korvette takes you up on your hint that he cancel the policy."

"If Korvette cancels our policy I'll put that on the year-end memo I write about how big my bonus should be."

"But we have to assume he won't."

"He won't. He got to be a billionaire by being a jerk, not an idiot."

"Okay." My turn to sit and think, which I did for ten seconds. "I guess we need a jail coach."

She shot me a puzzled look. I'd stumbled on something relevant to an insurance risk that Proxy Shifcos didn't know. This was one for the highlight reel.

"What's a jail coach?"

"It's someone who can train a soft, well-educated, upper-income felon in the skills he'll need to survive a stay in prison and come out with a reasonably whole skin. Started showing up after Watergate, when the courts began sending bushels of politicians and high-level executives to prison."

"How do you get to be a jail coach? I mean, is there, like, an associate degree you can get at a community college or something?"

"I expect you start by going to jail. That way you can say you've been there, looked at other people who've been there, and you have the credibility to guide someone else through it."

Proxy clicked off a good ten miles of streaming windshield time while she thought about that. She's smart and she has enough self-esteem for a Harvard Law School class reunion but, excuse me, she's twenty-seven years old. She joined Trans/Oxana thinking of insurance as the most Rotarian gig in the world. And up to three-million bucks or so, it is. When the stakes hit eight figures, though, insurance turns into an intersection between high finance and organized crime.

"How much does a jail coach cost?"

"Not sure, but it's gotta be less than one percent of thirty-six million dollars."

"Where do we find one?"

"I don't have the faintest idea."

"Well," she sighed, "if it were easy Aetna could handle it."

# Chapter Five

The first thing I saw in Trowbridge's sunken living room was Trowbridge snoring on a California Mission-style couch that looked a lot pricier than anything a Franciscan missionary would ever use. The eye candy had decided that Luci—that was apparently what Lucinda went by—was just the cutest thing in the world. They were on the living room floor with her, solemnly discussing her doll's adventures with Dora the Explorer. Levitt and the bruisers hadn't shown up yet.

Trowbridge must have collapsed before he could play Gracious Host. Thompson was foraging in the shelving of a wet bar, which told me that she didn't frequent circles where people had wet bars. It took me about three seconds to spot the liquor cabinet concealed behind a panel in a California Mission-style false beam just behind her under the ceiling. I didn't even have to jimmy it. A little push inward and it popped open.

"What are you drinking?" I asked.

"Anything you can mix with Coca-Cola."

Well, you can mix Pinch with Coke but I wasn't going to do it. I have some standards. Fortunately I stumbled over an almost full fifth of Jack Daniels in the back of the cabinet and hauled it out. Thompson had come up with Coke, ice, and tumblers on her own, and she promptly made good use of the bourbon. I filled another tumbler with ice, spritzed tonic water into it, and brought it over to Proxy. I kept the tonic water bottle for myself so that Proxy could think she was having a positive influence on me.

"What about you ladies?" Thompson asked the eye-candy.

"Diet Sprite for them, unless they show you government-issued picture IDs," I said. The blonder one playfully stuck her tongue out at me and giggled.

Proxy took a measured sip of her tonic water. Then she dove into her purse and pulled out a fistful of folded twenties.

"DDD said the charge was four hundred and I gave them a credit card for it." She said this to Thompson. "But I can give you eighty in cash for the tip."

"You got yourself a deal, sister." Thompson took four twenties and wedged them into the left side-pocket of jeans that she wore under the leathers.

"I'll need a receipt."

"The forms are in my scooter's saddle bags. I'll get one for you as soon as the tsunami out there has died down. The way it's going, though, I don't expect that'll be anytime soon."

"We don't want to inconvenience you."

"No problem at all. It's warm and dry in here, and Lucinda and her mama ain't taking a scooter home in the dark over slick pavement anyway."

"Too bad it's not a Harley." I thought I'd better jump in before Proxy dropped any more subtle hints.

"Oh, God, a *Harley*." Thompson closed her eyes like she was dreaming. "I would do anything short of a Class C felony for a Harley."

*Anything short of a Class C Felony.* Interesting way to put it. An intriguing little question started banging around in my head.

Tires squealing to a quick stop on asphalt signaled Levitt's arrival. Slamming doors. Then the bell rang and I opened the door to let Levitt in. Trowbridge suddenly woke up like Sleeping Beauty at the prince's kiss. He stopped snoring, started, blinked a couple of times, then swung himself to a sitting position.

"Hey, Saul. 'Bout time you got here. Fix yourself a drink."

"Later. Right now, you and I and Trans/Oxana Insurance Company have to reach an understanding about a few things."

"Ah!" Trowbridge jumped to his feet and thrust his right index finger into the air like a college professor in a Marx Brothers movie. "A confabulation! Confabulous! To the bat cave!"

He began to shuffle through the dining room toward a pitch-black room behind it. Levitt followed him, Proxy followed Levitt, and I followed Proxy. I suspected that "the bat cave" was a private screening room and I'd always wanted to see one of those. Maybe next time. At the doorway Proxy turned to face me.

"Jay, I think you can add more value out here looking for jail-coach leads."

She had a point, even if what she really meant was that we needed Levitt on our side in this little conference and he was never going to be best buddies with me.

"You got it."

I did my second about-face of the day and went back into the living room. I found the less-blond half of the Doublemint twins digging a pack of L&Ms and a lighter out of her purse. Luci's novelty value had apparently worn off. The two ingénue-wannabes headed for an open kitchen that might have been delivered yesterday morning fresh from a high-end home show, and exited through the back door onto what must have been a roofed porch. Thompson picked up Luci, who was holding her dolly's left arm with her left hand and sternly wagging her right index finger in the doll's face while she said, "If I *ever* catch *you* with a cigarette, young lady, so *help* me I will *wear you out.*"

"That's a good mommy, Lucinda," Thompson said. "Now why don't you and Annabelle take a little nap here on the couch until it's time to go home?"

Not a murmur of protest from Luci. Thompson laid the tyke on the sofa recently occupied by Trowbridge and fitted a throw-pillow under her head. Luci pulled Annabelle to her chest and wrapped her arms around her in a motherly embrace while Thompson dimmed the lights, fetched her biker jacket, and laid it over the eight-year-old.

Retrieving our drinks, Thompson and I made our way to the kitchen. It sparkled—clean not in the way well-tended kitchens are but in the way kitchens that are almost never used are. Thompson parked her hips against a massive Sub-Zero refrigerator-freezer and fixed her eyes on the living room. I hauled my 4G out of its holster with designs on surfing the net.

"Luci seems to feel very strongly about smoking." I said that just to say something. Break the ice.

"One of the only times I ever really prayed." Thompson kept her eyes on the living room, speaking in a low, intense voice that the girl couldn't have heard even if she were still awake. "Halfway to Tikrit we come under fire. I scoot my butt under the truck, and first thing you know it is *big time* hot. They have mortars and rpgs and twenties, and I am goddamn wet-my-britches scared. So I said, 'I am piss-poor at praying, but if you get my sorry ass out of here in one piece and back with my little girl, so help me I will never smoke another cigarette the longest day I live.'"

# Chapter Six

"Marines?"

"Three tours in Iraq." Thompson glanced at me as I whistled. "You too?"

"Army National Guard. Federalized after nine-eleven. One tour in Afghanistan and one in Iraq."

"Infantry?"

"MPs."

"Yeah, you look like an MP, come to think of it. No offense, but I would take any MOS in the book before MP."

"That's what Sergeant Rutledge told me before I shipped out." I moved to the other side of a cabinet-counter island, where I could lean over and park my forearms. "Rutledge was this crusty old African-American sergeant in charge of our National Guard unit. Day before we shipped out he pulled me aside. 'Davidobitch,' he says, 'soon as some officer gets a look at the build on you, he's gonna tab you for MPs. Davidobitch, do *not*—say again *not*—take this assignment. I would rather spend all day stirring shit in a vat than pull an MP detail.'"

"Bet you wish you'd listened to him, boy."

"Bad things happen in war." I shrugged. "Thing is, when my detailer came to me with that MP gig, I was literally stirring shit in a vat."

"Been there. You'd think that if we can zap a guy in northern Pakistan by watching him on television while we pull a trigger in Virginia, we'd have something more high-tech than a private with pole to keep the latrine goop churning while chemicals do their thing. But *nooooo*."

"'You go to war with the army you have.'"

That got a chuckle. Quoting the Busher's Secretary of Defense to an Iraq War veteran usually will. Thompson pulled out her own mobile phone, punched up a game app, and started thumbing the keyboard. I began Googling "Jail Coach." The two blondes reappeared and headed upstairs.

"Jail Coach" produced a quadrillion hits or so. I started methodically going through them. A lot of fetish come-ons, natch. Hit number sixty-one sucked slightly less than the first five dozen. I was about to click on the link when I realized something: any jail coach I found on Google was, by definition, the wrong guy for this job. The first bullet point on his job description had to be, "Can't figure out he's a jail coach by Googling him." Setting the blogosphere abuzz with rumors about prepping Trowbridge for the slammer was *not* my assignment.

Now, don't ask me why, but somewhere in there I started doing math. Not sixty-one divided by a quadrillion but twenty-twelve minus eight equals twenty-oh-four. I looked up at Thompson, who was intensely focused on killing angry birds or breaking bricks or whatever she was up to. I politely waited until her deflating shoulder sag signaled the end of round.

"When did you punch out?"

"Last year."

"So you signed up in, what, oh-six, when Iraq looked like it was headed right down the crapper? What was that all about? Bush fever?"

She clicked her app off and turned to face me. People like to talk about themselves. They think they're a fascinating subject.

"Allergy to the Harris County hoosegow." I could tell from her eyes that she was thinking about whether to cut it off there. She decided to go on. "Grand jury in Houston wanted to know where Luci was. I wasn't saying. They kept me in jail for contempt until the grand jury's term ended. Seven months. At the discharge hearing the judge told me they'd do it all again as soon as the next grand jury convened. Then he settles back in this good ole boy way and says, "Course, I don't have jurisdiction over Camp Lejeune.' And he winks. I took the hint."

"What are you doing now, besides Dial-a-Designated-Driver?"

"Little acting, little modeling."

I kept the smart-ass smirk off my face. The average fashion model in California has the body of an anorexic sixteen-year-old boy, which Thompson hadn't had since she was twelve. And I would have given you thirty-to-one on a rainy day that she couldn't act her way out a wet paper bag. What she meant was "acting" and "modeling"—the Simi Valley samba. Porn. Porn stills and porn films.

"Sounds like the rain has finally stopped," she said. "Guess I'd better be thinking about getting Lucinda and me home."

*No no no!* I only get one blinding insight a week. Couldn't waste this one.

"That's a forty-five minute ride on wet pavement in the dark. Tell you what. Maybe Trowbridge will let me borrow his Lexus long enough to drive you."

I had to follow her into the living room and say this to the back of her head. She answered me without slowing down her brisk pace.

"Nope. DDD is supposed to provide a service to customers, not inconvenience them. That's a nice little gig and I don't wanna blow it." I heard Lucinda gently snoring—scarcely more than a whisper—as Thompson picked up the leather jacket. "Wake up, wake up, Lucky Luci. Time to go home to your own bed."

"Absolutely not."

This came from Trowbridge, who was striding back into the living room trailed by Proxy and Levitt, neither of whom looked very happy.

"What are you saying?" Thompson asked Trowbridge.

"It's too late and too dark to make a trip like that with a child on a scooter that's two steps above a moped. I want you and your little girl to sleep here tonight. Plenty of room. Comfy beds. I promise to behave like a gentleman. And if you have to be somewhere in the morning you can get as early a start as you need to."

"Are you sure you don't mind? I can't say I was looking forward to the trip."

"I insist."

"Well that is just the *nicest* thing anyone has done for me in a long time. Mr. Trowbridge, you got yourself a deal—and if there's anyone you'd like to have killed, you just let me know."

Proxy and I said goodnight, and I had my mobile phone out before we were elbow to elbow in the Fusion's front seat. Proxy waited until she was pulling out of the driveway before she asked the obvious question.

"What are you looking for?"

"Hotel."

"We have a hotel. Less than an hour from here. Westin. Nice one, right at the top of Trans/Oxana's allowable expense range."

"We need one forty-five minutes closer, and as long as it has a bed and a bathroom I don't care how many stars it gets from Zagat." I glanced over and had no trouble reading her this-better-be-good expression. "You look like you and Levitt ran into a brick wall with Mr. Hollywood Royalty just now."

"Not smooth sailing for sure. Did you find a jail coach?"

"As a matter of fact I did. Right at the first light around this curvy road. There's a Ramada ten minutes away."

# Chapter Seven

"Two things I can't stand: Clerks who give you this does-your-mother-know-you're-buying-that? look and—"

"You know something, Davidovich? You say that a lot. 'Two things I can't stand.' Third or fourth time around, I get the feeling there are more than two things."

I couldn't blame Proxy for the attitude. She'd had to get up at five, she hadn't had her workout or her mucho grande latte whatever, and she'd had to put up with me. She'd actually been a reasonably good sport about it until the trip to the twenty-four grocery store with the snarky cashier. I climbed out of the Fusion, cradling the paper sack from Von's Grocery around the bottom. Instead of slamming the door and yelling through the window, I leaned inside and did my soft-answer-turneth-away-wrath thing.

"Just cruise around until you find a Starbucks. I'll give you a call when I've got the trail blazed."

"Why don't I just park here while you blaze it?"

"That would probably qualify as loitering with intent. I suspect it's a misdemeanor even to be in possession of a Ford Fusion in Malibu."

The car rolled sedately away. I did *not* cross the street to the speaker on the gate that protected Trowbridge's place. I stayed on the other side of the road, worked my mobile phone out, and punched in the number I'd memorized when I'd glanced at Thompson's phone last night. Four rings took me to voice-mail.

I gave my watch a puzzled glance. 6:38. *Hmm.* Someone less than a year out of the Corps shouldn't still be in bed.

"Hey, Hurricane Katrina," I said after the prompt, "this is Jay Davidovich, the tall dude you met last night. I'm outside Trowbridge's house. I brought some groceries by in case you're in the market for any."

I signed off and waited. Could she possibly already be headed back to Simi Valley on that scooter? That would be unfortunate.

My phone vibrated on my hip.

"Davidovich."

"Jay? Jay?"

Not Thompson. The voice was trembling which isn't exactly unheard of for this particular voice. I heroically suppressed a sigh.

"Yes, Rachel, this is Jay."

"Jay, he beat me. He actually *beat* me."

I straightened up and automatically started scanning the perimeter, as if I were back in Iraq. Pure reflex. The beginning of Rachel conversations often has that effect on me. I asked what struck me as the most urgent question.

"Where is he?"

"I don't know."

"Is he in the house?"

"No. He stormed out last night and hasn't come back yet."

*Yet? Hasn't come back YET?*

"Does he have a key?"

"I guess."

"You *guess*?"

"Well, I mean, he's had one for awhile. Unless he didn't take it with him or something."

She started to sniffle because the sarcastic emphasis that I put on "*guess*" constituted yelling at her. No doubt she'd be hearing soon from her therapist that this represented emotional abuse. I tried to think of a constructive follow-up.

"Can you get the locks changed?"

"I suppose, but…I mean, I have to work today."

"You just said he—"

"I know. I mean, it's not like he punched me or anything. He just slapped me around a little."

"Oh, well, that's okay then."

"No, I know. I'm not saying it's okay. I'm just saying…Jay?"

"What?"

"Could I just go to the apartment tonight?"

*Shit.* I didn't suppress this sigh. Didn't even try.

"I'm sorry," she said. "I mean, if it's too much trouble…"

"Yes, you can go to the apartment. I'll call Hal and tell him to let you in. You, but not Denny."

"It's Nick."

"Oh, you've moved on. Nick, then. Nick doesn't set foot in my apartment. We clear on that, Rachel?"

"No Nick, got it. And would it kill you to be a little less condescending?" Then her voice softened. " I was hoping maybe I could stay through the weekend."

"You can, but that's it. I'm shooting for Tuesday night to get back and I'm not in the mood for a roommate. You get your locks changed or get a restraining order or buy a gun or something between now and Tuesday morning."

"Is there any way you can get back tonight or maybe tomorrow night?"

"No. Look, Rachel, the deal hasn't changed. We can stay married or we can get divorced, but we're not gonna get divorced and sleep together on weekends. It's one or the other."

"Okay. Bye. Thanks."

"*De nada.* Bye."

I was a little distracted on the "bye" because I'd just noticed the cop. He cruised up on the other side of the street, stopped, and looked at me with what I would call pointed and conspicuous interest. At that moment a piercing west Texas screech from across the street preempted whatever follow-up the cop had in mind.

"Is that really food, Tall Dude?"

"Sure is, Hurricane."

"Well just you bring it on over here."

Thompson was standing right inside the driveway gate, which she'd managed to open. She'd presumably wheedled the code out of one of the Doublemint twins, which was probably where she'd also gotten the jogging shorts and halter top she was wearing, because they were both one size too small. Not that the cop or I had any complaints. Wet sand caked her bare feet, and sweat glistened on her body.

"I tried returning your call, but you must have been on the phone with someone," Thompson said as I crossed the street.

"I was."

She led me around the house to the back. Funny thing, it didn't look all that big in the daylight. Proxy's briefing book put the value at three-point-two million and I wondered why. Then we got to the back of the house and I had the answer: the Pacific Ocean. Right *there*. Forty feet from the back porch where Lucinda was offering breakfast to her doll.

Thompson gave Lucinda a peck on the top of her head and paused at the back door to towel off her feet. She led me into the kitchen, where she relieved me of the Von's sack and set it on the counter.

"Milk. God bless you for that. Lucinda's got to have milk with her cereal and there wasn't a drop of it in this house. Bitty boxes of cereal; that's sweet; there'll be something she'll like in there. Grapefruit and bananas, good. Bacon! And bread! Wonder enriched white bread! Thank you, God! I mean, you too, Jay."

"No, no, give God the credit. I'm just his humble instrument."

"Would you believe there wasn't more than three or four bites of solid food in this entire kitchen?"

"Yes, I would." I'd been kind of counting on it.

"Unless you're really into nuts, strange fruit, and brown bread. Lucinda! Come on in here and get yourself some cereal, honey. Mommy's gonna fry up some bacon and make a little toast."

Taking one of the bananas for myself, I parked on a stool at the counter-island and watched Thompson get to work. I made sure that Lucinda had trudged back out onto the porch with her cereal, and that the door had closed smoothly behind her.

Even then, I waited until Thompson had eight slices of bacon sizzling on a stove-top griddle before I spoke.

"Can I ask you a question, Hurricane?"

"Shoot."

"Do you have any acting or modeling work that will tie you up for the next couple of weeks, or are you up for a gig?"

She looked at me like a Vegas pit boss might look at a tourist who'd doubled down on face-six three hands in a row and won all three.

"Depends on the gig."

"Legal and you get to keep your clothes on. But it would involve some travel."

"How much would this legal, fully-clothed, traveling job pay?"

Tricky question. I could get her twenty-five hundred a week without breathing hard. But if I said *that* she'd assume it was drug smuggling which, if I had her sized up right, would be a deal-killer.

"Depends. Say, eight-hundred a week. Plus room and board—and we're talking nice rooms and nice boards."

Now she looked at me like I was a cat who'd missed the litter box. She flipped bacon, popped toast, put in more toast, and started spreading margarine on the toast she'd popped.

"What do you do for a living, Tall Dude?"

"I work for an insurance company." I started to pull out one of my cards.

"Skip it. I didn't ask you who you worked for. I want to know what you *do*."

"Well, it's like this. Insurance companies make bets with lots and lots of people that certain things won't happen. If they win ninety-eight percent of those bets, they pay off the other two percent and make a lot of money. What I do is, I go into situations where it looks like my company might lose one of those bets, and I try to get them from the two percent column into the ninety-eight percent column."

"Oh. Okay. I get that I wouldn't be hooking or showing off my birthday suit. What *would* you want me to do for two weeks for—oh, just for fun, let's say for a thousand a week?"

Before I could get a word out, Trowbridge's pitch-perfect baritone voice echoed resonantly through the kitchen.

"He wants you to be my jail coach."

# Chapter Eight

Trowbridge was wearing a black-and-white silk robe that came down to just above his knees. One of the almost-twins, still wearing what she'd had on last night, came into the kitchen right behind him. Working her way around his body, she pulled an industrial-sized blender out from the wall next to the refrigerator.

"Jail coach?" Thompson shot me a look.

"Something like that," I said.

"Yep," Trowbridge said.

"I forgot where you keep the celery," the almost-twin said.

"So." Trowbridge put his hands in the pockets of his robe and gave Thompson the kind of attention the cop had given me. "Let's say you were my 'jail coach.' I already know not to bend over in the shower. What else could you teach me?"

"I guess I'd have to think about that."

*Hmm.* Trowbridge had decided that we were going to do a little improv, which isn't the first thing you think of when someone says 'Simi Valley.' Thompson would need some help. I turned toward Trowbridge.

"How about this? First full day in the zoo. You're in the day-room with your new neighbor, Hurricane Thompson here. Go."

"Okay." With a shrug, Trowbridge sauntered over to Thompson. "So, Hurricane, is it? So, Hurricane: what are you in for?"

"No." Thompson wagged an index finger back and forth in front of her face, like a very shapely windshield wiper. "No, no, no. You do *not* ask anyone on the inside what they're doing time for."

"Why not?"

"Don't know, don't care. Just don't do it. It's a fresh meat move, and fresh meat is something you do *not* want to seem like—especially if you are."

"And you know that...how?"

"Not from reading it in a script. Mama has been a guest of the county."

Thompson put four strips of bacon and two slices of toast on a plate. Trowbridge glanced at the blender, where something that looked vaguely like a pea-green smoothie was shaping up. Thompson held the plate out to him.

"Uh, no, thanks."

Trowbridge said this about the way you'd say it if someone offered you toxic sludge. Thompson handed the plate to me.

"Would you mind taking this out to Lucinda? Oh, and remind her to say her grace, in case she forgot?"

Lucinda had *not* forgotten to say grace. By the time I got back Thompson was jail-coaching Trowbridge with both barrels.

"Here's the deal. I can tell you the do's and don'ts in five minutes and you won't have to pay me a penny. Don't accept anything anyone offers you, whether it's a joint or a library book or something in between. Don't tell the guards you have a big, scary lawyer who can sue them. Don't snitch on *anyone*, including the bruiser who puts your face into the wall. Don't take the bait when someone starts jawing at you. Don't fight unless there's absolutely nothing else you can do. If you do have to fight, do it like your life depends on it, 'cause ain't no director gonna yell, 'Cut!' Don't promise anyone a job on the outside. He'll know it's bullshit. If a guard starts playin' with your head, just swallow hard and take it. Don't say a word, don't shift your eyes, don't move a muscle. Just take it. Find something in the vending machines that you can stand to eat. Mind your own business, do your own time."

"Okay." Trowbridge did a little exhale take that I vaguely remembered from two movies ago. "Got it. So now I'm ready?"

Thompson now offered me a plate with four slices of bacon and two pieces of toast. I started nibbling the part of the toast that hadn't touched the bacon. Strolling over to Trowbridge, Thompson looked at him with a kind of brutal pity.

"Mr. Trowbridge, from everything I can see, you are a really decent person. Letting Lucinda and me stay here last night—that was just real nice. But there's one thing you definitely need to know if you're gonna spend more than twenty minutes in jail. Something way past those dos and don'ts I just rattled off."

"Tell me." Trowbridge spread his arms and flashed his million-dollar smile.

"There's somethin' *about* you that makes people just wanna kick the livin' *shit* outta you. That's your problem, right there. Every time you walk ten feet across the exercise yard two or three guys are gonna have this sudden urge to whip your ass just for the exercise."

"Oh." Trowbridge didn't spread his arms. The smile he attempted wouldn't have brought ten cents at a junior high slumber party.

"Now, that's what I think Tall Dude here wants me to work on with you if I take on what you call this jail coach gig. I'm not for sure I can do anything about it, but if you wanted me to give 'er a try that's what I'd zero in on."

Thompson glanced over at me. Her eyes said, "Am I hot or what?" I gave her the eyebrow equivalent of a thumbs-up. She noticed the untouched pigs' bellies on my plate.

"You don't like bacon?"

"Not kosher. I looked it up."

"Oh my Lord!" She blushed tomato red and her hands went to her cheeks. "I'm *sorry*. I had *no idea*."

"No way you could have known. I left my prayer shawl back at the hotel."

Thompson suddenly turned back to Trowbridge. She looked like the basic concept for the next generation of smart phones had just popped into her brain.

"Say, I just got an idea! A place we could start."

"All ears."

"How about if you go to the studio sometime today, look up that kid you sucker-punched, and say you're sorry? No photo-ops, no publicity, no press release, no posse, just by your lonesome. Don't give him any money, don't promise to make it up to him. Just say, 'Look, I was way out of line. No excuse for it. My bad. It's on me. I'm really sorry.' Do you think you could handle that?"

That had to be the world's easiest question, right? I mean, you've got to at least *say* you could handle a decent apology.

Trowbridge didn't say this. For a good five seconds he didn't say anything. Then he said, "I've gotta call Saul."

I had to call someone too. I speed dialed Proxy as I walked out onto the back porch. My one-minute recap ended with, "So it seemed like a good time to call you."

"It sounds like ten minutes ago would have been a good time to call me."

"I had a fluid situation on my hands."

"Let me get this straight." She had that little pant to her voice that you sometimes get when you talk on a mobile phone while you're doing complicated driving. "We're about to lay a thousand bucks a week on a high school dropout porn actress who's an alumna of the Harris County Jail so she can play Doctor Phil with pretty boy—am I clear on the concept?"

"Just for the upcoming tour. As soon as that's over, I'll have a Rhodes Scholar who's done time in some classy federal penitentiary replace Thompson."

"If you're joking, Davidovich, I'm pissed off—and if you're not I'm scared."

An hour later we were two fingers from a deal. Proxy had somehow managed to jack Thompson's stipend up to twelve-hundred a week—negotiating isn't her strong suit—but that was still chump-change on Planet Trans/Oxana. Trowbridge said he was okay with apologizing to the kid he'd punched out. Levitt had signed on. Thompson was on board. Then Proxy almost blew it.

"And we'll be happy to arrange twenty-four/seven child care for Lucinda while you're gone."

"Uh-uh." Thompson shook her head gravely as something close to shock washed over her face. "Luci comes along with mama."

Lucinda nodded vigorously, jumping into her mother's lap. She clutched the doll like it was a seat on the last life-boat leaving the *Titanic*. Proxy looked at me. I nodded. What could possibly go wrong?

# Chapter Nine

By 9:45 Monday morning we had been in the air for an hour, and we'd made up enough time to be only forty minutes behind schedule. We had a cozy little group: Trowbridge, Thompson, Lucinda, and yours truly; a flack from Levitt's office named Jeff Wells and a go-fer for him; Jennifer Seawright, a studio flunky, and her go-fer; a guy who knew how to replace toner and ink-cartridges and make computers behave; another guy who looked to me like he could mop the floor up with a gunnery sergeant and who was Trowbridge's personal trainer; a person whose gender I had to guess at but who carried a massive make-up satchel with him or her at all times; and a couple of short-necked knuckle-draggers.

No Proxy. She was back in Hartford, telling the suits not to worry about the Trowbridge policy—or something like that. Proxy has three rules: (1) Don't lie; (2) Back up the people who are working with you; (3) if Rule (1) conflicts with Rule (2), Rule (2) wins. So I wasn't worried about her.

First stop would be Nashville. That's right: not one of the East Coast biggies, not Atlanta, not even Miami. Nashville.

"Nashville is the single best per capita market for westerns east of the Mississippi." This from Wells, who had decided that he and I should be good buddies. "No one knows why. Maybe just because the entire city lives on hat-acts."

I shrugged. I was concentrating on figuring out which members of our merry band had illicit pharmaceuticals stashed in their Travel Pros. Also, I couldn't get Rachel out of my head. No question about it, the chick is a drama magnet. Always has been. But things got way weirder after my return from Iraq. Had she cheated on me and then gotten fucked up guilt-tripping herself over it? Don't know. Something huge had gone down, though, and I had no idea what it was. Wells interpreted my indifference as ignorance and explained his comment.

"A 'hat-act' is a country-western singing group? Because they all wear cowboy hats?"

"He knows what a 'hat-act' is." Trowbridge beamed down at us.

"I do now."

"Look, Jay, could you maybe join me for a few minutes while I do a little cardio?"

"Sure thing." I stood up and stretched, then threw Wells a bone. "Interesting dope about Nashville."

I followed Trowbridge to the rear of the main cabin, where the exercise stuff waited. He had on a plain white tee and blue shorts, with a regular white towel around his neck. He climbed onto the stationary bike, fussed with the settings, and started pumping away with the effortless steadiness of a guy who really does keep himself fit. He nodded toward pairs of twenty-pound and fifty-pound weights locked into the weight bench near the bulkhead.

"You ever do free weights?"

"Twice a week." I found a seat that I could swivel toward the middle of the plane so that I could look at Trowbridge while I kept my legs at full length.

"Katrina says you were an MP in Iraq."

"Guilty."

"You sign up after nine-eleven?"

"Nope. Joined the Connecticut National Guard for help with college tuition. I figured basic training would be a breeze after basketball practice, and then I'd just have a month of summer camp and an occasional natural disaster. Nine-eleven came as an unpleasant surprise to Bush and me."

"You got called up?"

"Yep. Ended up doing the college thing in bits and pieces."

Trowbridge pedaled away, leaning forward with an intense expression as he glanced at what must have been pretty good numbers on the screen between the handlebars, seeming to glow from the fine sheen of sweat he'd already worked up. Cord-like muscles pulsed rhythmically in the thigh and calf that I could see.

"Saul had a workup done on you."

"That doesn't come as a complete surprise."

"It says your real name is Davidson."

"My parents' name is Davidson. I changed it back to the original family version when I turned eighteen." My look was supposed to tell him that I wasn't exactly fascinated by me. Didn't work.

"Why did you do that?"

"So mom and dad wouldn't feel disgraced if I ever got caught humping underage girls."

That worked. Trowbridge's mouth formed a little O as his head snapped in my direction.

"You're talking about Kathy and Cathy, right?"

"We were never actually introduced."

"You know how old they are?"

"My guess is they should get grounded for smoking."

"Twenty-three. That fifteen-year-old Lolita deal is their thing. Their look."

"Their art."

"Well, let's not get excited." Trowbridge threw me the patented grin.

"Well, they sure fooled me."

Trowbridge leaned into the bike and did a good three minutes of serious pumping. Not quite *Tour de France* stuff, but he had his legs moving. Then he dialed it back closer to normal and returned his attention to me.

"You don't think much of me, do you?"

I thought about that for a second. I've learned the hard way to cut people some slack. There have been times when I didn't think much of myself. Bad things don't just happen in war. They also happen in peace.

"You know what? I won't say that. You don't exactly get a gold star for punching out a kid who couldn't defend himself. On the other hand, you were drunk. On the other hand, knowing that you do stuff like that when you get drunk is a good reason not to get drunk."

"I told Dex I was sorry. I tracked him down and did the apology thing, like Katrina said."

"I'm glad you did that. Strikes me as the right thing to do."

"And I came to get you myself just now, instead of sending someone for you."

"Another Katrina suggestion?"

"Yeah." The *whirr* of the well-oiled pedal gears picked up again, heading back toward something just short of a whine. "It seems lame, hearing myself say that just now. As if it's something special to act like a regular human being. Like I'm in some kind of twelve-step jerk-rehab program."

"For what it's worth, I don't think you're a jerk. To someone on the outside looking in, it seems like you've had everything handed to you, without having to work for it. People hate that. They see the great bod, but they don't see the three-hour work-outs that keep it great."

"What can I do about that?"

"Beats me." I pushed my shoulders into the back of my seat. "Probably nothing. I thought I was going to go through college on rebounds and lay-ups and then find a job somewhere as a civil engineer if I couldn't get into coaching. Didn't work out that way. So what? There are five billion people in the world who'd love to have my problems."

"So, just sort of accept things?"

"That's not what I'm saying." I tried to pinpoint what I *was* saying, exactly. "Certain things we can control. When your unit gets into a scrap you can shoot or take cover or run. That you've got control over. What the overall plan is, whether there's enough troops in-country to make that plan work, whether you've got decent armor or pot-metal on your vehicles—those things you can't control. So you don't worry about them. Focus on the choices you do have, and make the right one."

"You know what's funny?" Trowbridge was panting a little now, and he had to mop streaming sweat from his face. "Katrina said almost exactly the same thing just before I came back here. Not in those words. She said a lance corporal told her once that the life of a Marine grunt is tactically rational and strategically random—so get the tactical part right."

"Good advice. Speaking of which, I'd better get back to mid-cabin and start deterring recreational drug-use again. If Ms. Thompson gets a whiff of pot near that little girl of hers, she'll probably take a powder as soon as we land."

"You go deter all you want to." Trowbridge said this with his grin back in place at full wattage. "But I wouldn't work up too much of a sweat about it if I were you. Saul put the word out: This little junket is a clean and sober operation. What they do in their hotel rooms is between them and their rabbis, but if they indulge on the plane they'll never take a meeting west of Reno again."

So as we flew over flyover country, I was feeling pretty good about things. Saul Levitt hated Trans/Oxana's guts but he was scared of us—not a bad combination. Proxy had told me to stay overnight in Nashville and then fly from there back to D.C. Tuesday morning. Trans/Oxana charges eight-hundred-dollars per day against her budget for my services if I'm working on one of her matters. So I wouldn't have to put up with this too long.

Two hours or so into the flight, after Trowbridge had a shower—they'd rigged up the plane with one of those, too—the make-up person started doing his or her magic and made Trowbridge look like a *People* magazine cover. We landed in Nashville just before three. This was a charter flight, so no jetway. We'd land and stairs on wheels would roll up to the door. Trowbridge would do a star stroll down the stairs and across the tarmac to a limo with a couple of lucky local reporters waiting for him in the ample interior. He'd do sound bites flogging the upcoming flick while the limo took him to the biggest Nashville TV station, get some face-time with the on-air talent, and hit his hotel in time to watch himself on the tube.

Everything went according to script. Tons of people and plenty of cameras waiting on the tarmac. Plane taxis to within twenty yards of the limo. Stairs roll into place. Door opens. Trowbridge comes out, grins, waves, basks. The cameras start translating Trowbridge into digitized pixels and sending them who knows where. When Trowbridge is three steps down the stairs, the publicist appears on the scene, carefully inconspicuous and staying three steps behind Trowbridge as he descends. Yep, everything was perfect.

Then Thompson and Lucinda came out. All those cameras kept right on humming and snapping. And I didn't think a thing about it.

# Chapter Ten

"It sounds like Thompson is good for Trowbridge." Weather between Hartford, Connecticut and Alexandria, Virginia made Proxy's voice sound a little tinny over my mobile phone. "But the flip-side risk is Trowbridge becoming psychologically dependent on Thompson, like people sometimes do on their shrinks."

"Why 'risk'?" I slam-dunked three pairs of pink satin panties into Rachel's suitcase, which lay open on my bed. "Dependent would be fine with us, right?"

"Until something goes wrong. Then it wouldn't be fine with us anymore."

"Little Mary Sunshine strikes again." I scooped a bunch of crap in plastic tubes into a small, quilted bag and tossed the bag into the suitcase.

"You sound like you're panting, Davidovich. You're not sneaking in an Elliptical workout while we're talking, are you?"

"I wouldn't have an Elliptical on the end of stick. I'm packing Rachel's bag. She missed her check-out time from my apartment this morning."

It sounded like Proxy was munching on a celery stalk or something while she thought that over. I probably should have called her on it after the Elliptical crack, but I believe in having only one female pissed off at me at a time. She politely swallowed before she talked again.

"Okay. For now I can live with the idea of letting Thompson do her thing and hoping for the best. But where is the tour supposed to be by Friday?"

"Omaha. Why?"

"Because New Paradigm is holding a major test screening for *Prescott Trail* on Thursday. If it tanks you're on your way to Omaha."

"Understood. I can stay with them until they get back to LA. Should have a pretty tight idea by then about whether the Thompson idea is tenable."

"Is somebody on the tour keeping you up to speed between now and then?"

"Levitt's dog-robber is supposed to give me a call every night."

"How much is that costing me?"

"Nada. Levitt knows which side his bread is buttered on."

I stuffed a curling iron, a pair of size-seven Nike running shoes, and two of those cute little anklet socks with balls on the heels into Rachel's suitcase while Proxy thought things over. I was zipping the thing closed by the time she was ready to converse again.

"In case the jail-coach thing falls apart, what's Plan B?"

"Plan Bs are for pessimists."

"Cracks like that are for people who don't have Plan Bs. I get paid to be a pessimist. Think about it and call me tomorrow."

"Will do."

After re-holstering my mobile phone I pulled Rachel's bag off the bed and headed for the bedroom door with it. Rachel had made the bed that morning, with military corners as tight as any I'd managed on active duty. At the same time, she'd left clothes and cosmetics and other chick-shit scattered all over the room. Which meant that she'd thought she was going to be sleeping in it again tonight. Which she wasn't. I waited until I had the bag in the bay of my Ford Explorer and was halfway to the house before I punched Rachel's speed-dial number on my mobile phone.

"Now, Jay, you can't be mad at me. I just had to get in a run this morning and I didn't have time to pack after my shower before I left for work."

"I packed for you."

"Plus…I was kind of hoping I could stay there one more night."

"That would be no. I'm betting you didn't get the locks changed, either."

"Not yet. I mean, I have a life, you know?"

"Also okay. I'll just pick up your extra key from whoever. Nick, is it?"

"Please don't hurt him, Jay. Please. I mean, about three months ago you almost broke Denny's nose."

"He hit me first."

"But you hit him back harder than he hit you."

"That's my policy. I'll need Nick's description and his three favorite bars."

"I have a picture of him at the house. That's where you're going, right?"

"No, I thought I'd drop your suitcase off at the Air and Space Museum."

"Jay, I just hate it when you're sarcastic. Doctor Keefe-Atkinson says it's a verbal form of domestic abuse. It's very hurtful."

"Three favorite bars, Rachel."

"I'll text you."

She hung up. Just in time, too, because five seconds later I pulled into her driveway—which used to be our driveway. I still had a key, so less than a minute later I had her suitcase stowed in the front hall and was looking on the mantle for Nick's picture. Let's see: ballerina-Rachel in mid-air, lithe and supple as a dream; ice-dancer Rachel with one of those glorious, sleekly muscled legs at almost a ninety degree angle to the other. Even smiling Rachel next to Jay in digi camis and black beret. No Nick. Then I heard a peevish voice from the kitchen.

"About time you got back. You about done with the psycho bitch number?"

"I'm guessing you're Nick," I said as he strolled into the living room holding a tumbler of orange juice and a lettuce-and-something sandwich on brown bread.

He hadn't combed his curly brown hair yet, but aside from that he looked about as good as a guy can look when he's still in pj's at eleven o'clock in the morning. He had a good six feet on him and a pretty trim build. Plus he sported that I-enjoy-being-a-goy cool that southern boys are so good at. As soon as he saw me, though, his eyes went to roughly the size of TV test patterns.

"Shit! Oh, shit!"

Yep, definitely Nick.

He high-tailed it back into the kitchen. I followed, in no particular hurry. I heard the back door slam as I stepped from hardwood onto linoleum. Pulled up a chair at the butcher's block kitchen table that Rachel and I had spent five bloody hours shopping for together, and took out my phone. By the time Nick remembered that he didn't have clothes, phone, car keys, or options, I'd gotten through the entire morning's worth of corporate communications. I looked up when I heard the distinctive squeak of the back door re-opening.

"I've called the police." He stayed just inside the door so that he could bolt again if I got too adventurous.

"Sure you have. Tell you what. Sit down. We gotta talk."

I could tell from his twitching upper lip that he wasn't too sure about that. Then I guess he decided that he'd better switch into show-them-no-fear mode. He came over and sat down across from me.

"Congratulations, Nick. You got the crazy chick."

"Look, Rachel said you were separated. She—"

"That's right. We're separated. Plus, it's not the first century BC, so she can hop in the sack with someone else without getting stoned to death." I waited two seconds. "She says you beat her."

"Bullshit!" A seriously indignant expression blasted across Nick's face. "I just smacked her a coupla times, to calm her down. No real rough stuff."

"Okay, here's the deal, Nick. You can fuck Rachel if she wants you to. You can sponge off her and play house with her and smoke pot with her when she's channeling her inner earth mother. That's all fine. But you don't get to hit her."

Nick looked like he was having trouble processing this information. I didn't think it was all that complicated, but I wanted to move things along so I explained it to him.

"The reason you don't get to hit her, Nick, is that I love her. Period. End of issue. I love Rachel. Therefore, you don't get to hit her. No matter what she does. Whether she's having a bad case of all-about-me or whining like a spoiled eight-year-old or playing head games or doing any other Rachel shit, you don't get to hit her, No punches on the arm, no slaps across the face, no smacks on the fanny, no grabbing her and pushing her onto the floor. No hitting. We got that, Nick?"

"But, man, *she hit me!*"

"She will do that, dude. That's her Ukrainian blood for you. But that is not a loophole. Not an exception to the rule. The rule is, you don't hit Rachel. Period."

I could sympathize with Nick. It isn't an easy idea to grasp. The stakes were high, though, especially for Nick, so I decided to hammer the point home.

"Tell you what, Nick. Take a swing at me. Hit me as hard as you can."

Terror filled his eyes and total fear bleached his face.

"This isn't a setup, Nick, I promise. If I wanted to crease you up you'd already be on your way to the hospital. Just take a swing at me."

Give him credit. He found the guts to do it. His right fist shot toward me as he half rose from his chair. Had some meat to it, too. I snapped my left arm up. His fist was still a good half-inch from my face when the outside of my left forearm smashed the inside of his right forearm. I should mention that the outside forearm bone is roughly four times bigger than the inside forearm bone. His arm flew sideways and upward as he grunted in pain. He brought the arm down onto his lap and hunched over it.

"Jesus H. Christ! That hurt! Jesus!"

"Well of course it hurt, Nick. I'm harder than you are. Just like you're harder than Rachel. So when Rachel takes a swing at you it's okay to block the punch. She's a smart girl, and after you've blocked a couple she'll find other ways to dump shit all over you."

A glimmer of understanding brightened his eyes. Time to close the sale.

"Lemme tell you about a boyhood experience of mine, Nick. True story. Josh, and I are out shopping with mom. Josh being my younger brother. I'm, what, maybe eight. Josh does something that annoys me, so I clock him one. Unfortunately for me, mom sees me do it. She grabs my right hand and pulls my arm out to full length. This is in a shopping mall, right in front of everybody. She smacks the back of my hand three times. Not slaps, *smacks*. I mean I *felt* it. With each smack she says, 'Don't HIT. Don't HIT. Don't HIT.' All three smacks landed at the precise moment I heard the word 'HIT.' Kind of ironic. Are we communicating here, Nick?"

After a couple of seconds he managed a nod. I glanced at my watch.

"Let's say twenty minutes. At ten minutes of noon, I want you down here, dressed and packed and ready to go, with your key to this house in my pocket."

"But, man, this is where I *live*, man."

"Yeah, I can see where that would be a problem. But you've gotta get Rachel comfortable again with the idea of living under the same roof as you before you can go back to doing it. I'd suggest groveling, abject apologies, 'I am so, *so* sorry, I'll never do it again, I promise'—that kind of shit. She's a Jewish girl, very big on atonement. If you're convincing enough, maybe she'll give you the key back. Or not. Personally, I could give a shit. Bottom line, though, no way I'm turning my apartment into a battered women's shelter."

While Nick went upstairs I texted Rachel not to bother with the list of bars.

# Chapter Eleven

On the East Coast you think of Omaha as—actually, on the East Coast you don't think of Omaha at all. At least I didn't. Warren Buffet lived there. That's about ninety percent of what I knew about Omaha. So what I saw out of the MD-80's window surprised me. Not sure any of the buildings qualified as skyscrapers, but some of them were pretty tall. Houses spread all over Hell's half acre. Had to be something between half-a-million and a million people living there.

The test-screening report shook Proxy, so I was rejoining the tour. Even so, I wasn't feeling too bad about things. Had a couple of leads for Plan B in the jail-coach department. More important, I'd gotten last week's expense report in. To me, expense reports are a profit center. The Trans/Oxana meal money per diem is $35. If I spend more than that, I put in for $35 and the rest comes out of my pocket. Fine. But if I spend less—I always spend less—then I still put in for $35 and the rest goes *in* my pocket. I mean, I like the symmetry. Plus, I call the close ones in my favor. Also the ones that aren't close. I call those in my favor too.

Jeff Wells, the Levitt flunky who'd been giving me nightly updates, picked me up at the airport. I liked the nightly updates, because either he was a twenty-four carat bullshit artist, or Thompson was getting the job done.

"Trow thinks she walks on water," he told me as we hit Interstate whatever on the way downtown. "Last night one of the roadies toked up in the same area code as the little girl, and Trow said he was almost fired."

"Man, that is *strict*."

I glanced out the window of the comp car Wells was driving. Some local Ford dealer had provided three loaners to Trowbridge and company for their twenty-hour Omaha stay. Just short of four in the afternoon and we were moving at a cool sixty-two miles per hour. This would not happen in metro Washington, D.C.

"How is the tour going over all?"

"The locals all seem thrilled. Interviews get monster numbers. But does that mean butts in seats? No *idea*, man. Uncharted waters."

"Sounds exciting."

"Korvette's theory is, no dream-factory bullshit. He's into *regular* factory bullshit. What can't be measured can't be managed. A movie is a product. A product is supposed to make a profit. If it doesn't, people are accountable."

We pulled into the semicircular driveway of something called the Hotel Devo XV in downtown Omaha. I spotted the guy before the car stopped. He was standing in the smoking area, not smoking, looking everywhere. His body hardly budged. But his black eyes moved constantly, scanning the area around him. His face—nut brown and smooth under a bald head—showed nothing.

I made it a point not to look at him as I climbed out of the car. Wells traded the keys for a piece of stiff brown paper and gave the valet a five-dollar tip. Pity the poor schlub from Kansas City who blows in here next week and thinks he's a big shot when he hands the car caddy two bucks.

"Is that a Levitt boy over there? The one who looks like a cop?"

"I don't see any cops." Wells swiveled his head like a farm kid getting his first look at Broadway.

"Skip it. But if Levitt has some private heat on this thing I need to know."

"I'll ask."

In the lobby, Wells gave me a mini-envelope with a key-card in it and a room number written on the inside flap. New Paradigm was allocating me a room from its block-booking package for the tour and billing Trans/Oxana directly.

"Where's Trowbridge?"

"Getting ready to do 'Live at Five' with KOMN. Due back at six."

"Am I on the same floor he is?"

"With Trans/Oxana's expense cap, you're lucky to be in the same hotel."

"Is Thompson with him?"

"Yep. He treats her like a good luck charm. Takes her wherever he can. She parks the kid in Trow's room when she goes somewhere with him. And every place we've been, Trow has put the porn-blocker on the room TV."

"Is Trowbridge on the top floor?"

"Yep."

"Floor security detail?"

"No, it's a key-access floor and we have all the rooms." Wells looked mildly annoyed. "Why are you getting all Yellow Alert of a sudden? No one has spiked Trow's latte grande since you bailed Tuesday morning. How did things suddenly get scary just because you showed up?"

"Thanks for the ride." No sense spending forty seconds of my life teaching shady-guys-for-dummies to a civilian. "ETA is ten tomorrow, right?"

"Right. On to Denver."

I dialed Proxy's number as soon as I got to my room. Four-twenty-five in Omaha equals five-twenty-five in Hartford so Proxy figured to be at her desk. She was. It took me thirty seconds to give her the gist.

"If it's Levitt double-teaming the tour that's not a problem because our interests are congruent." That's Proxy-speak for 'We're on the same side.' "Could be an Omaha cop just making sure the city doesn't get embarrassed. But he could also be a free-lancer with an angle we don't know."

"Or he could be Korvette's boy."

"What would Korvette be up to?"

"A movie is supposedly just a line of soap to him. You told me the test-screening graded out to b-minus/c-plus. Maybe Korvette wants to sabotage Trowbridge, trigger the policy, and cut his losses."

By the time Proxy was through thinking that over I'd finished unpacking. Of course, it doesn't take long to take four changes of socks and underwear, one clean shirt, and a shaving kit out of a gym bag.

"Not buying it. New Paradigm has a hundred million in this movie. Korvette has plenty of cards he can play before making a high-risk move like that."

"Well, Proxy, my degree is in civil engineering so I'll go with you on the business strategy stuff. Question is, do we throw an extra eight-hundred bucks a day at this thing for the rest of the tour to get on-site security?"

"Can't see it. Strike that. I'll think about it. Getting me a little more dope on the bald guy might help me to sell something like that upstairs."

"Understood."

"Anything else? I'm late for pilates."

"Nada. Sweat well."

The room service menu beckoned, but it would have to wait. "A little more dope on the bald guy" came first, starting with whether he was still outside. Before I left to check on that, though, I punched 0 on the room phone and asked the operator to put me through to Trowbridge's room. She did.

"Yo." The voice providing this answer sounded male, edgy, and pot-deprived.

"Davidovich from Trans/Oxana. Listen, would you be a good bro and put the little girl on the phone? Tell her I'm the one her mom calls Tall Dude."

He grunted something that didn't sound too happy, but apparently being almost fired works motivational wonders. After about ten seconds Luci's voice piped over the phone.

"Hello, sir."

"Hello, Luci. How are things going?"

"Fine, sir." Mix southern and Marine and you get lots of 'sirs.'

"What are you doing right now?"

"Powdering Annabelle, sir. And working on the computer. And waiting for mommy. Do you know when mommy will get back, sir?"

"Six o'clock, I think. Do you know when six o'clock is, Luci?"

"Yes, sir. When there's a six on the screen, with two zeroes after the dots."

"Okay, Luci, can you do me a favor?"

"Yes, sir."

"In case I'm not there when your mom gets back, would you ask her to call me on my mobile phone if I give you the number?"

"Yes, sir. I'm ready."

"Okay. Here it is." I'd barely gotten the area code out when I heard a male voice over the line, muffled but clear enough to make out the words.

"Luci! What are you doing? Where did you get that?"

"From the bathroom, sir. I borrowed it."

"Okay. You really shouldn't have that. Why don't you give that back to me?"

"Yes, sir. I'm sorry."

"That's okay. Just give it to me and I'll put it back."

I counted to five as seconds ticked off in silence. I was about to prompt Luci when she chimed back in.

"Could you say the numbers again, sir?"

"Sure I can, Luci." I did. She repeated it.

"That's right, Luci. Thanks a lot."

"Okay, sir."

I hung up and headed for the elevators. Time to check out the bald guy. Before I'd gotten two floors closer to the lobby, though, he dropped to number two on my list. I realized that I had to get to Trowbridge's room in a great big hurry.

# Chapter Twelve

I went down to the lobby. Within two minutes a guy wheeling a Stratus suitcase came by and punched the UP button. Door opened. I got on with him. He punched ten. As in not eleven. Shit. I banged the inside of the closing door and got off, muttering something about the wrong elevator.

Three minutes later, same routine. This guy was going to eight. I couldn't bull my way off again without attracting attention, so I rode up with him, stalled until he was out of sight, and then went back down to the lobby.

Third time's the charm. My free-pass to the top floor turned out to be a cheerful South Asian in a Saville Row suit. I followed him into the elevator. He put his key in the magic slot and punched 11. He asked which floor I wanted, I said same as yours, and the elevator started going up. That's how airtight a key-access floor is. His attaché case, by the way, had Something-or-Other Nanotechnology stamped on it in gold. Which meant that he was *not* part of the New Paradigm traveling party. Which meant that New Paradigm had *not* block-booked the entire top floor like Wells said it had.

I'm no genius, but it didn't take a genius to figure out that Trowbridge's suite was the one with double doors at the end of the hall farthest from the elevators. The maid was just leaving, pushing a cart loaded with maid stuff. I thought she looked a little white for a hotel maid, but I chalked that up to East Coast stereotyping. I got to the doors maybe eight seconds after she started trudging away from them. My knock brought a grumpy "Who?" shouted from the inside.

"Davidovich, Trans/Oxana."

The door didn't open right away. I could make out indistinct voices going back and forth—apparently a lively little debate about letting me in. The door finally opened. I walked in to a welcoming committee consisting of Wells and the studio flunky, Jennifer Seawright. She was giving me that it-would-be-so-wonderful-if-you-weren't-here look that chicks learn in second grade.

Luci sat at a table about twenty feet away—this was a *big* suite. Eyes riveted to the screen, she pecked at a computer with her left index finger while she clutched her doll in the right arm. Her feet didn't quite reach the floor. She swung them rhythmically under the chair. A couple of other entourage types sprawled on a sectional, their eyes fixed on the suite's biggest TV.

"Great to see you, too, guys." I nodded at each of them. "Which way is the bathroom?"

"Who the *hell* do you think you are?" Seawright demanded. "You—"

I brushed past her and started looking around the suite for the head. It wasn't hard to find. I wondered whether Wells or Seawright or one of the other two would be the one to follow me. Turned out to be Wells.

There must have been fifteen damned bottles and cans of men's toiletries on the counter around the sink and on the shelf above it. Even in a suite-sized bathroom it looked uncomfortably crowded. I probably could have picked out the one I needed, but I didn't know how much time I had. When I played basketball in high school a clock ticked inside my head, sort of a sixth sense about when we were about to timeout on the five-second rule or run out of time to get the ball past half court. I felt it ticking now. I turned to Wells.

"Which one is the powder Luci was using on her doll?"

"Hell if I know, man. I just—"

I grabbed a fistful of his FUBU burnt orange shirt in my left hand and shoved his back against the wall. Didn't quite slam it, but I definitely pushed him harder than I absolutely had to.

"Now listen, you sniveling little shit, we don't have time to screw around. I need it and I need it right fucking *now*, bro."

Wells got that queasy look you see on guys who haven't been in a fight since they were nine when you put a little muscle on them. He managed to nod. I let go of his shirt. He staggered over to the counter, picked up a short, plastic cylinder marked Hotel de Coronado Talcum Powder in cursive on a retro label, and handed it to me. I sprinkled a little on my palm. Looked a lot more like snow than powder to me. A dab on my tongue confirmed it. Nose candy. Cocaine. Not even crystal meth or something halfway original.

Suddenly I figured out my clock. The maid. It wasn't just that she was white, or that after 4:30 is pretty late for maid service. Might have been a little ex-military in her bearing, or maybe just the way she carried herself, like she wasn't making any minimum wage and hoping for tips from generous Anglos to make ends meet. My MP instincts told me that, if cops in a place like Omaha were thinking about executing a high-profile search warrant, they might send someone in under cover first for a little scouting report, just to make sure they wouldn't drill a dry hole and end up with egg on their face. Someone disguised as, say, a maid.

I slammed out of the bathroom. Wells was saying something about, "Look man, I didn't," but I wasn't paying a lot of attention.

Into the kitchenette. Turn the water on full blast in the sink. Steak knife from the drawer. Start hacking and slicing through the plastic maybe a quarter of the way from the top. Nick myself on the left thumb. *Damnation*, you call this piece of shit a *knife*? It couldn't cut hot butter! There, got it. Big, gaping gash almost all the way through the bottle. Pour everything in the bottle down the drain. Seems like it takes forever. Part of the stuff clumps in the sink and I have to push it toward the drain so the cascading water can take it the rest of the way.

Finally the damn thing was empty. I rinsed it out.

"Hey!" one of the entourage sofa spuds yelled. "Could you cut the water, please? Trow's about on!"

I walked away from the sink, leaving the water going full blast. Not out of the woods yet. Not by a long shot.

I headed for Seawright. The eyes she showed me when I got within six feet stopped me cold. She was *scared* of me. Flat out terrified. She hadn't seen me rough Wells up, so that wasn't it. Some chick-instinct was telling her, before I'd raised a finger, that I was major bad news. *Dial it back, buddy. Just turn it down a couple of clicks.*

I stopped and took a deep breath. Don't think about that ticking clock. Just like a jump shot when you're one point down with four seconds left. All the time in the world. Square up. Get the wrist right. Eyes on the basket. Bend the knees. All the time in the world.

"Excuse me. Jennifer, right?"

"People call me Jenny." Her voice was a little shaky, but at least she'd answered with words instead of a primal scream.

"Okay, Jenny, there's something I need you to do. Take Luci back to her mom's room and help her give her doll a nice bath."

"*What?*"

"Just in the sink. You know. Little sponge bath."

She took a couple of steps toward me—good sign—and stared at me like I'd just started babbling about the president's birth certificate.

"Why?"

"Well, Jenny," I said, lowering my voice to a whisper so that she had to lean forward to hear me, "between you and me, we're about to have company—and right now that doll has the most expensive plastic ass east of Cher."

I showed her the hacked up plastic bottle. Then I put the pieces in my left trouser pocket. She got it. After a quick nod she walked over to Luci, squatted, and started cooing at her in a soothing voice that would have charmed a pit bull.

I tensed again as I approached the suite door, thinking that I'd open it to a squad of Omaha's finest. A look through the peephole showed me nothing but an empty corridor. *Hmm.* I opened the door. Empty corridor all right. Was my internal clock going paranoid on me? Flipping the manual lock-bar out so that the door couldn't close all the way, I walked out into the corridor. Strolled all the way to the other side of the elevators, trying to spot the surveillance cameras. Had to be some, but I couldn't find them. Concerning. My plan was to drop the remains of the bottle onto a room service tray set out in the corridor for pick-up. That wouldn't accomplish much if a hotel camera recorded me doing it.

Down the intersecting corridor on the other side of the elevators, to my left, I spotted a sign saying SODA ICE. That at least provided halfway decent cover for my walk. I stepped into the room, noisy with the hum of the ice machine. There, just inside the door, stood an answered prayer: a bright green plastic bin saying, "WE RECYCLE! Thank you for helping the Hotel Devo's Green Initiative Project!" God bless your good green soul, Hotel Devo. Fishing the plastic bottle out, I dropped it in the bin.

Back to Trowbridge's suite. Luci and Seawright and, most important, Luci's doll weren't there anymore. Good. The only thing I couldn't figure out was where the cops were. If the "maid" was a scout she had to have spotted the coke. She'd had plenty of time to get word to whoever was waiting with the warrant.

"Whoa, man, Trow is *killing!*" This came from half the guys on the couch.

I walked all the way to the back of the suite. Pushed a heavy, glass sliding door to my right and walked out onto the balcony. Worked my way around a metal table painted with green enamel. Across the street I saw a white Ford Crown Victoria. Eight to one that was an unmarked cop car. *What are they waiting for?*

"Go, Trow, go! Go, Trow, go!" erupted from inside the suite.

It hit me: *that's* what they were waiting for. Trowbridge. They wanted to make the bust after he got back, turn it into a media stunt that might come in handy at budget time.

I turned my back to the street. Clenched both fists. Looked up at the overhanging eave. It was high, but it looked like I could just about reach it. I lifted both arms, casual as you please, with a clenched fist at the end of each. *Don't ham it up.* My hands reached just over the lip of the gutter. I rested them there for just a second, opening both fists. Then I brought my arms down, glanced furtively over my shoulder, and went back into the suite.

The raps on the door came in less than four minutes. "Open up! Police!"

Wells got to the door first. I was in no hurry, and the two guys on the couch were busy not soiling their pants. A bullet-headed man in a tan sport coat led the way into the room. He looked like he was about five years from retirement. While he was flashing a piece of paper at Wells, the cop who'd posed as a maid streaked in behind him. She ran full tilt for the balcony, where people sitting in the unmarked car had to have seen me reaching for the gutter. As she reached me, though, she paused long enough to stick a finger in my face.

"You stay right there! Don't move an inch!"

I nodded, folding my arms across my chest. She probably didn't see the nod. She was already back on course for the balcony at flank speed. The second she got there she pulled the table closer to the doors and then scrambled up on top of it so fearlessly that I was afraid she might fall and break her muscular neck. She was pretty agile for a farmer's-daughter type, though, and before I knew it her head was out of sight as she presumably scanned the roof and the inside of the gutter, searching diligently for the contraband she thought I'd stashed there.

I swiveled my head to see what her colleague was up to. I caught a glimpse of him disappearing into the bathroom. I figured I had maybe six minutes between me and two cops in a bad mood.

More like three, as it turned out. The female cop came back in almost immediately and went to join her buddy in the head. That shortened things up. She knew what she'd found the coke in, and it didn't take her long to figure out that it wasn't there anymore. They came out together and converged on me.

"All right," bullet head said. "Are you going to tell us where it is, or do we have to tear the place apart?"

"Do you have a warrant saying what 'it' is, detective?"

"You bet your ass I've got a warrant." He showed it to me. It said something about up to three grams of cocaine, followed by what I assume is the chemical name for the stuff.

"Detective, I don't think there's anything like that in this suite."

"Well what happened to it, then?"

Red faced and squinty eyed, he yelled the question at me. He'd had pizza with green peppers and onions for lunch. I felt a belly drop. Icy little gut-chill. Fifty-fifty I was about to catch a cop-punch—and there's nothing you can do with those but take them.

"Detective, I'm trying to be helpful. All I can honestly tell you is that, no matter what you do, you're not going to find any cocaine in this suite because there isn't any here to find. The bald guy who gave you the tip was kidding you."

He started to snap a crack back at me. Then he paused for a second.

"Whaddya know about any bald guy?"

"I know he's about five-ten to five-eleven, weighs in at one-seventy or so, dark eyes, olive complexion. That's about it. But I plan to know a lot more before sundown tomorrow. Can I show you some ID?"

He turned that one over in his mind a couple of times. Then he backed up a step and gave me a three-inch nod. Maybe only two inches.

I broke out the military ID (inactive) and the Trans/Oxana card. The first was just for luck and he barely glanced at it, but he studied the T/O card like it was a winning lottery ticket. Then he looked back up at me.

"What's a 'Loss Prevention Specialist'?"

"Someone who keeps shady customers from planting cocaine in hotel suites."

"How did you stop him?"

"Guess I scared him off."

"You're what they call a scary guy back east, huh?"

I choked back a smart-ass comeback. Took a deep breath.

"Detective, we're on the same side. The bald guy just hit the top of my shit list, and I'm guessing he's pretty close to the top of yours now too. Let's be friends."

I was ready for anything from a left jab to a hug, but I wasn't ready for what I got. He started laughing. Just threw his head back and roared, like I'd told the knee-slapper of all time. He had a bit of a paunch, and it shook a little. I actually saw a couple of tears running down his cheeks. He turned to his colleague.

"He destroys evidence. He fakes us into jumping the gun on a search. And now he's going for Citizen of the Year. Can you beat that?" He shook his head as the laughter subsided. His voice suddenly ratcheted all the way down from semimanic to fairly normal. "Give him your card so we can blow this two-bit pop-stand."

The female cop and I traded business cards. The two of them did half-hearted ID checks of everyone else on their way out. At the door he paused and looked back at me.

"You have our number." I nodded. "And we have yours."

As soon as the door closed, the two sofa spuds started jabbering intensely at each other. *He wasn't getting NOTHIN' from me, man! Goddamn right! Goddamn cops! I wish he HAD come after me! Damn straight, man.* I looked at my watch. 5:34. More than enough time.

I found the ice bucket—classy thing; real wood on the outside, real plastic on the inside—and walked over to Wells.

"Let's get some ice."

# Chapter Thirteen

Wells turned roughly the shade of the plastic in the ice bucket. He looked like he was about to say something that would start with, "Hey, man." I wasn't in the mood for it.

"I can talk with you or I can talk with Levitt. Your call."

After thinking it over for two seconds or so he gave me a dejected nod and slouched toward the door. We made the trip in silence. He started to say something as we stepped inside the ICE SODA room. I waved my hand to shut him up.

"This isn't a dialogue." I put the bucket under the ice maker and pushed the handle, producing a rumble and a clatter and a lot more than a bucketful of ice. "I talk, you listen. Clear?"

He nodded.

"Don't know how the bald guy got to you. Don't care. Point is, I know he did. So I've now officially got your balls in my hip pocket. If I tell Levitt he'll believe me, and even if he doesn't he'll can you just to be on the safe side. You'll be lucky to get a job selling shoes in Oxnard."

I paused. He was looking down, licking his lips, flicking the bristles on his moustache with the tip of his tongue.

"But I'm not going to tell Levitt. You know why? Because having your balls in my hip pocket means I can use you. Here's the way I'm going to use you. You're going to stay on the tour. At some point between now and when the tour ends, the bald guy figures to come back to you. Now pay attention to this part. When that happens, play along. But you tell me. *Capice, paisan?*"

He looked up and managed to make eye contact with me. He nodded—the world-weary, nothing-more-to-lose nod of a defeated man.

"That's good, bro." I clapped him on the shoulder in a friendly kind of way. "That's real good. We're gonna get along just fine."

It's not that I particularly enjoy this kind of thing. Proxy says that perfect loss prevention means you never raise your voice, and I guess she's right. But two tours in combat zones will hard-wire something into you: *Nothing matters but the mission.* You can argue with that all you want to—but good luck getting rid of it.

Back in the suite we found Trowbridge. He'd returned a little early and was basking in the glow of his triumph. Luci had perched herself again in front of the computer. She held the doll in her lap this time, because the hand she wasn't using to peck at the keyboard was holding a phone to her ear. As far as I could tell, everyone in the traveling party was in the room now, most of them milling around Trowbridge and telling him what a great job he'd done. Everyone except one.

"Where's Katrina?"

"Freshening up." Seawright answered my question. "She said she'd pop back here in a few minutes."

*What's wrong with this picture?* I couldn't put my finger on it. I noticed Trowbridge looking at me.

"Understand we had some excitement while I was gone."

"Jumpy cops." I shrugged. "Hoping for six seconds of screen time."

Luci put the phone down and attacked the keyboard with both hands.

"Jenny was just about to take orders for room service. What are you up for? Bacon cheeseburger, I'm guessing."

"Yeah, except hold the bacon and the cheese. Fries would be good."

Seawright spoke this softly into a PDA. Meanwhile, Luci scooted out of her chair, trotted over to the credenza next to the television, picked up a green Crayola, tore a sheet of paper from a spiral notebook, and scurried back to her chair.

"Carrie is going to be happy," Trowbridge told me.

"Your costar?"

"Yep. They're going to put her chick-fight back in to punch up the numbers on the next test-screening."

"Mud wrestling in her underwear?"

"Yep. Gotta admit she looked good in that scene. Can't blame her for being pissed about the first cut."

Knock at the door. Wells jumped to answer it. Thompson came in. Thank you, God. I hadn't realized how much I'd been sweating it.

Trowbridge bolted for her but Luci beat him, yelling, "Mommy, mommy, mommy!" Trowbridge managed to give Thompson a worldclass hug, but he had to compete with Luci, who jumped into her mother's arms, squealing with delight.

"You were *wonderful*," she told Trowbridge after she'd rubbed noses with her little girl.

"So I've heard. What do you want Jenny to get for you and Luci when she calls down for room service?"

"Actually, I've been thinking about that very thing. Luci, you've been in this hotel room for hours, and you've been eating room service all week. How would you like to go out, just you and mommy, for some McDonald's or KFC?"

"And Annabelle?" Luci asked.

"Of course, and Annabelle."

"Yayyyy!"

Thompson swiveled her head back toward Trowbridge.

"That's okay, isn't it? She needs some fresh air, and I need some time with my girl. We'll only be forty-five minutes or so."

"Sure. Of course it's okay. You two have a great time."

Exit Thompson and Luci. This was the first time I'd seen Luci really excited. I didn't blame her. I would have *loved* to have gotten out of this gilded hothouse for a thick, juicy steak someplace where the locals ate, even if I'd had to blow my whole *per diem* on it. But the Asset was here and I didn't know where the bald guy was, so that meant I was here too.

The Hotel Devo probably set some kind of record by getting the most complicated room service order I've ever heard of up to us in less than half-an-hour. I was grateful for the effort because it was after seven-thirty on my east-coast biological clock and I felt hungrier than a nun in Lent. No doubt we got the quick service because His Royal Highness Kent Trowbridge made us a priority.

While we chowed down we watched a TiVo of the interview. I'm no judge of this kind of thing, but he looked plenty good to me. Everyone *oohed* and *ahhed* through the thing—everyone except Trowbridge himself. He focused intently on the screen, occasionally giving his head a slight shake. When it was over he looked up. He didn't have to snap his fingers. Seawright and Wells hopped over to him.

"This guy gets a fruit basket or something, right, Jen?"

"Yes. Premiere collection."

"Good. He did a nice job with me. Jeff, make a note. Need to get a sunshine yellow dress shirt exactly like the one I wore today— except no button-down tabs. Have them pick it up at Calvin's and Fed Ex it to whatever hotel we're going to be in tomorrow."

"Got it." Wells thumbed something into a palm-sized something-or-other.

"The button-down makes me look like a high school English teacher."

"Got it."

"Where's the script Levitt is going to have kittens if I don't look at?"

"In your bedroom. On the shelf right underneath the TV. "

"All right." Trowbridge stood up, half of his order still on his plate. "Hermit time. Tell me as soon as Katrina gets back. Anyone else, you don't know where I am and you can't reach me."

"Got it."

The suite had two bedrooms. When the door to the larger one closed behind Trowbridge, the answer to *What's-wrong-with-*

*this-picture?* popped into my head. No toys. As in 36-24-32 toys. Trowbridge hadn't brought the Doublemint Twins, and he hadn't had anyone pick up any local talent for him.

*"Tell me as soon as Katrina gets back."* More than an hour had gone by since mother and daughter had left on what was supposedly a forty-five-minute jaunt. Chicks, as a class, can be real flexible about time, but this was right on the edge of worrisome. I dialed Thompson's mobile phone number, got voice mail, and didn't bother leaving a message. Instead I looked around for Wells, so that I could get the second key to Thompson's room that I knew he had.

He was two moves ahead of me. He was already heading out the door when I spotted him. My first impulse was to go along with him, but then I remembered what I had in my hip pocket. He made it back in a little over three minutes. One look at his face and I knew we had a Problem. I hustled over to him.

"What is it?"

"Gone. Suitcase is gone, closet and drawers are empty. And I found this."

He held up a cream-colored, letter-sized envelope with **HOTEL DEVO** imprinted in the upper left-hand corner. "Kent" was handwritten in a girlish scrawl in the center. It was sealed and there was something inside. Seawright bounded over. I could tell she'd figured out what the deal was.

"Should I open it?" Wells looked earnestly from me to Seawright.

"Is your name Kent?" I didn't try to hide my sarcasm.

"I've gotta phone Saul," Wells said, shaking his head.

"Phone Saul after you've given Trowbridge the letter."

"Are you crazy?" Seawright asked me in a furious stage-whisper. "We can't just drop a piano on him like this. We have to think things through."

"Think what through?" The question came from across the suite.

We all snapped our heads to see Trowridge standing there.

# Chapter Fourteen

I've gotta hand it to him. Impeccable timing, perfect entrance—
pro moves. He held out his right hand and snapped fingers to
palm twice.

"Gimme."

Wells sheepishly handed over the letter. Taking his time about
it, letting the suspense build, Trowbridge tore one end open. He
took out a sheet of Hotel Devo stationery, folded three times.
After a quick scan, he looked like a guy in a rom-com would
look right after the only woman he'll ever love tells him that
she's already married/in love with someone else/dying from an
incurable disease/lesbian. Then, looking up and closing his eyes,
he favored us with a not-bad impression of Thompson's west
Texas drawl. "'Trow: You have just been *so* wonderful and I will
never forget all you did for me and Luci. We have to go now,
but don't worry. You're gonna do *just* fine, I just *know it*! Good
luck! Love, Hurricane.'"

"Okay, Mr. Trowbridge," Seawright said. "I know you're
upset, but you can't let this throw you off your game. You did
absolutely fantastic today. If you finish up the tour like you've
started it, you'll be killing on opening weekend."

"I don't think it makes a lotta sense to keep talking to Rotar-
ians in third-rate loservilles who haven't bought a movie ticket
in twenty years." Trowbridge collapsed into a white armchair.
"Only three cities left anyway. Screw it."

If Trowbridge just had the hots for Thompson, this was an overreaction. He could have almost any B-list actress in Hollywood and half the A-listers. Had he actually fallen for her? Oh shit. That would explain a lot, starting with everything he'd done from the moment he laid eyes on Thompson and ending with no toys in the suite. Which would mean that Thompson, who was *my* brilliant idea, was about to trigger breach of the MPA contract that Trans/Oxana had insured.

"Okay." I slapped my hands together like a coach in pep talk mode. "Our jail coach took a powder on us. We don't know why, or where she's going, or how she plans to get there. Looks pretty hopeless. Perfect job for Trans/Oxana."

Trowbridge flashed me a genuine grin. Shared the grin slowly with the rest of the room, as if he were milking a bow. Cocked an eyebrow at me.

"This oughta be good. Go."

"You're supposed to be in Denver tomorrow, swing through Santa Fe on Sunday, and then head to Tucson. You keep up your end of the deal, and I'll meet you in Tucson with Thompson Monday morning."

"How are you going to manage that?"

I turned toward one of the sofa spuds.

"When Jeff and I came back into the room after our ice-run this evening, Luci was talking on the phone. Did Thompson call and tell you to put her on?"

"Yeah." He shrugged.

"And then Luci went on the computer, right?"

"She was already on. She spends half her time on the computer."

"What I meant was, she stopped playing *Hello Kitty* or whatever and clicked on the Internet. Am I right?"

"I wasn't really paying all that much attention."

I nodded decisively as if that was exactly the answer I was looking for. Quick stroll over to the computer table. The loose-leaf Luci had scribbled on was still there. In laborious green crayon I read: 1050. The computer had Google running. I checked search history. Amtrak, Hertz, Greyhound. Called up Amtrak. Nothing leaving Omaha at 10:50, p.m. or a.m. Called up Hertz. 1050 didn't appear in the phone number or the address. Called up Greyhound. Bus leaving Omaha for Phoenix at 10:50 tonight.

I looked back up at Trowbridge. I was smiling like a confident bastard who knew exactly what he was doing, instead of like a madly improvising hustler who might be looking for work by Monday.

"It would be helpful if Mr. Wells here would get a list of the calls made from Thompson's room since five o'clock this evening."

"That's all?" This snarky little question came from Seawright

"Not quite. I'll need a rental car down front in about forty-five minutes. Mid-size or larger. Not red. Not a Ford."

# Chapter Fifteen

So that's how I happened to stroll into the Jim Thorpe Café at the Omaha Greyhound Bus Depot shortly after eight o'clock that evening. In addition to Greyhound's 10:50 run for Phoenix—and you don't have to be Sherlock Holmes to connect *those* dots—there was this: at 5:48, Thompson had called a number with Simi Valley's area code. She had spoken for seven minutes, which is longer than you can talk to a voice mail recorder. I hadn't fit the call neatly into my Thompson-making-a-run-for-it theory, but I'm guessing she wasn't calling about a dental appointment.

I figured Thompson would get to the bus depot nine-ish. After supper, she and Luci would kill as much time as they could in a downtown mall or department store, because no one wants to sit in a bus depot any longer than they have to. As closing time approached they'd look for a cab to the depot. I got there way before then so that when they arrived I could approach them with my customary finesse.

The Jim Thorpe Café didn't really have a door. More of an arching entryway separating a darkened area where you could eat and drink from the garish fluorescence of the depot waiting room where you couldn't eat but could *really* drink. I mean, there were three guys on the waiting room benches who didn't even bother with brown paper bags. Just chugged Wild Turkey or Thunderbird straight from the bottle, then pulled the rotgut back down until it was time for the next hit.

Before going in, I scoped out an empty table in the right front corner. By then I was close enough to hear bells and bongs and other arcade music coming from the alcove where they'd stashed Pac Man and its cousins. From that table I'd be able to see the depot entrance, the ticket counter, and most of the waiting room. I sauntered in, priming myself for a sixty minute-plus wait.

"Tall Dude!" Luci's voice from maybe twenty feet away. "That's Tall Dude!"

I'd thought this through very carefully. Wrongly, but carefully.

I glanced in the direction of the voice. Thompson and Luci each sat behind a can of Dr. Pepper. Sitting next to Thompson I saw the bald guy. He had a cup of coffee. And next to Luci sat a black dude. Thin, wiry, maybe five-ten/one-sixty-five, looking like he could dance with Alvin Ailey or bulk up a little and play linebacker for a Division II school. The bald guy stood up, waving his arm at me and grinning like he was running for president of the Kiwanis Club and needed my vote.

"Are you Davidovich? Katrina's friend? Come here, Davidovich!"

He scrounged a chair from another table and put it in place for me as I ambled over. I was about to say that I couldn't place the guy's accent, but he didn't really have an accent. Maybe a little hint of a deep-south drawl in there, without any western twang to it like Thompson had. But only a hint. No northeast stuff at all, no melodic Spanish or Italian lilt to the syllables.

"I am Stan Chaladian." He held out his hand, I took it, and he pumped mine vigorously. "Katrina and Luci of course you know. That is Marcus Plankinton."

I shook hands with the black guy and started to murmur my name.

"Jay Davidovich, I know," he said. "Katrina here has been telling us about how you walk on water."

*Katrina talks too much.* I sat down. So did Chaladian. Plankinton had never gotten up. Chaladian nudged Thompson with his elbow.

"Tell him."

"Well it's just the most *incredible* piece of luck." She gave me a Crest-commercial smile. "Stan has a reality TV show in development about the Simi Valley scene. Now Stan and myself go way back, you understand. *Way* back. And when he happened to see me in the background of one of the stories about the tour, he actually *remembered* me. Doesn't that just beat anything you ever heard? He thinks I'd be perfect. Because of Luci and everything."

"That's fantastic, Hurricane. I'm thrilled for you." The next Snooki.

"You can't believe what a shot this is for Katrina." Stan sounded like he was trying to sell me stock in the thing. "TruTV. Okay, it's not HBO. I know this. But you have to walk before you can run."

"I feel bad about running out on Trow like this." Thompson was trying out a don't-be-mad-at-me look, which wasn't working. "But you know, I think he's gotten about everything I could give him along the lines of what you were worried about. It's mostly just common sense and attitude, you know?"

It seemed to me that Trowbridge was still about six bricks shy of a hod in both areas, but why say so? I wasn't buying a word of this. Thompson couldn't act. Or at least if she could, she wasn't doing much of a job of it right now. Chaladian had spotted her and Luci leaving the hotel and intercepted them. That much was crystal clear. Chaladian was studying me like the Torah the day before his bar mitzvah. I figured he wanted to know how much of this bullshit I was swallowing. Naturally, I tried to look like he had me hook, line, and sinker. And you know what? With just a little more luck, I might have brought it off.

Chaladian's eyes had shot warily toward Luci while Thompson was dancing nimbly around the Trowbirdge situation. Now they lit up as he reached into his pocket. He peeled a five from the bottom of a wad and reached behind Thompson and Luci to hand it to Plankinton.

"Marco, do me a favor. Huge favor. Take the little one here over to the games and let her play whatever she wants to for awhile."

"You got it, Mr. Ten." Plankinton apparently noticed my blank look. "Folks call him that sometimes. Mr. Ten Percent. Come on, darlin'. Let's go chew some dots or whatever."

Luci looked questioningly at Thompson, who gave her a nod and an indulgent smile. Clutching the doll under her right arm, Luci took one more sip of Dr. Pepper, then slipped to the floor and took Plankinton's hand so that he could lead her to the arcade. As soon as they were out of earshot, Chaladian locked eyeballs with me.

"This Trowbridge deal. Katrina hasn't told me a thing, you understand. Not one word. But I know what the Trowbridge deal is. Everyone knows."

"Arrests are public record."

"In some countries." Chaladian grinned at himself. "But let's talk business."

"Okay." I shrugged. Mr. Cool, that's me.

"What if the whole problem goes away?"

"Depends on how it goes away."

"It just goes away. You don't know how. Who cares how?"

"Well." This sounded a lot like what Proxy and I had heard Korvette pitch to the lawyers. "I have a limited imagination. But you seem to be enjoying yourself, and I don't want to spoil the party. So just to be a good sport, I'm supposing."

"I like this Davidovich!" Chaladian thumped the table and shared a megawatt beam with Thompson before turning back to me. "You heard what Marcus called me. 'Mr. Ten Percent.'"

"I picked that up."

"So. Ten percent of thirty-six-million is three million six hundred thousand."

"Can't argue with that."

"So. What do you think?"

*I think I'm right on the edge of being in very deep shit, that's what I think.* If Chaladian's idea was to run off with Thompson and Luci, why was he still tamely sitting here with them when I finally got to the bus station? Don't tell me Chaladian and Marcus planned on hopping any damn Greyhound Bus to Phoenix. Therefore, he'd been waiting for me. Why? To try to sell me this lame pay-me-ten-percent-and-I'll-put-in-the-fix scam? In other words, Thompson was just bait for yours truly? Really? Seriously? Well, I sure hoped so, because I could only come up with one alternative and I didn't like it.

So Job One was to make Chaladian believe he was about to reel me in. And I was bringing it off. I had Chaladian thinking that I might actually try to line him up for a big time payday. Problem was, I also had Thompson fooled. She decided that I was the dumbest Jew in Ukrainian history and I needed a hint.

"Stan, darlin'? Do you have a cigarette?"

"You got it." His right hand disappeared beneath the table top and came back up with a gold cigarette case. "But you'll have to wait until we're outside. If you light it in here some busybody will send you to bed without dinner."

He'd tried to hide his reaction when Thompson asked for the smoke, but he wasn't quite fast enough. I could tell that he knew it was her way of telling me he was bad news. Which meant that I was now officially up to my ears in fertilizer.

"Tell you what," I said, as I scooted my chair back and stood up. "Talking high finance is thirsty work for a ninety-nine per-center like me. Excuse me a sec."

I made my way over to the counter. The matronly black woman behind it—let's just say she was ample. She looked at me with world-weary wariness. I read her name on the tag cheerfully riding her left breast.

"Hi, Rayette." I took some of Trans/Oxana's money out my trouser pocket and put a twenty and a ten on the counter. "How are things goin'?"

"Gotta job, gotta husband, and the rent's paid. So things goin' just peachy. Whachoo want, darlin'?"

"A chocolate malt. And a roll of quarters. Keep the change."

"This place look like a soda shop to you?"

"I was kidding about the malt. Coke is fine. Or Sprite or whatever. But I meant it about the quarters. And about keeping the change."

She gave me a long, long look as she turned toward the cash register. Bottom line, though, "keep the change" meant seven bucks-plus to her and seven bucks is seven bucks. I stuffed the tightly-rolled sleeve of quarters she gave me inside the front of my shirt, grabbed the can of Coke Classic that she slapped on the counter, and headed back for the table. As I sat down I gave Chaladian a tight little smile that was supposed to combine crafty with credulous, like a rube being offered a gold watch for ten bucks and getting set to bargain.

"Okay." I licked my lips, took a good, long slug of Coke, and wished it was Vodka. "Two things. One. No one gets killed, no one gets threatened, no violence, and no blackmail. Those are off the table."

"Understood."

"Two." More Coke. "Anything close to seven figures is above my paygrade. I need to take this up the ladder. How do I reach you?"

"You don't. I reach you. How long will you need."

"Say a week." I started to reach for one of the business cards in my pocket.

"Skip it. Trust me—I will reach you."

I tried some more Coke. I glanced at Thompson. She looked a little like the Chevy had just parked by the river bank and she'd forgotten to take her pill that morning.

"So what's the plan?" I asked her instead. "Back to Simi Valley while the development deal shapes up?"

"Oh, we have *tons* of work to do. All I have to do is look pretty and be myself, but Stan will be workin' like a PFC on KP."

"Katrina got that right." Chaladian switched from smiling to earnest. "People think everyone in the entertainment business gets super overpaid, but in development we earn every penny."

"Well, Hurricane, unless Stan buys a policy from Trans/Oxana, I guess this is goodbye, huh?" I drained the Coke.

"I hope not. You've just been *wonderful*."

"Well, maybe I'll see you on down the road. Tell you what, though. I don't want you to leave before I have a chance to tell

Luci adios, so don't run off. I'll hit the head and blow by you one more time before I go back to Trowbridge country."

"You got it."

I got up, stretched across the table to give her a hug, then hustled toward the men's room. And I mean hustled. I figured I had about sixty seconds.

On the wall just inside the men's room door, I found exactly what I expected: a vending machine stocked with one-packs of condoms. They were cheap suckers, so I bought two, just for luck. Opened the first one. Unfolded it. Cracked the roll of quarters out on the edge of the sink counter. Fit the condom's mouth over the break and pushed quarters into the thing as fast as I could.

I heard the men's room door squeaking as it opened. No time to double-bag the two-bit pieces, no time to tie a knot in the condom I'd filled. I just pulled the open end back as far as the elastic would go and wrapped my right paw around the empty part as tightly as I could. Soft-soled shoes made the tiniest little pop as they shuffled on the tile floor. I dropped my right hand down beside my thigh. Marcus Plankinton came the rest of the way into the men's room.

"Everything come out all right?"

"No complaints."

"That's good. That's real good."

So much for foreplay. He pivoted cat like on the ball of his left foot. Next thing I knew his right foot was spinning toward my head in a bent-knee windmill kick that started somewhere behind his rear end and arced upward at blistering speed. If I were six-two instead of six-four he would have nailed me. Ditto if he'd gone for my ribs instead of trying to knock my block off. As it was, he had to come all the way off his left foot reaching for elevation. The extra couple of inches took just enough time to save my life.

I choked off an almost irresistible urge to flinch backward. Instead I lunged forward, snapping my left forearm up to catch his ankle. I barely got it, and I thought I'd broken my damn arm for my trouble. I didn't block it so much as slow it down and push it up and out just a smidge. The heel of his shoe smashed my left shoulder on the down-stroke and sent searing pain lancing diagonally through my torso until it reached my right hip. But pain I can handle. It's death that's a bitch.

For a fraction of a second Plankinton was off balance and in mid-air. Swinging my right arm back I sidearmed forward with the loaded funbag. I caught him on the inside of the right knee, exactly where I wanted to.

He landed on his left foot, then almost fell when his right foot hit the floor and his right leg nearly collapsed under him. I snaked a left jab at his face. He crossed his arms to parry my punch, slamming the underside of my wrist. Hurt like a bastard, but it gave me the opening I needed. My right arm had the condom right about six o'clock at that point. I swung it clockwise back behind me, up, over, and down until it hit the top of Plankinton's head at exactly two o'clock.

I heard quarters clanging all over tiles. The condom burst like it had been designed by an abortionist. Blood oozing from his head, Plankinton dropped to the floor. He didn't scream, but that was because he was taking a nap.

Naturally, one of the winos would pick that moment to come in. He was a gray-skinned Caucasian, with the ancient, vacant look that ex-prize fighters sometimes have, his face littered by silver whiskers that were a little more than stubble but not quite a beard. His mouth gaped. His eyes opened wide.

"Sweet Jesus!" he whispered.

He dropped to the floor and began scooping up quarters. I stepped around him to reach the door. I told Rayette she'd better call an ambulance because a guy had fallen in the men's room and hurt himself pretty bad. That wasn't mitzvah. That was tactics.

# Chapter Sixteen

When you've just cold-cocked a guy and cops might be there soon, you don't want people telling them that someone who looked like you was in a hurry. So I wasn't exactly running when I left the depot. But I wasn't wasting any time, either. If Chaladian drove off with Thompson and Luci before I could at least get a license number, I figured to be short one jail coach in Tucson Monday morning.

Thank God for Luci. She had apparently gotten drowsy enough for Thompson to pick her up and carry her, slowing things down just enough. When I got outside I could just see the tops of their heads on the far side of a wedding gown white Lincoln Navigator across the street. Chaladian had the rear passenger door open. Thompso's and Luci's heads disappeared as I imagined Thompson laying Luci on the back seat.

"Stan!" It was almost dark now, but I could see unpleasant surprise in Chaladian's face as his head jerked toward my voice. "It's Marcus! He's hurt!"

Chaladian hesitated for barely a second. I was busy snaking across the street without getting run over, so I didn't make out what he barked at Thompson. The tone, though, sounded like the one Sergeant Rutledge used with me. Then he sprinted toward the depot. I heard his yell as he was about to pass me.

"Where?"

"Men's room!"

I panted up onto the sidewalk. Might as well start with the obvious.

"We can't count on cops showing up any time soon. If you want out, we're in your basic now or never situation."

"Tall Dude, you don't know what you're gettin' into." I'd never seen Thompson scared before, but the look in her eyes right now was can't-make-my-legs-move terrified.

"I just dealt with the B-team at close quarters, so I've got a pretty good idea."

She suddenly brought her hands up as her mouth opened and her face looked like she was about to scream—but no sound came out.

An instant later I felt pain like I've never felt before in my life. Something hard and sharp—turned out to be Chaladian's elbow—smashed the middle of my back. Every atom of breath exploded from my lungs. Needles of agony radiated toward my shoulders and my gut. I felt bile rising in my throat. I started to turn around, but before I'd made much progress I'd gotten a left-right combination in the kidneys. Chaladian's fists felt like concrete.

I'd taken his fake. Totally taken it. Actually thought he was racing back to the depot to see about good old "Marco." Hadn't dreamed that he'd double back as soon as I was on the sidewalk side of the Navigator and ambush me. What a schmuck.

I danced away a couple of steps and completed my turn. I figured he'd go for my ribs and he did, so I got my forearms down there and he hit them instead. Which wasn't any picnic, but beat having my lungs fill up with blood.

Then came the one and only punch I contributed to this little fracas. I'd call it a first-rate effort. A jab, but a good one. My right fist moved about six inches and got the bastard right in the teeth. I've put guys to sleep with that punch.

Chaladian barely blinked. His head snapped back, but he didn't retreat. No fear in his eyes. While he contemptuously spat blood from his mouth, he waded right into me. He shot a left at my throat. I moved to block the punch and that left me wide open for his right fist. He caught me right below the heart with it.

I stumbled backwards two steps. He put his left into my gut and when I bent over he planted a worldclass uppercut on my jaw. I catapaulted backward and smacked the pavement with my head, shoulders, and hips in that order.

It was pretty much luck that Chaladian's ankle caught my knee as he sprang forward to pounce on me. That sent him sprawling and cussing to the sidewalk a few feet away from me. The five seconds or so that that bought me struck me as pretty academic. The few muscles that I managed to move during the respite did nothing to keep Chaladian from scrambling up, planting his left knee in my diaphragm, and cocking his right fist for the kill shot. I knew he'd be going for my throat, and right offhand I couldn't think of anything to do about it.

The gunshot took me even more by surprise than the dull explosion that followed it. They seemed to have the same effect on Chaladian, who put the kill shot on hold while he jerked his head around to look at Thompson—or, more likely, at the muscular automatic she was holding. Her voice had that oddly calm, slightly distracted quality you sometimes hear from people who are in clinical shock.

"Now, Stan, you know I can shoot this cheap-ass Russian gun you keep in your glove compartment, 'cause I just put a nine-millimeter hole in your tire. You need to stay down there on the sidewalk, but get off the big guy so he can stand up. Just do it, now."

It took him about three seconds to decide which way to go, but he ended up playing it safe. The pressure came off my diaphragm, and Chaladian slid very carefully on his knees to a point about three feet away from me. About then I heard a siren wailing. I figured that if Omaha sirens sounded like sirens back east, it was an ambulance rather than a police car. I wasn't sure how I felt about that.

"Now, Tall Dude, can you get up?"

"Gimme a minute and we'll both know."

The upper half of my body screamed in protest as I dragged myself to my feet. I made it, though. Not by any large majority, but I made it. Out of the corner of my eye I spotted an ambulance screeching to a stop in front of the bus depot.

Thompson was licking her lips. I could tell that it wasn't the first time she'd ever held a pistol, but she seemed to me to be right on the verge of going shaky. Couldn't blame her for that. Her voice quavered when she spoke.

"Okay. Now I'm not real sure how we're going to handle this, but we need to get some real estate in between Stan and the rest of us."

"Can I make a suggestion?" I asked this question standing right where I was, because I thought the next thing that moved might get shot.

"What's on your mind?"

"Why don't I walk over there so you can hand that toy cannon to me?"

"Sounds okay, I guess."

I pressed against the side of the Navigator to make sure she'd have a clear shot at Chaladian in case he changed his mind. Then I circled around behind her so I could take the gun with my left hand without having to reach across her body. I looked straight at Chaladian while I did it. I made sure he understood how happy it would make me to drill him. If he thought about trying something while I got my paw wrapped around the automatic, he came down on the side of staying alive. The pistol felt comfortable in my left hand.

"There's a set of car keys in my right pants pocket. Why don't you fish it out?"

It seemed to take her forever, but she finally got it done.

"They're for a rental car, so there's a tag on the ring with the make, model, and license number. Do you see that?"

"This ain't my first time at the swimmin' hole, buddy. You don't have to talk to me like I'm ten years old."

"Sorry. Now I have a job for you, Stan. Using fingers only, no thumb, pull the fob for these fancy wheels out of your jeans and toss it over to Katrina here."

"What if I don't?"

"Well, Stan, put yourself in my position. We've just established that you can beat the crap out of me in a fair fight, and I can't outrun you if I have a woman and a little girl along with me. So what options would I have at that point?"

"Have you ever killed anyone, Mr. Judas Maccabeus Davidovich?"

Looking down the barrel of his own gun, he said "Judas" with lip-curling contempt. I involuntarily winced. But Dr. Phil wasn't in the neighborhood, so I figured I'd have to handle the psychological trauma all by myself.

"I did tours in Iraq and Afghanistan, and I killed more of them than they did of me. And one time I shot a fella in the knee to discourage him from coming after me. It worked real well."

Chaladian smiled at me. I kid you not, the sonofabitch actually smiled at me. Then he dipped the fingers of his left hand into his pants pocket. I kept my eyes peeled for a derringer or one of those mini twenty-five-caliber jobs that they call "ladies' guns," but what he came out with was a fob. He tossed it at me instead of Thompson. I took a side-step to my left and let the fob fall on the sidewalk. Just as it hit, the siren cranked up across the street and the ambulance sped away. I stayed focused on Chaladian, though. He didn't move a muscle.

Thompson picked up the fob. She dropped it into the palm of my right hand. I worked it a couple of times to be sure I knew which button locked the doors. Then I let out a deep breath that I didn't realize I'd been holding.

"Now, Hurricane, get Luci up. You'll find the rental car if you walk carefully around this block. Get Luci in the car, U-turn, straight for two blocks, take a right, park, wait for me. Give me five minutes. If I'm not there, go to the police. Got it?"

"Uee plus two, ralph, park, wait five. Can do."

Luci was wide awake by now, of course. I had no idea how much she'd seen, but I switched the gun to my right hand so I could hide it from Luci with my body while Thompson walked off with her.

Thompson retrieved Luci from the street side. Then, cool as a Miles Davis riff again, she took her own sweet time getting her luggage out. She and Luci were four steps down the sidewalk when Luci realized that he'd forgotten her doll. So back they came while Jay Davidovich stood there in the gloaming working really hard at not shooting Chaladian, at least while Luci was there to see it. If Chaladian was sweating over that possibility, I couldn't see it in the glow of the one Omaha street light in the vicinity.

Once Thompson and Luci were finally under way, I counted to ten to give them some time to make tracks. The idea of just putting a bullet in Chaladian's knee at that point did more than cross my mind. It stopped right in the middle of my brain and did an impatient little dance to make sure it had my attention. Thing is, though, if I plugged him he'd be talking to cops soon, whether he wanted to or not. Which meant that, well before midnight, Kent Trowbridge would be sitting in a squeal room at Omaha police headquarters doing Q and A about how someone in his entourage had shot the guy who'd fingered him for coke possession. And *that* meant you could just put his Major Performing Artist contract in the shredder. Loss prevention specialists are supposed to prevent losses, not cause them.

So it seemed crystal clear I had to go another route. I did, resuming my dialogue with Chaladian.

"What you want to do now, buddy, is get into your truck. Back seat."

Chaladian favored me with a five-second wait, just to show that he was the one in charge even though I was holding the gun. Then he slowly rose. Keeping his eyes on me, he sidled over to the Navigator and climbed into the back seat. I then used the fob to lock the doors and roll down the back window.

"If you wait ten minutes before you unlock the door and get out, you'll find the fob and your unloaded gun five paces down from the corner of the street behind us. Less than ten minutes, and you can kiss them both goodbye."

With a thumb click I rolled the window up. I backed away until I reached the corner. I waited sixty seconds to see if Chaladian would jump the gun. He didn't. I took five paces down the intersecting sidewalk and dropped the fob on the sidewalk. Then I ran like an Alabama virgin with her uncle behind her.

Thompson had found the Dodge Charger that Wells had gotten for me and done exactly what I'd told her to with it. When I slid into the passenger seat I still had the gun. I lied about that.

# Chapter Seventeen

"Thanks for gettin' my fanny outta that mess." Thompson took the Charger from zero to forty in about five seconds. "But no flat tire is gonna hold Stan Chaladian up for long, so we need a plan in a big hurry."

"Step one: slow down to the speed limit. Getting pulled over with an unauthorized driver behind the wheel would slow us up considerably."

"Well, that's a start."

"Step two: turn left on the first street you come to that has a traffic light and head back toward downtown."

"No way I'm goin' back to the hotel."

"You got that right."

"What's step three, then?"

"I'm working on that."

I was, too. I did some touch-screen magic on the GPS that came with the Charger, hoping that the damn thing knew the name of Omaha's airport. It did.

"Eppley Airfield," the pert, sultry voice said. I decided to call her Ariane, just for fun. Thompson gaped at me.

"Honey, you think if I could fly two people anywhere you woulda found me at a bus station?"

"I'd say we'd better not plan on you flying anyone out of Omaha tonight. The airport is the first place Chaladian will look for us."

Thompson looked like I'd asked her to help me with a calculus equation.

"Well, Tall Dude, what do they do at the airport except fly people places?"

"They rent cars." I'd found Avis on my phone and was about to punch it in when, on pure impulse, I went with Alamo instead. "We have to assume Chaladian spotted this car. We need to switch vehicles. Then we need to drive."

"Drive? To *Phoenix*?"

"Wouldn't be my choice, since Chaladian knows that that's where you were going. If I were you, I'd call your girlfriend and tell her to meet you in Tucson."

I could tell she was about to pretend she didn't know what I was talking about, but Ariane decided to say something about getting ready to enter the freeway in "two-*tenths* of a mile," and Thompson obediently whisked over to the right lane.

It took me seven solid minutes to talk a counter boy at the Airport Alamo into reserving a Buick for me. That was because, unlike Avis, Alamo didn't have my name and account data in its computer—which meant that even if Chaladian made it to the airport before we did, and even if he got the bright idea of checking rental car alley instead of the terminal, he wouldn't see "DAVIDOVICH AISLE 3" on the Preferred Customer board. I decided not to call Enterprise to tell them about dropping the Charger off at its airport office. I figured I'd just let that be a surprise.

I risked a glance back at Luci. I was hoping she'd be asleep. Not a chance. She just sat there in the back seat, hugging her doll. No trembling lip, no wide eyes. Stoic, as if this kind of stuff went down all the time in her world.

When I looked back at Thompson, I saw her left hand on the wheel and her right hand in her lap, with her thumb moving madly. For a crazy instant I thought she was being insanely self-indulgent, playing with herself at sixty-two miles an hour. Then I realized it was worse: she was texting.

My phone chimed. I glanced at the screen. She was texting *me*.

"Cn u tk L where I say?"

"What about her mom?" I did *not* text this. I just said the words, in a normal tone of voice.

*Chime!*

"Tk my chnces."

If I'd been Rachel I would've burst into tears. As it was my throat tightened a bit. Thompson cared more about Luci than anyone or anything else in the world. And Stan Chaladian, Mr. Ten Percent, was by three orders of magnitude the baddest ass I had ever run into—and that is *saying* something. Yet she was willing to separate herself from Luci so that Luci would be safe even if Chaladian caught Thompson—which it was eight to one he would if she were running on her own.

"I think we can do better than that."

She glanced over at me with her eyebrows arched and her lips in an oh-sure oval, the way you might look at a ten-year-old boy who's just confidently repeated something he heard about sex from the eighth graders.

"Davidovich, it took a lot of guts for you to take Stan on."

"Not really. Taking him on the second time would be guts. This time it was just being dumb enough to let him catch me from behind."

"Point is, you didn't give up. Most guys do with him, when they see that look in his eyes. But guts ain't enough. If Stan is in the game, the odds aren't just in his favor—the fix is in."

I chewed that over for thirty seconds or so.

"I suppose I should say something macho right about now, something about how I've been in tougher scrapes than this and next time I'll see him coming and so forth. But I'll skip all that. You're right. Stan is one tough *hombre*. But I'm already in the soup. Tell you what. Let's just talk this over again once we get to Tucson."

It was Thompson's turn to think things over. She looked like she wasn't sure what to do with a guy who didn't bullshit her. Then her expression got crafty.

"I'll take you up on that, on one condition."

"Name it."

"You said your first name is Jay. But Stan called you 'Judas Maccabeus,' and it rattled you. And it takes somethin' to rattle you. So why don't you tell me what the deal is with that—and make it the truth."

*Oh-KAY.* That was your basic gut punch.

"My parents are rack-jobbers. You know what that is?"

"No idea."

"You know how when you're in a supermarket you sometimes see a metal tree with plastic bags of junk toys on it, like plastic soldiers and mini-rolling pins and jacks and so forth?"

"I guess. Still see those every once in awhile."

"Well, the metal trees are called racks, and the people who buy the junk and put it on them are rack jobbers. Rack-jobbing is the stirring-stuff-in-a-vat equivalent of distribution work in the United States."

"But mom and pop do this because—why?"

"Because rack jobbers own their own business. They aren't wage slaves. Which is very important to mom and dad."

"You're sneakin' up on Judas Maccabeus, aren't you?"

"Yes. When you own your own business, once every two or three years you owe money you can't pay. If you're a PEP Boys or a McDonald's you go to your bank for an emergency loan. If you're AIG, you go to Congress for a bail-out. But if you're mom and dad you go to Uncle Morty for a *mitzvah.*"

"That's like a Jewish good deed, right?"

"Close enough. Anyway, three months before I was born, Uncle Morty's *mitzvah* came with a string attached. Namely, that I would be named after a Jewish hero. The hero he had in mind was Judas Maccabeus."

"Oh." Thompson stared through the windshield. "Is that the Judas who betrayed our Lord and Savior, Jesus Christ?"

"No. Different fella altogether. Couldn't get along with the Greeks, who were running Judea about that time."

"Well, I can see that. 'Cause the Greeks I'm guessin' weren't Christians yet."

"No. No one was yet. Thing was though, lots of Jews back then got along just fine with the Greeks. Forgot to have their kids circumcised, for example. So JM and his posse, when they saw some Jewish men in their early twenties who were wearing Greek clothes and speaking Greek, they'd check to see if they were circumcised. Just sort of do a little street-inspection."

"In front of *everyone*?"

"Pretty much."

"*Oh my Lord!*"

"And if they weren't, JM would take care of it right then and there."

"*Ouch!* It hurts just to think about that! So that's how he got to be a hero?"

"Well, the main way he got to be a hero is that the Greeks eventually got around to sending an army against him and he kicked their butts. So the Greeks decided that maybe they should go back to Greece and get their butts kicked by the Romans, closer to home."

She took her eyes completely off the road and turned her head to give me a full, mouth-open stare.

"You are tellin' me the God's honest truth, aren't you?"

"I am. I could probably find it in the Bible, if you have one lying around."

"I don't, but no worries. No way anyone could make up a story like that."

"So we're good to Tucson?"

"We are good to Tucson. I have *got* to start readin' that Bible again."

# Chapter Eighteen

So, I'm thinking, worst case scenario: Chaladian hopped out of his Navigator the second my back was turned; found a cab; gambled that we were headed for the airport; got there and on his way to staking out the terminal somehow spotted us at Alamo; rented a car himself and managed to follow us without me spotting him in the ninety-seven minutes that we'd now been on I-80 West. All the while leaving a high-priced car sitting with a flat tire on a not-so-great street in Omaha, and an accomplice in the hospital with his head split open, both of which invite police attention that you've gotta figure Mr. Ten Percent wouldn't be anxious to have.

No. This did not happen. Electrons randomly colliding in a mindless universe to produce, oh, Katherine Heigl or Sandra Bullock? Yeah, maybe. Not a betting proposition, in my humble opinion, but I wouldn't totally rule it out. Stan Chaladian being on our tail right now, on the other hand? Not a chance.

Which meant that I would act like that was exactly what had happened. That's how you come home from an MP gig in Iraq with two of everything you're supposed to have two of and at least one of everything else.

I glanced over at Thompson. She had worked out a little niche for herself in the corner formed by the shotgun seat and the passenger door. She looked like she'd managed to drift off to sleep. Good for her. Let her be.

"I'm wide awake if you need somethin', tiger," she murmured drowsily.

"In about twenty miles there's supposedly a town that has at least four chain hotels just off the freeway. Odds are we'll pass an information sign maybe five miles this side of it. Keep your eyes peeled and let me know which ones are north of the exit and which ones are south."

"You got it."

Then she went back to sleep.

My phone buzzed. I pulled it up and took a quick look at the caller ID. Rachel. Shit.

"Yo."

"I am such a bitch!"

"No one gets to call you that, including you."

"I am! I took him back, Jay! I actually took him back! After what he did!"

"He hasn't hit you again, has he?"

"No." She almost sounded disappointed. "It's just…Why did I do that? Why do I do these things?"

"Well, Rache, you had one shrink tell you it's because you need to punish yourself for stepping out on me. And now you have another shrink telling you it's because you need to project less-threatening versions of me onto people who don't scare you the way I do."

"Jay! That's supposed to be confidential!"

"You put it on Facebook, Rache."

"I'd forgotten about that."

"Let's hope none of your clients stumble over it. Not a selling point for a small business lawyer."

"I am a very good lawyer!"

"You are a very good lawyer who should never mix wine with pot."

"Now you sound like my mother."

"I take that as a compliment."

"Well don't."

"Too late, I already have."

She started giggling. Either that or sobbing. It's sometimes hard to tell. Turned out it was giggling.

"You've always made me laugh, Jay. Goddamn you, you always have."

"Well, I've pretty much used up the A stuff, babe, so I'll just listen for awhile."

That triggered the monologue. Eight minutes that seemed like thirty. Pain, self-loathing, anger at me, anger at herself, anger at her mom and dad, anger at Jews, anger at *goyim*. This routine usually climaxes with a set piece about how I act so nice and everything but when you got right down to it I'm an even bigger shit than she is. Ending in sobs, that no one would confuse with laughter.

"Okay, babe." I sighed. "Try to get yourself a good night's sleep. And if you get the munchies, stick with rice cakes. No sense getting fat over me on top of everything else."

"Fuck you! Fuck you, you fucking bastard!"

She hung up.

"Wyndham, Red Roof, Ramada to the north. Best Western to the south." Thompson's hotel scouting report. She'd gotten her eyes open just in time.

"We'll be heading north."

"Yeah, I'm not a big Best Western fan myself."

"That's got nothing to do with it. Three times as many hotels means three times more light in the neighborhood, which makes it three times riskier to be nosing around looking for cars with rental plates."

Thompson nodded.

"What's the deal with that chick chewin' your ear off on the phone? Ex? Or would you just as soon not talk about it?"

"We're separated."

"Can't live with 'em, can't live without 'em. Boy, is that ever an old story."

"I guess it is."

"Sounds like she's got some baggage."

"We all have baggage." Any other time I would have left it right there, but something made me feel like I could unload on Thompson. "Thing is, if she was on chemo for leukemia or something and that made her cuss me out and treat me like crap, everyone would expect me to stand by her, no matter what. What she's actually got going on, though, is between her ears. So it seems like I should still stand by her, but it's a lot harder to explain."

"'Between her ears.' You mean that shrink stuff you were talking to her about?"

"That stuff is the closest I've come to anything specific."

"Well it sounded like b-s to me." Thompson turned her head to look straight through the windshield. "High grade b-s with four-dollar words."

"Can't really argue with that."

Exit one-half mile. I checked the rear-view mirror. Nearest headlights had to be a mile behind us. I waited until we went around a little bend, then nudged the Buick up to seventy-five and cut the lights. I braked barely enough to swoosh onto the exit ramp without laying rubber. As soon as we'd twisted far enough down the ramp that you couldn't see our car from the freeway, I put the lights back on.

"Did you spot him back there?" Thompson asked. Not an unreasonable question, under the circumstances.

"No. But I'm playing it as if I did." I stopped at the bottom of the ramp and just sat there, alternately checking the rear-view mirror and the road at the bottom of the ramp. "No way he'd figure on us stopping before midnight, so as long as we didn't advertise it our exit should have taken him by surprise. That means that unless he tries some *Fast and Furious* stuff to cross the median, he's stuck on the freeway at least until the next exit, thirty-seven miles down the road."

I eased onto the northbound lane of State Highway something-or-other, toward the garish lights of three hotels within half-a-mile of each other. My drive-past told me that all three had vacancies, but the parking lots were pretty full. Good. I circled back to the service station, spun the Buick around in the ample area next to the pumps, and backed into a parking space in front of the convenience store. That way I could look through the windshield and see any car headed north from the freeway before the driver had a prayer of seeing me. I scrounged two twenties from my shirt pocket and handed them to Thompson.

"We'll have at least ten hours on the road tomorrow, maybe more. Why don't you get some snacks, breakfast material, and some stuff to drink?"

"While you stay here and watch the road, just in case?"

"While I stay here and watch the road, just in case."

She whistled as she took the money.

"You are careful, aren't you?"

"I had a friend in-country who wasn't careful. I was the eighth rifle in the honor guard for him."

"You just might make it. You just might beat Stan Chaladian." She didn't sound like she'd give very long odds on it, but hey, it was something.

She came back in fifteen minutes with a bag of mini donuts coated with powdered sugar (that would be breakfast), chips, candy, and enough Dr. Pepper to make a sales rep's monthly quota. I picked the middle hotel—happened to be the Ramada— because it had the most floors and because it was the middle hotel. The desk clerk's eyes widened slightly in surprise when I asked for two rooms. She looked at me, looked at Thompson with Luci sleeping soundly on her shoulder, and shrugged.

"They're our last two. I'll need a form of payment."

"What brings so many people here this time of year?" I handed her two hundred-dollar bills, because you can't trace currency by hacking into a credit-card company's computer.

"This time of year?" She didn't bat an eye at the benjamins. "Hard to say. Hunting and football in the fall, and some overflow from Lincoln when the legislature is in session. But this time of year I guess we're just between where folks are and where they want to be."

"Thanks."

I took the keys and change from two hundred bucks. Thompson beat me to the elevator. I waited until we were inside before saying anything.

"In between where folks are and where they want to be. How about that for a business model?"

"Works for Stan Chaladian," she said. "That's why they call him Mister Ten Percent."

# Chapter Nineteen

As awkward moments go, the one that came about twenty minutes later was a corker. You don't see an "actress/model" blush in real life all that often.

We had adjoining rooms and we'd left the connecting door open. Thompson had Luci tucked into bed in pink jammies. She knocked shyly on the open adjoining door and walked in, holding a tube of something, a box of bandages, and a soaking face cloth from the bathroom. I had unbuttoned my shirt and was bracing myself for the ordeal of taking it off, because I knew that would involve several reminders of the numbers Plankinton and Chaladian had done on me. I aborted the removal operation when I heard her knock.

"Go ahead an' get that shirt off. We need to do somethin' for that shoulder and back of yours."

She was right. Trying unsuccessfully to hide the wince, I did as she said.

"Son of a *gun*, tiger. He got out the whoopin' stick for you, didn't he?"

"No sweat. Trans/Oxana has world class health benefits with modest co-pay."

After sponging my bruises with the hot face cloth, she started rubbing some kind of ointment into my shoulder and then onto my back. Not sure what it was—whatever you can find at a gas station convenience store, I suppose. It felt good and had a medicinal smell that comforted me. It was while she was putting the bandages on that her voice got hesitant and I sensed her blushing.

"Jay, you may have saved my life. For sure you saved me a smack down that would have laid me up for three days anyway."

I swiveled a bit on the bed to look her in the eye. Yep, blushing.

"Well you pretty much saved my life too. How did you know how to handle that pistol?"

"I picked up one just like it during my first tour. Tank—that's a Russian make—one-dash-thirty-five APS. Nine millimeter. Took it from an Iraqi officer who didn't need it any more and didn't look like he had any next of kin."

"I'd say we're even."

"I wouldn't say that." She recapped the ointment. "You stuck your neck out to save my sorry butt. And Luci. I really am thankful for that, Jay. I truly am."

"You're welcome."

She hesitated. The vibe I was getting was that if I wanted sex, she was willing. Out of gratitude for sure, maybe even desire. If I said no, I'd hurt her feelings. If I said yes and I'd read the vibe wrong, I'd piss her off.

I picked up her right hand, still smelling richly of ointment. I kissed it.

"I'm married."

"But you're separated."

"Separated. Not divorced."

"Most guys I know figure it's okay if you're separated. Even Methodists—and they're *real* strict."

"I'm not a Methodist. I took a vow. Married means married. Also, to be fair, there's one other thing, I guess. I love Rachel. I really, really love her."

Thompson's face slowly crumbled. She started sobbing, quietly at first and then really bawling with tears streaming down her face. She threw her arms around my neck and started to put her head on my left shoulder, then remembered my bruises at the last instant and switched to the right shoulder.

"That is just the sweetest thing I have ever heard in my whole life."

# Chapter Twenty

"America is one *hell* of a big country. Did you ever notice that?"

"Yeah," Proxy said. "That's why I mostly fly over it."

Ten-thirty mountain time Saturday morning. I'd gassed up the Buick while Thompson took Luci to the potty.

"It took us most of the morning just to get out of Nebraska. I mean, it's not like Nebraska is Texas or anything. Four bloody hours on I-80, plus the better part of two that we'd put in last night, and we're just barely into Colorado."

"So you still have, what, all of Colorado before you get to Arizona?"

"You're forgetting New Mexico. I could use a little sympathy, Proxy."

"Well, Colorado is *something*. I mean, at least it *sounds* Western instead of Midwestern, so you're, like, *psychologically* closing in on Arizona. Self-pity aside, Davidovich, how goes the battle?"

"As good as we have any right to hope. Wells reports that the pre-publicity tour is wheels up on its way to Denver. If we can avoid a temper tantrum for another forty-eight hours, we will have finessed our way through the first hurdle without a breach of contract."

"Dodging bullets. Speaking of which, you haven't actually killed anyone yet, right? Because if you have I really have to take it to Legal."

"Casualties but no fatalities. Any special reason you asked?"

"We got a call from a guy named Knapp claiming to be a detective with the Omaha Police Department. Said he wanted to verify your employment."

"I hope you told him the truth."

"Naturally. I just skimmed the report you emailed about last night. Do you think there was anything at all to Chaladian's pay-me-to-make-the-problem-go-away pitch?"

"Maybe at the start. If I'd convinced him that I was buying it, he might have figured that I wouldn't give him an argument about taking off with Thompson. He might even have followed up to see if he could shake a down-payment out of me. But then Thompson tipped our hand."

"And that's why he sent Plankinton after you?"

"Right."

"Hmm." A mental image came to me of Proxy tugging on her chin. "So why didn't he just yank Thompson and Luci off to wherever he wanted to take them right away, instead of waiting at the bus station for you to show up?"

Thompson and I had talked about that last night, during the first part of our drive. Turns out Chaladian had only gotten to the bus station about fifteen minutes before I did. He really was trying to sell her that reality show malarkey so that she'd come along quietly, without him having to use any attention-getting muscle. He'd already spotted me at the hotel, so when he saw me waltz into the bus station he figured out what I was doing there. I explained this to Proxy.

"So if Chaladian was going after Thompson to undermine Trowbridge, was that just to motivate us to pay him off?"

"Don't know, but my gut says there's got to be more to it than that."

"'More to it'—like what, for example?"

"Don't have a clue. Whatever Thompson meant about 'going *way* back' with Chaladian, she hasn't been very chatty about it since."

"Okay." Now I imagined Proxy uncapping and recapping a blue Bic pen. "For what it's worth, I think you made the right call in chasing Thompson instead of hanging around to watch the Asset pitch hissy fits. If this goes real wrong, though, it won't make any difference what I think."

"Noted. You're having someone do a total workup on Chaladian, right?"

"That's on my list for first thing Monday morning."

"Fair enough. Enjoy the rest of your weekend, Proxy."

Next stop was a Denny's about thirty yards down the frontage road. The waitress treated us like she thought Thompson and I were married and Luci was our kid. I couldn't help noticing that Thompson really got a kick out of living out that little fantasy. Not a fantasy of marriage to me, particularly. Just of being a regular wife and mom, traveling across country, instead of an "actress/model" who went way back with the likes of Stan Chaladian.

I've never seen Denny's screw up breakfast. Hamburgers or chicken can be hit or miss there, but short stacks and scrambled eggs they always nail. I was halfway through a waffle the size of an Olympic discus when my phone buzzed. Omaha number. I answered.

"Davidovich."

"This is detective-sergeant Knapp, Omaha Police Department. We met yesterday."

"Good morning. Almost good afternoon where you are."

"You mentioned knowing a lot more about the bald guy sometime today. Got anything for me?"

"His name is Stan Chaladian. Sometimes goes by Mr. Ten Percent. The last time I saw him he was sitting in a white Navigator. He pals around with some kung-fu muscle named Marcus Plankinton. I don't have an address for him yet."

"Someone whose insurance card said Marcus Plankinton took an ambulance ride to the emergency room last night with a hairline fracture in his right knee and a noggin cut that took eleven stitches to close."

"I'm betting that's the same guy. How does he say hurt himself—falling down some stairs?"

"He's not saying anything. You wouldn't have any ideas about what happened to him, would you?"

"I'd hate to speculate."

"Next time we see each other I'll update you."

He hung up. I was glad I wasn't in Nebraska anymore.

# Chapter Twenty-one

"'Rest area one mile.'" Thompson, sitting in the back seat with Luci dozing on her lap, read the words to me softly. "Let's pull over there."

Didn't like it. Sunday afternoon around two, only a couple more hours to Tucson. The deeper we'd driven into the vast expanses of New Mexico and Arizona, the harder it was to worry about Chaladian. Our Buick was a gas-guzzling pinpoint in open country with horizons that bumped up against infinity. One guy with nothing but guts and a fancy car didn't figure to find us. Getting to Tucson, though, would expose us all over again.

I pulled over anyway. In the last twenty-six hours, Luci had thrown up once and gotten cranky twice—not bad for an eight-year-old on a long road trip. At the second bout of crankiness, Thompson had pulled over to the shoulder. For sixty terrible seconds I thought she was going to smack the kid. But she handled it with a little heart-to-heart instead: *I know it's tough, Lucky Luci, but we've got tougher stuff than this to do, so we need to suck it up now.* Then she'd settled into the back seat, cradling the girl in her arms and nodding at me to take the wheel. If Thompson needed a break, how could I say no?

When we were ready to roll again, Thompson got into the driver's seat. I wondered if I'd somehow lost control of this little expedition. I had. Within a minute of getting back on I-10, Thompson handed her phone to me.

"There's a Best Western on Stone Avenue in Tucson. The directions are in there. As soon as we get within a mile of the exit, get ready to read them to me."

"Uh, yeah. But you know what? I'm thinking the money play would be to bunk at the Hotel Tucson—City Center. That's where Trowbridge and company will be pulling in sometime tonight."

"Stan's gotta know by now that Phoenix was a wild goose chase." Thompson shook her head while she spoke, and didn't sound like she was interested in a debate. "He can't be sure where we went, so he figures to re-connect with the tour and hope for the best. He probably has the tour hotel staked out already."

"If he has, then we should get in there as soon as we can and hunker down."

"Hunkering down ain't what I got in mind."

I dropped the subject. If I didn't show up with her in Trowbridge's suite on Monday morning, I'd be fresh out of credibility. Trowbridge would cop an attitude instead of completing the last day of his tour. All I'd have to show for about two weeks of expensive effort would be bruised kidneys and a rental car receipt.

We were almost three steps into the Best Western's lobby when I heard a screech that reminded me of the siren they used in Iraq for incoming mortar rounds.

"Trina! *There* you are!"

"Sue Ellen? Is that you?" Thompson matched the screamer decibel for decibel.

They scurried at each other across the imitation Navajo carpet and collided in a full-contact hug. Sue Ellen Whoever had hair a lot blacker than anyone that Anglo gets from nature. About an inch shorter than Thompson, she had roughly the same assortment of generous breasts and curves that would make an art director snicker if she called herself a model. She was wearing pink stretch pants and a black tank top. A big, four-wheel hotel luggage cart sat next to the chair where she'd been waiting. It featured a large suitcase, and about a dozen outfits hanging from its bar.

Thompson had called a friend in Simi Valley before flying the coop in Omaha. That figured to be Sue Ellen, who had apparently driven from LA to Tucson with what looked like a fair percentage of Thompson's worldly possessions.

With Luci in tow, I ambled over to the front desk and checked us in. Two rooms, paid for in cash. I got a little bit more of a fish-eye from this desk clerk than I had from the last two, and he wanted to see a picture ID. I thought about seeing whether a picture ID of Benjamin Franklin would improve his attitude, but then I just flashed the military card at him and that made him happy.

Thompson told me that the luggage cart was ticketed for the room that she and Luci would have. No surprise there. As soon as we got the cart on the elevator, Luci climbed onto it and hid herself in between the hanging outfits. She giggled the whole way up to the second floor.

"Thanks for coming all this way," Thompson told Sue Ellen. "Arizona isn't everyone's idea of a fun place this time of year, I know."

"By next year the whole industry will probably have moved to Arizona. Thanks to the People's Republic of California sticking its nose into—"

Sue Ellen cut herself off because Thompson shot her a look, accompanied by a nod toward the cart where Luci was innocently giggling. Thompson didn't want her little girl to hear a petulant complaint about California's decision to make actors in porn flicks start using condoms. Couldn't blame her for that.

We'd lucked into adjoining rooms again so my blood pressure dropped slightly. After plunking Luci in front of the TV, Thompson pulled the suitcase onto the bed and unzipped it. Sue Ellen, meanwhile, raided the minibar for a munchkin bottle of Jim Beam and busied herself making two bourbon-and-Cokes. Thompson looked up from unpacking long enough to ask Sue Ellen if she could stay for dinner.

Sue Ellen glanced at her watch as she sipped her drink.

"I'm gonna try to get to five o'clock Mass at Virgin of Guadeloupe. The desk clerk said it's about eight minutes away. So if you can wait 'til six-fifteen or so, I sure enough can stay for dinner—and lemme tell ya, girl, I could use some."

*Mass?*

"That works just fine. I was thinking we could just get a mess of pizza up here and chow down in front of the tube."

"You got it. See ya then."

I noticed Thompson burrowing deeply into the Lycra, silk, and cotton stuffing the suitcase as the door swung shut behind Sue Ellen. She glanced up at me.

"I'm hoping this is okay with you. I mean, I guess you have a vote—"

"Especially since I'll be paying for the pizza."

"—especially since you'll be paying for the pizza. But I don't see any other way to work it."

"I can live with it."

"Good. You still have that gun you took from Stan?"

"Yep. And I'm planning on keeping it."

Thompson pulled a hard-leather pouch from the suitcase, popped it open, and took out an automatic pistol. It looked a lot like the one I'd run away from Chaladian with, except without any chips in the bluing. She pulled the slide back to show an empty chamber. Then she popped the clip out of the handle.

"You go right ahead and keep the gun, bub. I just need the bullets." She held out her left hand.

If I was going to put my foot down, the time to do it was right now. If I didn't, then she was officially calling the shots. If I did, on the other hand, then it was eighty-to-one I'd show up empty-handed at Trowbridge's suite tomorrow morning. Two veterans from dirty, stinking little wars, we read each other perfectly. *Nothing matters but the mission.* For Thompson, the mission was Luci.

I unzipped my gym bag. Took Chaladian's piece out. Popped the clip free. Handed it to her. She gave me the empty clip from her gun. She slipped the loaded clip I'd given her into her gun's butt and clicked it home. She did this with smooth, practiced motions, without any wasted effort. She took a look at the weapon to make sure the safety was on. Then she looked past me at her little girl.

"Lucky Luci, look over here for a second, honey."

"Yes ma'am?" Luci's head swiveled as the words came out. If seeing her mom holding a loaded pistol startled her, she didn't give any sign of it.

"What's the rule about mommy's gun, honey?"

"I'm not to touch it, ma'am."

"That's right. What happens if you touch it?"

"You're gonna wear me out."

"Bingo, girl. And we don't want that, do we, honey?"

Luci solemnly shook her head. Then she turned back to the television.

I wondered if Thompson remembered that, even though I'd taken out the clip, there'd still be one bullet in the chamber of Chaladian's gun. I figured she would.

# Chapter Twenty-two

I didn't sleep with one eye open that night, but I did pull the mattress off the bed in my room and throw it on the floor. Sue Ellen Whoever—I never did get a last name for her—had left about an hour after we finished the pizza. I had the keys for the rental Buick, and its electronic ignition meant that Thompson couldn't hot-wire it. So unless Sue Ellen doubled back, the only wheels Thompson had in Tucson came with me attached. That meant the odds were against her sneaking off with Luci and leaving me looking like seventy-six inches of schmuck. But odds can always be improved. I spent the night with my head three inches from the adjoining door.

I woke up at five, about ten seconds before my watch would have started beeping. I'd slept fully clothed, just in case. First order of business was a cup of very hot coffee and a little recon. Before heading downstairs, I put my key card in the lock on Thompson's door and gently pushed. Moved maybe two inches and stopped. She had the security lock on. Good. She was still inside.

Coffee in the lobby, check; recon negative. Nothing suspicious outside the hotel, and no bad vibes. I paced around the sidewalk leading from the hotel's main entrance, nodding politely at a couple of crack-of-dawn smokers, sipped coffee from a cardboard cup, and enjoyed the most comfortable outside temperature Tucson was likely to have that day.

I'd been at that for about three minutes when a pick-up truck pulled into the parking lot. Ford F-250, black or dark gray, with Mexican plates. It drove past the entrance at a leisurely pace, then cruised to a parking spot on the part of the lot nearest the street. Dark canvas tarp stretched tight over the bed. Lever-action rifle horizontally mounted in the back of the cab and visible through the rear window.

In other words, *Oh shit.* You don't check into a hotel at five in the morning, and you don't park as far away from the back dock as you could possibly get if you're going to make a delivery. Unless it's newspapers, and the weathered, leather-skinned, Stetsoned gent in his fifties that I'd glimpsed at the wheel didn't look like any paperboy. I patted my shirt where it hung over Chaladian's gun, stuck in my belt near my left hip.

"Good morning." Thompson's voice came from behind me. She stood there with Luci and the baggage cart.

"Good morning. Sleep well?"

"Always do in the southwest. Almost like sleeping at home."

The driver started to get out of the pick-up. He took his time about it, as if his joints wanted to think things over before they decided to move. I spotted the six-shooter well before he was all the way out. Hard to miss. Old West-type hog's leg in a holster that went more than halfway down his right thigh. *Hoo boy.* He wasn't Chaladian, but no one was likely to mistake him for Mother Teresa, either.

After slamming the truck door, he stepped over to a mini-cactus just beyond the concrete and spat a long stream of brown juice onto the sand around it. Back to the truck. Loosening one of the bungee cords holding the tarp down and pulling up the driver's side front corner, he reached into the bed. He came out with two bottles of water joined at the neck by plastic collars, and a large Stanley stainless steel thermos. He began ambling toward us. Not as tall as I am, but not all that far off.

Without taking my eyes off him, I tilted my head toward Thompson because I was about to ask her if she knew who he was. Before I got my mouth open, Luci piped up in a delighted shriek.

"Grampa! Grampa!"

She pelted toward him, bright red flip-flops smacking the driveway pavement. He squatted, she jumped, and he gathered her up almost effortlessly with his right arm. Squealing happily, she buried her face in his neck as he stood back up. He reached Thompson and me in six more lanky, unhurried strides.

"Grampa, will you kiss Annabelle?"

"Sure I will." His eyes and face rounded comically as Luci lifted the doll. "Clarabelle, you sure have grown since the last time I saw you."

"Grampa! Not Clarabelle! Annabelle!"

"Ohhhhh, *Annabelle*. Why didn't you say so?" He planted a quick peck on the doll's face. "There's your kiss, Annabelle."

He let Luci slide down his body to the ground. The eyes he turned to me then weren't round and they weren't comical.

"You Davidovich?"

"Yep."

"Well I am Kirby Smith Thompson, and I want to shake your hand. Trina tells me that you got in between her and Stan Chaladian. I am much obliged, sir."

We shook. Firm, dry grip, and a hand that had done some serious work in its time.

"You know Mr. Chaladian?"

"Never met him. If I had, one of us would be in Hell or glory now. Back in the day we woulda just shot him down in the street like a dog. Or strung him up, maybe, if it was a three-day weekend. But I guess times have changed."

"I guess they have."

I got a funny little feeling in my gut just then. Sergeant Rutledge liked to say, "shooting too soon in self-defense is murder. Shooting too late in self-defense is suicide. Your call."

I'd had the drop on Chaladian. I could have put him away for good—could have killed an unarmed but very dangerous man in cold blood. The reasons not to do it looked just as good now

as they had then. But I couldn't help wondering if I was going
to regret the choice I'd made.

"Okay, then." He turned to Thompson. "You 'bout ready
to load up?"

Keeping my face bland, I choked back a protest. *Don't force
the issue yet.*

"Sure am."

"All righty. While I get started, why don't you be a good girl,
take this water up to your room and make me a thermos-full
of decent coffee?"

"Yessir."

Without a murmur, Hurricane Thompson obediently took
the stuff from her father and headed back into the hotel. First
time I'd ever heard her say "sir."

Luci hopped on the baggage cart. Kirby took the front and
I took the back. Getting the unwieldy thing across forty feet of
pavement single-handed would have been an adventure. Even
with two of us it wasn't any picnic, but we managed it.

"That a Colt on your hip there?" I asked as he started unfas-
tening bungee cords.

"No, sir. Starr Arms. Two r's. Confederate officers swore by
them in the War Between the States. That's where Trina's middle
name came from. I knew she'd be a pistol."

I swung the suitcase that Sue Ellen had delivered into the
Ford's bed. I gaped a bit at the truck bed when I got a good
look at it. There must have been seven-dozen bottles of water
back there, crammed into the area just behind the cab in blister
packs of six each. Kirby came around with two linen sheets that
he must have gotten out of the cab.

"Here, let's spread these out on the bed liner. We can lay the
hanging stuff on top of them."

"Fair enough. By the way, you think you have enough water
back here? Where are you headed, anyway? Death Valley?"

"Place we're headed has a well. It's 'tween here an' there that's
the problem."

"I know water isn't really plentiful in Arizona, but I didn't think they were about to run out altogether."

"Pink water." He spat as we laid stuff on hangers over the sheets.

"'Pink water'?" That was a new one on me.

He turned around and looked me directly in the eye. A fierce, chip-on-the-shoulder expression re-made his face.

"Pink water is what I said and pink water is what I meant. For fifty years American women have been pumping birth control chemicals into their bodies and then pissing all that excess estrogen into sewers all over this country. Well here's what nobody will tell you: sewage treatment doesn't break estrogen down or get rid of it. That stuff just builds up and builds up as the water is recycled. If you drink anything but well water or fossil water or spring water day-after-day, after thirty years or so you might just as well cut your balls off. Now that's a fact, mister. Don't let anybody tell you different."

"Got it."

"And don't get me started on fluoridation."

"I won't. That's a promise."

The last two things to load were the bag that Thompson had brought with her at the start of the trip, and Luci's overnight bag. Nothing to it. Kirby folded his arms and leaned against the tailgate, parking his boot heel in front of a license plate that had CHIHUAHUA stamped across the top. I couldn't think of any improvement on that, so I did the same thing. Luci took a good, long look at us. Then she folded her arms across her chest—over Annabelle—and leaned against the tailgate with a flip-flop heel planted on the bumper.

"That's why you gave Katrina the bottles? So you could have coffee made without pink water?"

"Dadgum right."

*Interesting.* Sometime in the last sixty hours or so, while I thought Hurricane Thompson was worrying about what makeup to wear at her next soft-core shoot, she had managed to coordinate an exit from Tucson that was all her own. She didn't need me anymore. Getting her here had exhausted my usefulness. She had found a hotel that Chaladian wasn't likely to stumble over. She'd gotten two different people there from two different places at the same time she was there. And one of those people sounded like he was for sure crazy enough to blow me away if I gave her an argument. She'd apparently learned something in the Marines.

I spotted her coming out of the hotel. Time for the show-down. Maybe I'd spent my whole life drinking pink water, but I wasn't going to take this lying down.

"Here's your coffee, dad."

"Thank you. Now, boots and saddles. We're loaded up. Let's get trucking."

I had an indignant *just a minute* right on the tip of my tongue. Thompson beat me to it.

"I already told you, dad. Six o'clock tonight. From the airport, unless I call you with a different plan."

"Trina, dadgummit, that's just not thinkin'. We're dealin' with a tough customer here. No law says he has to wait for twelve hours while you take care of unfinished business. You need to make tracks."

She locked eyes with him while five solid seconds ticked by before she spoke.

"Daddy, I gave Jay here my word of honor that if he got me to Tucson then I'd go see Mr. Trowbridge this morning. I can't go back on my word."

As if *word of honor* were a magic formula, Kirby gave up the fight.

"All right, then. Have it your way. But so help me, Katrina Starr Thompson, if anything happens to you or Luci, I'm not gonna wait for any dadgummed grand jury investigation before I do something about it."

She smiled at him. Leaning forward, she stretched her fore-arms up to rest on his shoulders, and kissed him.

"That's right, dad. Ride hard, shoot straight, and speak the truth."

# Chapter Twenty-three

"The real west is here. Tucson, Prescott, Yuma, places like that. No way any movie will be more real than the real thing. What we've tried to do in *Prescott Trail* is get the *idea* of the west right."

The local talent whose question had pulled this answer from Kent Trowbridge leaned forward to take her next shot. Trowbridge was Segment One on *Daybreak!* in Tucson this morning. He looked and sounded perfect. The only other person I'd ever known who could do "perfect" at 6:35 a.m. was Sergeant Rutledge.

Along with Thompson, Luci, and Wells, I was watching Trowbridge's performance on a big screen in a soundproof room about eighty feet from the KTUX studio where it was happening. I'd called Wells just before six to let him know that we were on the way to the hotel. He'd told us to go straight to KTUX and hook up with Trowbridge there. We were in the lobby waiting for him—not that he saw any of us but Thompson. When he laid eyes on her his face lit up like a loose slot machine. The guy is an actor, but if he was good enough to fake that he wouldn't still be waiting for his first Oscar.

"How long does his segment go?" I asked Wells.

"Seven minutes. That's an eternity, in case you're wondering."

He nudged me and started walking toward a corner on the far side of the room. I grabbed a glazed donut and followed him.

"What did you think of Trowbirdge's answer just now?" he asked me.

"Bullshit in a silk stocking."

"Perfect. That's exactly what your demographic is supposed to think. Spent hours working on it. Did you notice his wink right there at the end?"

"Missed it."

"Trust me, it registered subliminally. Six weeks from now you'll be sitting in your apartment on Saturday afternoon and you'll think, *What the hell, might as well go see that western.* And you won't know why."

"Maybe." I shrugged. "You're remembering you were going to tell me when Chaladian got back in touch with you, right?"

"Hasn't happened." He managed to look me in the eye, but I could tell it was an effort. "Look, there's something I need you to understand about that."

"Shoot."

"Have you ever heard of my dad? Sydney Wellstein?"

"Nope. Sorry."

"He's made a sort of a name for himself in some parts of the industry by raising money for movies that can't get conventional financing. You know?"

"No, I don't know. I don't have the faintest idea."

"You put together a limited partnership or something, shares at, say, ten thousand each. Get a few dozen lawyers and doctors and dentists who wanna feel like big shots to chip in—you can actually make a halfway decent indie flick with that kind of dough. They tell their wives they're doing it for the tax loss, then they write the check and start having fantasies about starlets and casting couches."

"'Lawyers and doctors and dentists'?"

"And businesspeople. Entrepreneurs. You know."

"Yeah, I think I do."

"Anyway, dad managed to raise over two-million bucks for *Mars Implies/ Venus Infers,* this art-house flick that Trow made last year to buff up his I'm-a-Serious-Actor cred. Five hundred thousand from one group alone."

"Was the group named Chaladian?"

"He was a go-between. He ended up holding the paper."

"And Stan the Armenian didn't take kindly to having half-a-mil go down the crapper, I'm guessing."

Wells' face paled. He wasn't looking me in the eye anymore.

"Chaladian said it was a con and demanded that dad pay him back. He's been bleeding him—five thousand one month, two thousand another. A few weeks ago he told dad it had to go up to ten thousand a month."

"And then Mr. Ten Percent came to you."

"Right. He said if I planted the coke and the bust went down, he'd back off of dad."

"Pretty expensive promise." If he was going to keep it.

"I guess he just really hates Trow."

"Why?"

"Can't be sure. Maybe he blames Trow for the flick tanking."

I thought that over for a few seconds. Say Chaladian tried to put the squeeze on Trowbridge; Saul Levitt tells him what he can do with it and blusters about putting a contract out on him; so Chaladian decides Trowbridge and Levitt have to be punished. Meanwhile, all Wells knows is that dad is hanging out to dry. *What would you have done, Jay Davidovich?* Don't know. You never know until you have to make the choice.

"Okay, buddy." What did he want from me? Hell if I knew. "You're not a shit. You did what a lotta people would have done. Maybe me, for all I know."

"Okay."

"Eight to one you hear from Chaladian again. When you do, you call me. That's the deal. Okay?"

"Sure."

Fast forward over the next ten hours or so. Replay of Omaha. All I got out of it was that being a movie star is a lot like work. Actually, I got one other thing. I got ten minutes alone with Trowbridge. Heading to the day's last radio interview he said he wanted to drive the Buick. Faked a little diva stuff to back everyone off, and managed to get himself and me alone in the car.

"If you were me," he said as we cruised along, "and making Katrina fall for you were the most important thing in the world, what would you do?"

I was *not* ready for that question. I clicked into improv mode and tried to come up with something that wouldn't be complete bullshit.

"I don't have a silver bullet for you. But let me tell you about a conversation I overheard this morning." I fed him the word-of-honor story.

"No shit? Seriously? Really?"

"No shit. Seriously. Really."

"That's so, so—"

"Retro?"

He laughed at that. Fairly decent laugh, but just a little nervous.

"She can't go back to LA with you." Seemed like a good time to get that one on the table. "Maybe later, but not now. Nothing to do with you, nothing to do with commitment or 'we're-so-different' or 'I'm-just-not-ready' or any chick-shit like that."

"What is it, then?"

"There's a bad guy looking for her. She's scared of him—and he beat the living crap out of me, so I don't blame her."

"Holy bombshell, Batman! Who is it?"

"Skip it. Point is, you can't change that. The bad-news gent is a fact. So if I wanted to impress her, I'd be a man about it. 'Okay. I understand. Whatever it is, when you get it taken care of, I'll be waiting.'"

"Those lines are for shit, man." He looked straight through the windshield. "Where did you come up with *that* script?"

"Can't remember, but it probably starred Rhonda Fleming."

He shot me a surprised little smile. Surprised and little, but a smile.

I don't know whether the Tucson Airport has a special entrance for people flying on charter planes, but if it does the limo didn't use it when the tour was ready to leave Tucson. It pulled up to the loading area in front of the main terminal. As people started to pile out, a Ford F-250 with a license plate that had CHIHUAHUA across the top pulled around it and parked right in front of it. Trowbridge and company headed for the door, screened for about five seconds by the pick-up. And when they weren't screened anymore, Thompson and Luci were no longer with them. Slickest move I'd seen in two years.

# Chapter Twenty-four

"Stanislav Chaladian was born in Odessa, Georgia on July 16, 1963. The old Commie Georgia, not the one here." I figured this was Andy Schuetz's idea of a joke and I chuckled, but the other five people at the table didn't. "He got what Europeans call a 'licentiate' from something called the Novribisk Preparatory Institute in Odessa at eighteen. Then he went into the Red Army. Drafted."

I like Schuetz. Weathered face, sparse, gray hair, and the hard eyes that you often see on guys who used to put people in handcuffs. Retired from the FBI at fifty, now in his tenth year at Trans/Oxana, go-to guy if you need a data dump on someone ASAP. But why was I sitting in a gray and white conference room in Hartford, Connecticut listening to Schuetz instead of reading his report on a computer screen in my apartment? This was the Wednesday morning after Thompson and I had parted company in Tucson. So far I hadn't heard anything worthy of more than an email.

"Made sergeant six months in." Schuetz glanced at his notes. "Rooskies thought people from Georgia were natural-born sergeants, so if they found one with any brains they fast-tracked him. Deserted less than nine months before his five-year hitch would have been up."

"Political?" Proxy asked this question without looking up from her laptop.

"Not hardly. He'd been stealing gasoline from his base to sell on the black market. He was about to get busted for it, so he got out while the gettin' was good. Iced a couple of guys on the way. One of them was a KGB agent. Just goes to show there's a little good in everyone."

A puzzled frown marred Proxy's poker face. She was still skipping rope and playing jacks when the Cold War ended. I wasn't all that much older, but I had Ukrainian parents, so Schuetz's crack didn't puzzle me.

"When did he reach the US?" I looked past Proxy to the far end of the table, where Don Quindel had asked this question. Quindel says "metrics" a lot.

"First record we have is ninety-three, when he enrolled at the University of Georgia. That being our Georgia this time. Came in on a student visa from France. Visa expired but he didn't leave. If the Feds ever catch him, overstaying his visa will be, like, count thirty-seven in the indictment."

"What makes him so hard to track down?" This question came from Dennis Stepanski, who called Proxy "Foxy Proxy" the first time he met her and has called her "Ms. Shifcos" ever since.

"No one is trying all that hard to catch him, and he's good at what he does. His crimes aren't priority offenses. He started off as a con man with muscle. He's not running drugs or robbing federally-insured banks or helping terrorists. The guys in the Hoover Building have more important thugs to worry about."

"So mostly nonviolent crimes, then?" Quindel again. "Leaving aside his recent interaction with our Mr. Davidovich here?"

That was definitely supposed to be a joke. Everybody at the table laughed—except Schuetz, who answered with an absolutely deadpan expression.

"Four murders that we know of. But the victims were all thugs. N-H-I."

The only other woman at the table looked up. Veronica Galliano. Assistant General Counsel.

"N-H-I?"

"'No humans involved.' Not the kind of thing a cop skips a donut for."

"Four is a pretty high body count for a con artist," Stepanski said.

"He's moved on to other things. Call him a broker. That's where the 'Mr. Ten Percent' alias that Jay picked up comes from. You want a genuine snuff film, he'll find someone who sells them and handle all the details. You want exotic sex with people it's illegal to have sex with and you don't want a record of it on your computer, ditto. And if you want a hit man who'll take out your ex-wife while you're playing golf with the mayor, he could probably handle that for you as well."

"How about if I want a DUI charge to go away?" Quindel grinned.

"No, that's off the table," Galliano said, not grinning.

"Joke," Quindel sighed.

*That's* why this was a face-to-face meeting instead of an email exchange. We were going to talk about things that were off the table.

"Did Chaladian's proposition sound like a joke to you, Davidovich?" Stepanski asked, mispronouncing my name 'David-OH-vich.'

"He'd be happy to take the money if we were dumb enough to throw it at him. He wasn't joking about that. Whether he could deliver is a different story."

"Do you think he could deliver?" This from Quindel.

"No idea. But it's irrelevant."

"Why?"

"Because we're not going to do it," Galliano said.

No one else at the table paid the slightest attention to her. They all fixed their eyes on me.

"Because if we did somehow accidentally do it, and Chaladian actually brought it off, he'd just find another risk we'd insured and extort another million or so from us anytime he ran short of ready cash."

Quindel glanced down at an Xcel spreadsheet he had on the table in front of him. Stepanski snuck a look at it too. Quindel looked back up at me.

"Let's get some metrics. What's your assessment of the loss-risk?"

"I'd say we have a halfway decent chance of not having to pay on the policy. I've tracked down two professional penal consultants and sent Proxy a report on them. We can hire one of them to fill in any gaps in the little seminar Thompson has already given Trowbridge. Plus, he's not a cream puff, and he can stay clean and sober if he's motivated to. So, like I said, halfway decent chance."

Quindel and Stepanski looked at me like I'd been speaking Yiddish. Without making any sound, Stepanski mouthed 'half-way decent chance' while rolling his eyes. Proxy elbowed me.

"They want a number, Jay." I shrugged. I could tell that she was shrugging too, but she was doing it mentally.

"I'd put the odds at four to one in our favor. So call it eighty percent that we don't write a check."

Quindel found the calculator app on his mobile phone and attacked it. He showed the number to Stepanski.

"Seven-point-two million."

My dad could have computed twenty percent of thirty-six million in his head without missing a pitch at a Red Sox game. I didn't mention that.

"Not necessarily," Galliano said. "We don't automatically have to pay the policy limit if Trowbridge craters. We just have to pay whatever loss New Paradigm Studios can prove—and Trowbridge has already made one of the three pictures."

Stepanski swiveled toward Galliano.

"If *Prescott Trail* ends up netting, say, sixty million, then New Paradigm could argue that it lost more than the policy limit on *each* of the unmade movies."

"Right. But if *Prescott Trail* tanks, claiming that New Paradigm lost anything at all would be a tough sell. I've prepared a pro forma exposure analysis."

She passed a chart around the table. It had three columns: dollar amounts, percentages, and lower dollar amounts, with a total at the bottom of the third column. But I didn't pay any attention to it because 'pro forma' meant it was just Fun with Numbers—assumptions plus arithmetic. The important thing I'd just learned wasn't anywhere on Galliano's chart. It was that Trans/Oxana Insurance Company should be very happy if *Prescott Trail* became a colossal flop. Stepanski has your basic glass head. I could practically see the pieces of the puzzle falling into place as he turned his gaze to Proxy.

"Ms. Shifcos, what are the movie's prospects?"

"Improving. New Paradigm added some scenes over the weekend and had another test screening last night. Much better numbers. We have to assume grosses will triple costs after foreign and digital distribution are factored in."

Americans like chick fights. Who knew?

"I guess that brings us to Citadel Re." Quindel said this to Stepanski as if they were the only two people in the room. Proxy reminded them that they weren't.

"What does Citadel Reinsurance Company have to do with anything?"

"Citadel Re has offered to take everything over ten million off our hands." I think the thing that Quindel then did with his lips and teeth was a smile. "For a two-point-six million dollar reinsurance premium."

"That guarantees a loss on the policy, even if there's no payout at all."

"True." Stepanski nodded earnestly. "But I didn't sell the policy."

"Or rate the risk," Quindel added.

A quick rap on the conference room door drew my eye to it just in time to see a dark-haired woman stick her head into the room.

"Mr. Davidovich? There's a call for you."

*Rachel? Again? Screw it.*

"Take a number and tell her that I'll call back as soon as I can." I snapped that without meaning to, so I added "please" as an afterthought.

"It's him, not her. A Mr. Chaladian. He says that it's urgent."

"Send it in here," Quindel said before I could open my mouth. "Put it on speaker."

# Chapter Twenty-five

"Good morning, Jay Davidovich! Thank you for taking my call. Who's in the room there with you?"

"You don't need to know that, Mr. Ten." I paced back and forth between the conference table and the credenza. "What's on your mind?"

"I follow up on my proposals. You have a problem. For ten percent I will make this problem go away."

"I have a lot of problems. One of them is getting feeling back in my left arm after the kick in the shoulder I got from your buddy Marcus."

"I do not apologize for that. An apology would insult you. That was an operational necessity. Like shooting prisoners in the first hours after D-Day. Katrina said that you were tough and determined, so I knew you would follow us if you could. Therefore I had to make sure you couldn't, at least for the rest of the night. You're a professional, you understand this."

"I'm not sure Marcus understood it. He aimed that kick at my head. I think he had something more permanent than the rest of the night in mind."

"Perhaps so. Marcus is not a precision instrument. Even so, no hard feelings, I hope. Now, what about my proposal?"

*No hard feelings I hope?* I took a look around the room, hoping for hints about where to go with this. Stepanski nodded. Galliano looked down at her legal pad. Schuetz shrugged. Proxy gave me a thumbs up and a smile. Quindel came through. He put the thumb and index finger of each hand together in front of his chest and then pulled his hands apart until his arms were stretched out full length: *Keep it going, draw him out.*

"Three things about that proposal, Stan. First, you're way high. We figure there's only ten million really at risk, and only a ten percent chance of losing that."

"Jay Davidovich, this is bullshit and you know it. But I like you. That was a good right jab you rocked me with. So I offer my special discount for people with good right jabs. One million dollars. I know, I give in too easily. I bargain like a pussy. But I like you."

"Second, there are a couple of red flags on your resumé. Like killing people."

"This I deny. But if I *had* killed anyone, it would only have been because this was absolutely necessary—or, at least, a really good idea under the circumstances. Not my business model. I'm not some two-bit Russian pig from Brooklyn."

"Which brings me to third. Felonies aren't Trans/Oxana's business model either. When I asked you how you were going to fix the problem, your answer was, 'Who cares how?' Not good enough. We need to know what the plan is before we sign off on anything."

"Jay, Jay, Jay. This is what I *do*. I *arrange* things. I don't know how I'm going to do it when I start, but I find a way. A legal way, I promise. Suppose you wanted a date with Ellen DeGeneres. How would I arrange that? No idea. But I would do it somehow, with no one under arrest at the end."

"One, I don't want a date with Ellen DeGeneres. Two, she's a lesbian."

"There are no lesbians. There are only women who haven't met me yet."

Galliano looked up open-mouthed from her notes. Outrage radiated from her violet eyes, and shock made her slender shoulders tremble. She didn't blow her cool over murder, but making fun of sexual orientation set her aquiver with indignation—which actually made her look pretty hot. But I didn't let that distract me.

"'Just trust me' is a deal-killer, Stan. No plan, no deal."

Seconds ticked by. I couldn't believe the bastard was actually thinking about what I'd just said. We had a good fifteen seconds of dead air before he spoke again.

"I will give this some thought. We have plenty of time before Trowbridge's next chance to breach his contract. So no rush. In the next few days I will think up your million-dollar plan."

"Think up a quarter-million-dollar plan while you're at it. The CFO here keeps saying that Trans/Oxana is in business to make money. He gets cranky when it doesn't And remember, keep it legal."

A dial tone abruptly sounded over the speaker, so I punched it off. Interesting to feel the vibe around the table. Schuetz gave me a quick, two-millimeter nod: *Nice job.* Proxy was as cool and detached as if we'd been discussing price-earnings ratios for a Fortune 500 company. Quindel and Stepanski were a little defensive: *Yeah, I could sound tough over the phone too.* Galliano looked a bit scared. I could sense her gut flutter from across the room. Not scared of Chaladian, scared of me. Not in the way Seawright had been, just scared on general principles. Dealing with guys like Chaladian meant I must be at least a little like him—and I was right here in the room. I actually got kind of a kick out of it. Guilty pleasure. I made a mental note to feel ashamed of myself when I had time.

"What did he mean about time before the next possible breach of contract?" Quindel directed this question at Proxy.

"*Prescott Trail* is scheduled for release in August. Under his contract, Trowbridge has to show up at the premiere and do at least three promotional appearances on national TV. He's also supposed to do a little meet-and-greet at the advance showings for critics, the week before the official opening."

"When does filming on the second movie start, the retro-spy thing?"

"Set for next February, but that's tentative."

"I thought you already saw a clip."

"That was just a tease to use when they're shopping the concept to backers."

Quindel looked at Stepanski. Stepanski looked at Quindel. No one looked at Galliano. Or at me. Then Quindel snapped his head around, sweeping his gaze over Proxy and me.

"Stall Citadel Re. We're not laying off any of the risk at this time, but keep them interested while we try to get harder numbers on the Thompson variable. You hear anything from Chaladian, I want a report pronto. Also from your boy Wells."

"Written report?" I hated to ask that, but I had to.

"Yes," Galliano said. "Addressed to me. That makes it privileged."

"No," Quindel said. "Oral. To Ms. Shifcos or directly to me. Real time, no voice mail. I'll handle liaison with Legal."

"Got it."

Quindel stood up. So did the rest of us, maybe two seconds behind him. Proxy took her and my copies of the Galliano chart and slid them across the table to Stepanski. He folded them up with his spreadsheet and Quindel's. Quindel started for the door, then turned back to us.

"Thanks for your time. Good work so far."

Quindel and Stepanski went out first. Galliano, obviously smarting from Quindel's spanking just now, waited for a good thirty seconds before she followed them. Schuetz smiled at her exit, shaking his head. Then he was gone too.

Proxy walked over to make sure the door had closed all the way behind Schuetz. Then she sat down in the chair nearest the door. In other words, not the chair where she'd been sitting during the meeting, where her laptop was: *I'm not taking notes. This is off the record.* I took the hint and sat back down. She looked up at the ceiling, as if she were thinking out loud instead of talking to me.

"I can't see Chaladian solving this problem for us."

"Neither can I. Not by sabotaging *Prescott Trail* and not by putting in an imaginary fix."

"What are you going to do if he calls again?"

"Report to you and ask for instructions."

Now she looked back to me.

"I'm not going to tell you to go in harm's way."

"Instructions are strategy. Going in harm's way is tactics. Chaladian isn't going to solve the problem for us, but if we string him along for awhile we might be able to keep him from making it worse."

Proxy picked up a pencil and started fiddling with it. She reminded me of Carrie Deshane playing with her cigarette that first night. She put it down again when she had her next question ready.

"How sure are you that Trowbridge has fallen for Thompson?"

"Hundred percent."

"How can we use that?"

"To start with, we can try to keep Thompson alive. After that I'm like Chaladian: I'm making it up as I go along."

"You think Chaladian might kill her if he gets frustrated?"

"No. I think he might kill her if he thought that would make us pay him a million bucks. So it makes sense to string him along."

Proxy frowned. Again with the pencil. For a second I imagined her actually smoking the thing. Then she put it down. No, she didn't "put it down." She smacked it against the table top with an audible pop.

"Okay, Jay, here it is. I don't care what Galliano's little exposure analysis chart says, I've got thirty-six million at risk. One-half of one percent of that is a hundred-eighty-thousand. I can get approval to spend that much on loss prevention without raising any eyebrows—as long as it prevents the loss. But I don't think that road runs through Chaladian. I think it runs through Thompson—and so does Quindel. That's what his 'harder numbers' crack meant."

Time for me to think things over. I didn't have a pencil to play with, but I managed to think without it.

"The Chaladian road and the Thompson road intersect. You're right: our best shot at avoiding a Trowbridge meltdown is getting Thompson on board. But Thompson is hiding in a Mexican border state in a *casa* with an old man who shoots first and asks questions later."

"Okay. Next step?"

"Find out what the deal was between her and Chaladian and see if we can do anything about it."

"Makes sense." Proxy nodded. "I'll get Schuetz to start digging."

"Suit yourself, but I wouldn't bother. If checking public records and calling in chits from old buddies at the Bureau could dig it up, Schuetz would already have it."

"So what *are* you going to do?"

"I'm going to start by talking to Sydney Wellstein, Jeff Wells' dad."

# Chapter Twenty-six

Two things were waiting for me when I walked into my apartment just after seven-thirty that night.

The first was a thin, midnight blue vase holding a single red rose and a single yellow rose. The note attached said, "I'm sorry. I'm so, so sorry. Rache." The roses had come from her garden—technically, our garden—not from a florist. The vase was one I'd given her for the Valentine's Day before I left for my last tour in Iraq. I found them just inside the door, which meant that she'd had to leave them with the building superintendent so that he could actually put them in the apartment. If she'd talked him into letting her in, she would have set them on the kitchen table.

The second was a message on my answering machine, left by someone with a California area code. I'd called Wells on my way to the Hartford Airport and asked him to put me in touch with his dad. Hadn't muscled him or threatened him. Just a polite request. Really. I hadn't expected a response until the next day, at the earliest. But this figured to be it. I pushed PLAY.

"This is Sydney Wellstein." The voice seemed a little labored, like someone elderly and chronically short of breath. "My son informed me that you would like to speak with me, and gave me your number. I'm sorry that you aren't there to take my call, because I'd prefer to respond to you directly. But so be it. Here's my answer: Go to hell. Don't call me again. Don't ask Jeff to call me again. Don't ask anyone else to call me again. Don't write. Don't drop by."

"I'm going to have to take that as a no," I muttered out loud as I hit ERASE.

Okay, time for Plan B. I'd picked up a big roast beef sandwich and chips on the way home from National, because until I hit my front door I was technically still traveling and I could charge them against my *per diem*. Pulled out a plate for the sandwich, just so Rachel's roses wouldn't think I was a complete slob. Grabbed a Miller Genuine Draft from the refrigerator. Didn't bother with a glass. Then, while I ate, I thought about what Plan B might look like.

After I'd worked it out, it seemed pretty obvious. As soon as I'd finished my dinner I emailed Proxy, because I'd need her approval for the money and her assistant's help with the logistics:

> Need to fly to Houston Friday morning; reservation for a *smoking* room at the Embassy Suites–Galleria for Friday night and Saturday night; $3,000 cash advance.

Once I'd launched that missive into cyberspace I called Rachel to thank her for the flowers. I reached the voice-mail prompt.

"Hi, Rache. Got the flowers. Beautiful. Classy. Thanks. No problem about last week. Apology accepted. Don't beat yourself up."

By the time I hung up, Proxy had replied to my email:

> "Smoking? Seriously? Why Houston? And $3,000 for what?"

I was about to hit REPLY when the phone rang. Rachel. I answered.

"I just got the door unlocked when you finished leaving your message. Sorry I'm late getting home. I was tied up on something. A good client just had a customer go bankrupt."

"Ouch. Big bill unpaid?"

"Opposite. The customer paid the client almost a hundred-thousand dollars over the last three months before bankruptcy. The bankruptcy trustee is demanding that we give it back."

"How does that work? You got paid fair and square, right?"

"It's complicated. Basically, anything you get paid by someone who files for bankruptcy within ninety days is vulnerable to getting clawed back into the bankrupt estate by the trustee. It really sucks."

I shook my head. *Thank God I'm not a lawyer.*

"Well, I hope it works out for you. Good luck with it."

"Thanks. Uh, Jay? I threw Nick out. That guy you talked to."

"He didn't hit you again, did he?"

"No. But after you talked to him, he couldn't get it up anymore. With me. He's fine with other women. At least that's his story."

*Win-win, then.* I self-censored fast enough to keep from saying that. Barely.

"Well, I think you're better off with him out of the picture."

"Jay? Do you think we could get together this weekend? We don't have to make love if you don't want to. Maybe we could just be together and you could hold me a little."

"I'm heading for Houston Friday. Tell you what, I'll call you from there."

I braced myself for an f-bomb, but it didn't come. Instead I heard a tiny, little voice with a hint of a catch in it.

"Okay." Then she hung up.

Back to Proxy's email. REPLY: "Seriously. Smoking. Houston is the only important thing I know of in Harris County, Texas, and that's where Thompson spent seven months in the slammer. The $3k is for a call girl."

Seventeen seconds after I hit SEND my phone rang. Proxy.

"Davidovich! I can't approve $3,000 for a hooker!"

"Not a hooker. A call girl. Different thing altogether. Mistaking a call girl for a hooker is like confusing Miller Genuine Draft with Bud Light."

"I guess I've led a sheltered life. When you explained your plan yesterday, I was picturing something a bit more corporate.

Why don't you cut the crap and give me a little primer on where you're going with this?"

I did. When I'd finished she almost said, "Oh, shit." But she caught herself and whistled instead.

# Chapter Twenty-seven

I worked my ass off on Thursday. Sat in my apartment all day long, keypunching on my laptop and my phone, just like one of the drones at the Trans/ Oxana cubicle farm up in Hartford—except with better coffee. I called every buddy from Iraq and Afghanistan who was now working as a cop or a bouncer or a bodyguard for unknown bands without finding one who knew who to call for a good time in Houston. So I did the obvious thing: I called Wells to lie to him for his own good. Got him on the first try.

"Still no Chaladian." He said this groggily, and I realized I'd probably gotten him out of bed.

"I'm calling about something else. Has Levitt asked you about Omaha yet?"

"No. I reported the search to him and he shrugged."

"Well some stringer for an entertainment e-zine that I never heard of left a message saying he wants to talk to me about it. *Me*. And I'm nobody. I doubt that Levitt will shrug about that."

He bought this little piece of fiction without thinking twice about it. Didn't ask me the name of the e-zine or the caller or the number or anything else. Just swallowed my story.

"Shit. When they get around to calling Saul he'll launch the nukes. Shit shit shit shit shit shit shit."

"So make sure he hears it from you. When you go see him, know one thing: I've got your back. I will *not* throw you under the bus on this thing."

"Okay." Wells didn't make the word sound very enthusiastic.

My brainstorm came around one in the afternoon, when I was wolfing down a pizza I'd had delivered. The Harris County Clerk of Court files are available on-line. There were tons of women named Thompson who'd found themselves in court down there during the time frame I cared about—but only one of them spelled her middle name "Starr" with two r's. A complainant who claimed to be the kid's father had somehow gotten an assistant DA interested enough in a kidnapping investigation to try to force a DNA test for the baby. He didn't call himself Chaladian, but that meant nothing. Three judges had their fingerprints on the case that came out of all that. It took me thirty solid minutes to figure out which one had winked at her with the hint about joining the Marines. That turned out to be the Honorable Samuel Trinity Bosworth—or "Trinity Sam," as Google said he periodically presented himself to voters.

He had retired in the meantime, and even serving judges tend to have unlisted numbers, so I needed a little help from Schuetz to get a current telephone number for him. By two o'clock, though, I was on the phone with his former honor. Fortunately, if you spend more than fifteen minutes in the United States armed forces, you learn to talk southern.

"Good afternoon, your honor. Jay Davidovich with Loss Prevention at Trans/ Oxana Insurance. I'm hoping you remember a case several years ago where a young mom went to jail for not telling a grand jury where her daughter was."

"What's 'Loss Prevention'?"

"People who try to keep insurance companies from having claims made under policies they've issued."

"Well I bet your mama's proud you're doin' that. You a reporter?"

"I can barely spell 'reporter,' judge. You can call me back through Trans/Oxana's general number if you want to."

"No, skip it. Assuming that I do remember that case, why should I tell you a blessed thing about it?"

"Here's my theory, your honor. I think you were pulling for the young lady. The guy who got her into that scrape is trying to find her, and I don't think his intentions are altogether honorable. If I find out what he was up to with her back then, I might be able to stop him."

"Is that so?"

"Yessir, that's a fact."

"Well, I surely have no idea of any scam he was trying to pull. For all I know he really was the father and just wanted a look at his baby girl."

"I know you wouldn't know about anything dodgy, judge. I figure, though, that there are probably some people who do know, and they would have been known to the Harris County courts."

"Young man, if your intention is to ask me who was in the high-end skin trade in Houston several years ago, why don't you quit beatin' around the bush and just come out with it?"

"I guess that's about the size of it."

"Well, I don't rightly see how I can help you. I assume you are aware that it is a violation of federal law to use instrumentalities of interstate commerce to arrange for the exchange of money for sex."

"That doesn't come as a complete surprise to me, judge. Sex trafficking isn't exactly what I have in mind."

"Sure it isn't, son. You know, I didn't just get to town last week. You have yourself a good day."

Click. Shit. Now what? Fly to Houston and try to find a vice squad cop who didn't hate yankees? Or, even worse, start nosing around on my own?

The only thing that went right for the next hour was the arrival of a bonded messenger. The envelope he had for me held a boarding pass for a flight out of Reagan National tomorrow at 10:20 a.m., the code for a confirmed reservation at the Embassy Suites—Galleria in Houston, and thirty hundred-dollar bills. I was surfing Houston smut sites on the web when the phone rang.

"Davidovich."

"Hi, Davidovich. This is Molly. I'm a Houston-based entrepreneur doing cold calls in your area. I wonder if you might have any use for our services in Houston this weekend."

*Thank you, judge.*

"Well, I just might at that."

"Were you looking for anything in particular? We don't do SM or anything creepy, but we have a number of positions you might be interested in."

"Something very particular, as a matter of fact. You see I have a bet with this friend of mine about someone named Katrina Starr Thompson. He bet me a thousand dollars that I couldn't find anyone who could tell me what she was up to in Houston eight-to-ten years ago."

"Are you sure he only bet you a thousand?"

"Now that you mention it, he may have said two thousand."

"And how much of this two thousand would you be willing to spend to get the information you need to win your bet?"

"Well, Molly, this might sound strange, but I think I'd spend the whole two thousand just for bragging rights with him."

"That's all you want for your two-thousand dollars? The lowdown on a minor-league scam that went down eight-plus years ago? Because that is the flat-out weirdest kink I've run across in seventeen years as an entrepreneur."

"You know what they say, Molly. It takes all kinds."

"Where can I reach you tomorrow?"

"My flight gets in from Reagan National around twelve-thirty local time, so I should reach the Embassy Suites—Galleria by one-fifteen or so."

"Got it. Have a safe flight."

# Chapter Twenty-eight

I was tying my shoes when I heard Chaladian's voice. Down on one knee about thirty feet past the security area at Reagan National, knotting my size twelve Nikes, when the four words registered.

"I have a plan."

I stood back up. I'd emptied my pants pockets into my windbreaker to clear security efficiently. Now I started reversing the process.

"A million-dollar plan or a quarter-million-dollar plan?"

"A million if it works, nothing if it doesn't."

"You have my undivided attention."

I resisted an urge to walk toward my gate. I didn't want to tip him that I was headed to Houston.

"The prosecution has a problem with a key exhibit. Big problem."

"And Trowbridge's lawyers don't know about it?"

"Not even the prosecutor knows about it. No one knows about it except me."

"So the plan is to hope they don't find out and then ambush them in court?"

"No. The plan is to make sure the prosecutor finds out about this problem. Because then she will try to fix it. And when she does, she will catch her tit in a wringer and get the case against Trowbridge thrown out."

"That's brilliant."

"No, that is average. But for me, brilliant is average." He grinned. "You see the problem, of course."

"You can't tell me what this mysterious evidence issue is because you don't trust me—and why the hell should you?—and as soon as I know it we don't need you anymore."

"This is true. But if I don't tell you, and Trowbridge is acquitted, then how do you know I wasn't just blowing smoke up your ass?"

"Right. After all, it could be just a coincidence."

"I have thought about this." Chaladian glanced up and down the concourse, then turned his onyx hustler's eyes back to me. "Here is my idea. I write the evidence issue down and put it in a sealed envelope. We give this envelope to someone who will hold it until the trial is over. After the case against Trowbridge goes away, we open the envelope."

"Sounds foolproof."

"You give this person a million dollars. If the reason for dismissal matches what I wrote, the money goes to me. Otherwise, it goes back to you. No-brainer."

"I'll bump it up the line and see if I can get to yes."

"Very good. This is all I ask."

"Later." I nodded—meaning *Go away now*.

"One more item."

"Shoot."

"I believe in free markets. No one has to do business with me if they don't want to. Another thing I believe in, though, is not getting fucked with."

"Got it."

"You don't want to deal with me, you say, 'No thanks, Chaladian, go to hell.' No hard feelings. But you do not string me along and play games with me."

"We are communicating."

His face split into a wide grin. He slapped me on the right shoulder, which was the one Plankinton hadn't kicked.

"Excellent. No misunderstandings then."

"Right."

He turned away, then looked back over his shoulder at me.

"By the way, I may need a lawyer here in Virginia. Do you know any?"

He laughed and sauntered off.

# Chapter Twenty-nine

I hit the highlights of the Chaladian chat in a message I left for Proxy before boarding my plane. I heard back from her in Houston, while I was trudging toward where signs promised GROUND TRANSPORTATION.

"Your message didn't sound like you think this is a risk-free proposition."

"I don't. What's that noise? Are you calling me from a wind-tunnel?"

"Helicopter. I got off one of Trans/Oxana's planes ten minutes ago, in a place where taxis are scarce. What's the risk you see?"

"Either Chaladian is going to fiddle with the documentation of the Trowbridge breathalyzer test, which would make us criminals; or he's going to pull a switch with the guy holding the money and walk off with our cash while Trowbridge heads for the hoosegow—which would make us patsies."

"All right. I'll pass that on to Quindel."

"Fair enough." I stepped onto an escalator going down. "Gotta find a cab."

Actually, I didn't. The first thing I saw at the bottom of the escalator was a matronly blonde in black chauffeur's livery. She held a piece of white cardboard with DAVIDOVICH scrawled in black felt tip across it. I caught her eye and pointed an index finger at my chest. She nodded.

"Molly sent me. This way."

Ten minutes later I was in the back seat of a black Chrysler Imperial, zipping along a freeway past bank signs that flashed the up-to-the-second population of Houston. I don't think I heard three words from her during the thirty-minute drive until I offered her a tip as we approached the sweeping drive in front of the hotel.

"All taken care of." She waved her left hand dismissively.

I blinked at that. This is the kind of treatment you get in Vegas if they think you're going to want fifty thousand in chips for starters

Checked in and started for the elevators. On the way I noticed a great pair of primly-crossed legs whose owner's face hid behind a *Wall Street Journal*. I was getting a little sixth sense tingle about them for some reason. Molly? Maybe. Before I could speculate further, though, I noticed the chauffeur coming into the hotel through the front door. She headed for the same elevator bank I was aiming for, and she wasn't being shy about it. We got there in a dead heat. Sensing someone behind us, I moved to the call buttons and punched UP. Then I glanced at the chauffeur.

"Did you decide to go for the tip after all?"

"I'm Molly." She nodded toward just beyond my left bicep. "Who's your friend?"

I looked over my shoulder. Proxy. I should have remembered those legs, even without the face that went with them. She now had her *Wall Street Journal* folded under her left arm. She blushed like an honor student caught sneaking a Marlboro on her way home from choir practice.

"Davidovich, I'm *really* sorry about this. It wasn't my idea."

"Molly," I said, "this is Proxy. Proxy, this is Molly."

The elevator came. We all got on. The two women exchanged last names. Molly gave hers as Engleiter.

"So, Ms. Engleiter, you're the uh—"

"Entrepreneur. Call me Molly. And you'd be the…what, exactly? Not wife, I'm guessing. Chaperone?"

"Babysitter," I said.

"Now don't get snarky on me, Davidovich. I got you the advance, didn't I?"

"Yes you did." And some stiff in Hartford spent twice that much flying her down here on a company plane and then bringing her downtown by helicopter to make sure I didn't blow the whole wad on a gin-soaked orgy.

"*I* sure didn't want to spend my day this way. They just—"

"Skip it. Not your fault."

Give Proxy credit. Room 803 was *definitely* a smoking room, but she didn't gasp or even wrinkle her nose when we walked in. In no time at all she'd gotten a whiskey-over-ice and brought it to Engleiter, who lit a Virginia Slim to keep it company. Proxy contented herself with tonic water, and at one-thirty in the afternoon I did the same thing. Engleiter settled into the chair she'd grabbed and gave me a hey-you look. I nodded to show I was listening.

"I met you at the airport because I wanted to size you up. The judge told me he wasn't all that sure about you. He thought you were probably on the level, but he warned me to check you out."

"I hope I passed."

"If you were a Vegas punk or an East Coast thug I would have had you made before you'd finished your escalator ride. You aren't. Plus, you look a lot like your picture on the Trans/Oxana website."

"Glad to hear it."

"The second thing you need to know is that digging up that information you wanted was a lot of goddamn work. I've been involved in top-tier hookups in Houston since my hair was naturally blond, but this isn't *Guys and Dolls*. I don't just absorb dope about sexy scams by cruising down Broadway. So when you give me that two grand—and you *will* give it to me, by the way—I'm going to feel like I've earned every penny."

"Wouldn't have it any other way."

"You *do* have the money, right?"

I pulled the folded sheaf of hundreds out of my shirt pocket and held it up where she could see it.

"Okay. One last thing." She took a long pull on the cigarette and held the pose, with her green eyes locked on my baby blues. "The judge asked me to call you because he remembers Thompson. He said she had a lot of spunk and 'an acre of Texas in her,' which is the best thing he can say about anybody. He figures she's in a tight spot and hopes you're on her side."

"She is and I am."

"I pray you are. Because if you're not, you'd be best advised not to let the sun set on you in Harris County, Texas. If you get crosswise of Trinity Sam you will be one hurtin' yankee—and *no one* in Harris County, Texas will give a damn."

"I'm duly warned. It's easy for me to understand how someone could have a soft spot for Katrina Thompson. That's why I came all the way to Houston to hear a two-thousand dollar story. But I need to hear the story—and I need to believe it."

"You'll believe it all right." She stood up and drained her drink. "You're going to hear it first hand from a girl who knows it by heart. I think I can get her here by seven o'clock tonight."

"Seven it is." I glanced at my watch. "That'll give Proxy time to check my expense reports."

Before heading for the door Engleiter pulled a card out of her left jacket pocket and handed it to me. It said RIDING WITH MOLLY, with a phone number underneath.

"That's in case you get bored between now and seven. Not comp, though. It would be on a professional basis."

The door took about five seconds to close all the way after she stepped into the hallway. That was long enough for Proxy and me to hear an exchange between Molly and what I guessed was a bellboy.

"There's no smoking outside the room, ma'am."

"Shove it up your ass, Roy."

That raised Proxy's eyebrows a good quarter-inch.

"Apparently not her first time at the hotel." She pulled out her laptop and set it on the worktable. "Look, I brought plenty of stuff to do. You can put the tube on if you want to kill some time. It won't bother me."

"That's okay. I'm not in the mood for ESPN right now."

"Are you just sulking about them sending me down here, or is something really bothering you?"

And just like that, without giving it any thought at all, I told her about Chaladian threatening Rachel.

# Chapter Thirty

"Trina was my mama." The woman who said this had a chocolate brown face that looked twenty-nine and chocolate brown eyes that looked thirteen. "My inside mama, I mean. When I was in the jail."

"You'd better tell them what an 'inside mama' is, Ladasha." Engleiter spoke these words slowly, almost soothingly. "They might get the wrong idea."

"Okay." Ladasha shook orange and purple bangs that matched a tattoo on the inside of her right thigh, peeking from under the hem of very short white shorts. "Like, my first week inside, see, I was like *this* close to just losin' my shit all the time. I figure I gotta show a lotta attitude and use my mouth."

"Ouch." Engleiter covered her eyes with her right hand.

"So, like, my third day, okay? I'm workin' the lunch line. And this one bitch be pickin' through this cheap-ass shit they be feedin' us, like mosta them weren't good enough for her. An' so I say somethin' like, don't just stand there, bitch, pick one and move your fat ass down the line."

"That's using the mouth, all right." Engleiter shook her head.

"And this bitch just stares at me. She don't say *a word!* Just give me this look. An' I got no idea what to do! I be scared totally shitless. Even if I coulda thought of somethin', I couldna got the words out. Then Trina saves my butt."

"What did she do?" I asked.

"She be workin' in back, okay? Breakin' down boxes and keepin' the shit straight on the shelves. And 'tween her an' me there's just this long metal storage cabinet comes up to our waist. So she leans over and says, 'Ladasha, honey, can you give me a hand with somethin'?' So you best believe I hustle my black butt back there 'bout as fast as ever I could."

"I'll bet." Engleiter offered a cigarette to Ladasha, who took it and leaned over for a light almost mechanically, as if she didn't realize she was doing it.

"So I get back there, an' Trina just hand me a box to break down. She don't be getting' in my face or anything. She just start talkin' to me, like talkin' 'bout what be on MTV last night, you know?"

"Sure." I gave her the best encouraging smile I had.

"And she say, 'Ladasha, now, you're new here, you know? That lady you're runnin' your mouth at, she's been here six months an' knows the score. So you don't wanna be dissin' people like her, or they gonna haul your butt into a storage room an' smack some act-right into you.' So I don't say nothin'. An' Trina, she wait 'til I get the box she give me busted down. Then she say, 'Now, Ladasha, I'm gonna walk out there with you, an' I would surely like to hear you tell that lady you're sorry 'bout what you said and you didn't mean nothin' by it. Would you do that for me?'"

"And—" Engleiter prompted.

"Well I done it. I hated it, but I done it. So after that, she was my mama. She just let me know the way things was, you know? I be a little worried at first, you know? 'Cause I thought maybe she want me to be her wife, you know? An' lie with her an' shit. An' I don't hold with that shit. That be against my religion. But she never done nothin' like that. Just kinda looked out for me, an' had some good talks with me. Some good, long talks."

"Did what Trina was doing before she went to jail come up in these talks?"

"Oh yes it did. It surely did."

My gut tingled. I was just about to get what I'd come to Houston for. I was starting to lean forward when two sharp raps sounded on the door. Proxy jumped up to get it, stepping over a white envelope on the floor that I hadn't noticed before. She looked through the peephole. When she reached for the doorknob, I assumed she was going to tell whoever it was to go away. Instead she opened it all the way.

Rachel walked in. *BOING!* She had her blond hair pulled back hard and then wrapped around the crown of her scalp in rope braids so tight you could have used them in bondage porn. She wore a black dress and a pair of black high heels. She did a classic Rachel take: a nice, slow look around the room. Proxy, Ladasha, Engleiter, and me.

"So. Should I take a number?"

# Chapter Thirty-one

"You've got 'wife' written all over you, honey." Levering herself from her chair, Engleiter strode toward Rachel. "And you look like you could use a cigarette."

Rachel stretched twitchy fingers toward Engleiter's Virginia Slims.

"You are absolutely right." She bent forward to accept a light and then straightened and sort of spat smoke over her left shoulder. I knew she was getting ready for a riff that I've heard a dozen times. "Cigarettes and I have flirted with each other since high school, but we've never gone steady. An occasional weekend fling, a quickie now and then over the lunch hour—but no commitments. Tonight the occasion demands smoking."

Ladasha glanced over at me with widened eyes.

"She talk funny."

Hard to argue with that, so I didn't. Instead I looked at Rachel.

"What are you doing here?"

"You said I couldn't see you this weekend unless I came to Houston. So I came to Houston. I actually beat you here. I got a flight out of Dulles first thing this morning. I had to fast-talk the name of your hotel out of Proxy's assistant."

"Please tell me she didn't give up the room number as well," Proxy said.

"No. I sent a FAX to Jay from the business center here and then followed the bellboy when he brought it up."

God, I love this woman.

"That tells us how. My question was why."

"I noticed someone creepy checking out my office yesterday."

Eight to one she was lying. But even a one-in-eight chance of Chaladian casing Rachel was something I couldn't blow off. I shrugged.

"Okay. You're here."

"Sorry about interrupting. It looks like it was about to get interesting."

Ladasha swiveled her head toward Engleiter.

"Does she think we're here to do him?"

"No, she doesn't." I answered the question. "She's pretending to think that."

I thought I read "fuck you, Jay" forming on Rachel's lips. It turned out that she had a different f-word in mind.

"Fair enough. I probably deserve that."

"Okay." Proxy finally moved from her position by the door into the middle of the room. "We were having a confidential discussion, and we were just coming to the most sensitive part of it."

"So I guess the polite thing for me to do would be to go down to the bar for an hour or so." Rachel took another hit on the Virginia Slim. "But I'm guessing that your discussion involves the creepy guy who was stalking me, so I think I have some skin in the game."

I expected Proxy to give that one a close-but-no-cigar. She surprised me.

"Describe the creepy guy."

"About my height. Dark eyes. Not overweight. Solid build, but not a brick shithouse or anything. Somewhere in his forties. And bald as a cue ball."

Proxy showed me one of the better poker faces I've ever seen.

"All right Jay's call, but as far as I'm concerned, you can stay."

Rachel helped herself to the bed, digging out two of the pillows to prop against the headboard and rest her back and head on. I nodded at Ladasha.

"As you were saying."

"What Trina be doin'. That what y'all want to know?"

"Yep."

"She say she an' this guy has this thing goin' on. Pretty slick shit. The guy would spot a young, minor league athlete—baseball, hockey, didn't make no difference. Some kid maybe gonna' make millions down the road. Trina would get him in the sack with her and do him. Tell him, 'Don' worry 'bout no rubber, I'm on the pill.' This goes on two, three times. Then she'd come runnin' to him, bawlin' like how she be pregnant, what am I gonna do, all that shit. An' of course he's like, okay let's get you an abortion, you know? An then she's like, 'I can't have no abortion, that's against my religion. You got to pay child support.' Now, see, child support, that's some percent of whatever this guy happen to be makin'. So right now it ain't nothin', but five years from now, that's maybe some percent of a million bucks, you know? An' he's thinkin', 'Shit, baby, I be fucked.'"

"I hope they didn't think they were coming up with anything new." Engleiter sipped her drink. "That was in the grifter's handbook before I was born."

"I don' know nothin' 'bout that. Anyhow, then Trina's man, he'd come into the picture. She call him Stan the Armenian. He's all, 'Look, you just write us a check for fifty thousand, sixty thousand, we'll call it even. So they'd go back an' forth for awhile. Finally, the kid's agent scrapes up whatever he can, they sign some papers, and everything be cool. Then Trina get herself an abortion, you know, an' they be ready to start again."

Ladasha paused. I happened to look from her face to Rachel's. The look in their eyes was oddly similar, kind of fatalistic and defiant at the same time.

"So, anyhow, they do this two times an' make a nice little pile. I mean, shit, nice work, you know?"

"Nice work for Stan the Armenian," Engleiter muttered.

"Then she go for the third time around. Got theirselves a prime target. Nineteen-year old baseball player in, like, Double-A or somethin', an' the Astros are real high on him. Trina gets herself knocked up an' the whole routine, you know? Except this kid's agent is one hard-nosed motherfucker. The back an' forth drags on an' on. They finally get theirselves a nice, big check, but by the time they get it Trina is more than six months along."

"So that complicates the abortion, I guess," Proxy said.

"Oh, she got an abortion all right. Stan found this place in Kansas that would do it. But that baby in Trina's belly, she be too tough to die from any damn abortion. She come out alive an' kicking, baby."

"Luci." I thought I'd whispered that, but I apparently whispered it loud enough for Ladasha to hear.

"Thass right. She name that little girl Lucinda, and she call her Lucky Luci. Say she gonna keep her. Not just that, but she say she out of the racket. She through with that shit."

"Stan the Armenian doesn't like it." Proxy started connecting the dots out loud. "He claimed paternity to try to pressure Thompson into staying with the scam. She isn't sure who the father is. Maybe Stan really is the guy. She gets Luci to gramps so that he can hide her in Mexico. Then she does seven months in the Harris County slammer and three tours in Iraq rather than give her up."

"That be about the size of it, I guess."

My eye strayed over to Rachel on the bed. She was hugging herself, chin down on her chest, shaking and starting to sob silently. If Ladasha or Engleiter noticed, they pretended not to. They stood up, Engelieter first and Ladasha a half-second behind her.

I took the wad of hundreds out of my shirt pocket, peeled off twenty, and handed them to Engleiter. She thumbed out five of those and handed them to Ladasha. Proxy followed the money changing hands with professional dispassion. I handed the unused thousand to her.

"We'll need a receipt," she told Engleiter.

# Chapter Thirty-two

I'm not a sucker for chicks crying. Sometimes it's real and sometimes it's fake, but it never moves the ball, so my general policy is to get lost while it runs its course. But Rachel isn't a weeper. Her standard pissed-off mode is ice queen, and Plan B is Psycho Bitch from Hell, which involves swearing and hitting and throwing things. So I figured something more than sisterly solidarity was behind the waterworks. I walked over and wrapped my arms around her.

She reacted first by trying to fight me, like a kid throwing a temper tantrum. That lasted maybe five seconds. Then she sort of collapsed against my body and just let the sobs come.

"Uh, okay, then." Proxy started edging toward the door. "Maybe I can answer some emails and we can hook up again around ten."

"No way." I looked up and made damn good and sure she saw my eyes. "We need to talk right away. All three of us. So just chill for about ten minutes."

Proxy didn't chill. She sat back down at the worktable, took a minilegal pad out of a pocket in her computer bag, and started drawing on it. Proxy Shifcos working with pen and ink instead of on a computer—imagine that. Rachel cried. I held her. While I did, I thought about Lucky Luci, with her blond bangs and solemn eyes, being dumped into a D&C pail like sloppy garbage.

I stopped thinking about that as fast as I could, because it wasn't doing anything good for me.

It took eight minutes instead of ten. After a lot of Kleenex dabbing, we managed to get three dry-eyed adults around the worktable.

"I paid two-thousand dollars in tuition." Proxy looked up from her chart. "Tell me what I learned."

"Thompson is off the table as long as Chaladian is in the picture." I settled back in my chair. "Doesn't make any difference how much money we throw at her. All Chaladian has to do is tell Luci that her mom tried to kill her in the womb, and he destroys Thompson's relationship with her daughter. So, no way Thompson can perform without putting Luci at risk. Therefore, she doesn't perform."

"Sounds right to me." Proxy doodled at the top of her chart, without looking at it. "Option one is paying him off, which you're against. So the question is, can we keep Trowbridge from imploding in jail without Thompson?"

"Not without neutralizing Chaladian. He took a six-figure hit on Trowbridge's indie-crap last picture. Trowbridge's agent probably dissed him when he made noises about payback. So Thompson or no Thompson, Chaladian will keep trying to sabotage Trowbridge unless someone motivates him not to."

"Suppose we motivate him?"

"Motivate him how?"

"Make good his loss. I mean, what is it, four-hundred-thousand something?" Proxy said the number as if it were chump change. "Say we give him, what, a hundred thousand up front. That's more than he figures to sweat out of Wells' dad anytime soon. Then, if Trowbridge fulfills his contract, we pay off the rest."

Proxy turned her chart around so that I could read it. It had four columns:

| $ | Risk w/Thompson | Risk w/out Thompson | Exposure Value |
|---|---|---|---|
| 36MM | 1% | 2% | 360M/720M |
| 24MM | 10% | 30% | 2.4MM/7.2MM |
| 12MM | 20% | 40% | 2.4MM/4.8MM |
| 6MM | 15% | 25% | 900M/1.2MM |
| 0 | 54% | 3% | 0/0 |
| | 100% | 100% | $6.06MM/$13.9MM |

DISCOUNTED EXPOSURE VALUE:

|  |  |
|---|---|
| w/THOMPSON: | $6,060,000 |
| w/out THOMPSON: | $13,920,000 |

"This is the way Quindel will analyze this issue," she said. "I don't know what risk percentages he'll assume, but it almost doesn't make any difference. The 'with-Thompson' percentages that I picked are a lot more conservative than the four-to-one shot you came up with, and even so it skews way toward payoff. If there's even a ten percent chance of getting Thompson back on the job by throwing four hundred thousand at Chaladian, it's a very good bet, because the difference in exposure value is twenty times higher."

"I get it. I can almost follow the math. But I'm sitting here telling you it's *not* a ten percent chance. It's zero percent."

"That's exactly what you're telling me, and I'm hearing you. But Quindel will say that you can't be objective because you have a conflict of interest."

"That would be me." Rachel socked my bicep with her fist. "I'm your conflict of interest. Call me 'Connie' for short."

"Meaning that I've got some macho male thing going on that makes me say we can't reward Chaladian for threatening Rachel."

"Basically, yeah."

"Best case, the only way this could possibly work would be to go through Wellstein," I said.

"And you hit a brick wall when you tried to reach him."

I really should have told Proxy that I had another baited hook dangling in the Wellstein pool. But I didn't. Instead I smiled at her.

"Selling starts when the customer says no."

# Chapter Thirty-three

"Ukrainians have been killing Russians for practically as long as there have been Russians, Rachel. You can do this. It's in your blood."

"Chaladian comes from Georgia."

"A Georgian is just a Russian with a suntan. Now work the pump and squeeze the trigger like I showed you."

She racked the pump on the Remington 870 twelve gauge back and then pushed it forward. Not the smoothest thing in the world, but it got the next shell into the chamber all right. Raised the shotgun to her right shoulder and acted like she was aiming it. If she actually had to use the thing in my apartment, of course, there wouldn't be a hell of a lot of aiming going on before she pumped goose load into everything in front of her. But I didn't want to discourage her. She pulled the trigger instead of squeezing it and flinched as she did it. Hard to blame her. That gun has a kick like homemade vodka. Naturally, her shot went way high.

I choked back a crack about how we weren't duck hunting. She'd never fired a gun before tonight. I had to cut her some slack.

"Shit. I'm pathetic."

"It'll come together. Do it again. Squeeze the trigger gently, and try to fire without jerking the barrel up."

She didn't argue, didn't cuss me out. Just started loading more shells into the magazine. A pump-action shotgun is practically an antique these days. Almost everyone uses automatics. But the problem with automatics is that you can fire them too damn fast. In your first actual combat situation you're liable to empty your magazine into the ceiling before you know it.

She focused again on the black-on-gray target rectangle thirty feet away. The shotgun roared. Bit of a flinch but not nearly as much, and a much smoother trigger squeeze. A respectable number of pellets actually peppered the target. Before I could even think about saying anything, she worked the pump back without taking the shotgun from her shoulder and squeezed off another shot. Then she did it again and again. She kept it up until she'd fired all five rounds. She'd shredded the target—and unless I missed my guess, she'd also done a pretty good number on her right shoulder.

When she brought the gun down and turned to me, her face was radiant. Glowing. Not with happiness or satisfaction, or anyway not just with that. She was turned on. Period. Ready to go at it, right then and there.

"Okay, let's get back to the apartment." I stretched out my right arm to invite her to hand the gun to me. "We still have some work to do."

Which was true. On the flight back from Houston Saturday morning, we'd talked the Chaladian situation through and agreed that for the time being she should move into the apartment with me. It was a lot easier to defend than the house. That would mean I'd be spending my nights in a sleeping bag on the living room floor for a while, but I'd rather do that than attend her funeral. So we'd killed that afternoon getting some of her stuff moved in, and then had our little Saturday night at the shooting range.

I didn't have any illusions about turning her into a self-defense machine by teaching her the bare basics of firing a shotgun. The point was to make her feel like she had some control, that she didn't have to just sit there and wait for something to happen. Probably an illusion—but illusions can be useful things.

On the same theory, I worked out a basic DefCon protocol with Rachel after we got back to the apartment. I had her practice picking the shotgun up from the coffee table, taking the safety off, and raising it to firing position. Then I loaded it, clicked the safety on, and set it on the table.

"This stays here, right?"

"Got it," she said.

I moved a floor lamp over to four feet from the door and turned it on high.

"The lamp stays on at all times, right?"

"Got it."

"If you hear someone trying to break in, every other light that's on in this room goes off, you pick up the shotgun, stand right at the table, and get ready."

"Got it. What about the bedroom window?"

"It's inch-thick thermal pane and can't be opened. Besides, this is the fourth floor in an eight-floor building, with the fire escape at the far end. Unless Chaladian gets Spiderman on his side, I don't see the window as much of a risk."

"Got it." She nodded firmly.

"Good."

I headed for the bedroom closet to dig out my sleeping bag. She didn't say a word, but something made me stop and look over my shoulder. She was giving me one of her patented Rachel-looks—in this case, the one that meant *I want it and I want it now.*

"Jay? This…stuff, this preparation, the gun and the rules and the getting ready. It excites me."

I turned around to face her directly. I put my fists on my hips. I think I saw a little flash of fear in her eyes, and I swear it looked like that "excited" her too.

"I thought the problem you had with me was that I'm walking around with all this violence coiled up inside of me, like some kind of bomb ready to go off."

"No. That was bullshit from my therapist."

"That's funny, because I didn't hear it from your therapist. I heard it from you."

"I bought into it. But it wasn't true. I knew you were a soldier when I married you. I knew you'd been in combat, I knew you'd killed people. I didn't think you were a chorus boy or a dancing master. It's complicated."

She shut up. She looked like she was trying to make more words come but couldn't quite get it done. I didn't know what to do, what to say, how to say it.

I didn't hug her. I put my hands on her shoulders. I tried to be tender about it, but I was probably a little rough. I could feel her muscles reflexively recoiling.

"Look, Rache, you don't have to flash guns to excite me. All you have to do is breathe. But whatever the problem is, we've gotta get it on the table and work it through. Or give up. All or nothing. I'm not going to share you with anyone. And I'm not doing any on-again/off-again crap. It's all-in, all the time, or we cash in our chips. That's the deal."

Rachel forced herself against my body and wrapped her arms around me. I thought that she'd start crying again, like she had the night before, but she didn't. She just kept murmuring *I can't-I-can't-I-can't*. I held her, not because I'm sensitive or romantic, but because I couldn't think of anything else to do.

# Chapter Thirty-four

I thought Chaladian might call on Sunday, but he didn't. He called on Monday. Everyone called on Monday. Monday was telephone day. I got Rachel to work around 8:15, and the only productive things I did after that were courtesy of Verizon 4G.

First came Proxy, at 9:23.

"We have a go on the Wellstein option. Now all you have to do is make it happen."

"And the million-dollar thing is out?"

"Definite no on Chaladian's pitch."

"Thank God."

"Thank God if you want to," Proxy said. "But if I were you, I'd thank me."

I made it to 11:45 a.m. before I got the call I'd really been hoping for—the one from Jeff Wells.

"I told him and the shit just hit the fan. Levitt went full postal."

"Did you tell him the truth?"

"Up to a point. He'll be calling you for sure."

"I'll be ready. Is there a company line ready?"

"Yeah. Search didn't happen. Absolutely did not happen. Nothing to see here, folks. Move along."

"Is that Levitt's bright idea?"

"If it works it is. Otherwise, not so much."

"I'll look forward to his call."

Chaladian rang through a little after one, just as I was finishing lunch. I answered with my last name, as usual.

"So, Davidovich. You have an answer for me yet?"

"Yep. The bad news is that they're taking a pass on your offer. Trans/Oxana will keep the million bucks and muddle through the Trowbridge trial as best it can."

"Eh, what bullshit. They want us to bargain like a couple of towel-hat rug merchants."

"'Towel-hat'? Seriously?"

"Slang term for 'Arab.'"

"Yeah, I know. I just haven't heard anyone use it since I got back from Iraq."

"Okay, okay, enough sociology. What's the counteroffer?"

"No counteroffer. Trans/Oxana isn't interested in your information about the problems with the evidence against Trowbridge. Hartford is taking a pass on your generous offer. Thanks for thinking of us, and good luck in your future endeavors."

"Trans/Oxana disappoints me. But you said that was the bad news. Is there good news?"

"Maybe. I understand you fronted for some investors who had a bad experience on Trowbridge's last movie. You've been trying to get the money back in nickels and dimes and it's slow going."

"Maybe you understand some things that aren't so."

"Maybe I do. Humor me, though. Pretend for a minute that it's true. How would you like to get that money back—not quickly, but guaranteed?"

"I'm listening."

"Two catches. First, Trans/Oxana has to work the deal out. Second, you're out of the Kent Trowbridge business. You get the money when we're off the risk on the Trowbridge policy."

"Translation: you want me to guarantee Trowbridge's performance without getting paid anything except what I'm already owed."

"I didn't say that." I switched the phone to my other ear and leaned my kitchen chair back. "If Trowbridge turns into a sniveling pile of puss and can't work anymore because somebody is mean to him in jail, that's not your problem. We pay off on the policy and you get your money. The only way you don't get your money is if you're the one who sinks him."

Long, *long* pause. I kept my mouth shut. Finally he came out with a question.

"How could you guarantee the payment?"

"That's some lawyer's problem. Back-to-back letters of credit with a Hong Kong bank or some crap like that, probably. There must be some country that doesn't have warrants out on you."

He cackled at that. A long, jagged, staccato laugh. When he spoke, his tone was almost jovial.

"Tell you what. Throw in my Katrina and it's a deal."

"I can't deliver Thompson. Don't know where she is, and I wouldn't have the balls to go after her if I did."

"Very disappointing. But you might actually be telling the truth. When will you know whether you can get this deal worked out?"

"By close of business tomorrow."

"All right. One more thing: my pistol. I want it back."

"Let me ask you something, Mr. Ten Percent. What are you smoking and where can I get some? You think I make it a habit to hang onto hot guns that have probably been used in murders? If you want that gun, call the Omaha Police Department and ask politely."

"You bullshit me, then. You told me you would leave the gun if I waited ten minutes."

"Yeah, I was kidding about that. I don't like to lie, but some-times it's an operational necessity. Like shooting prisoners."

"At least we speak the same language. We will talk tomorrow."

I barely had time to catch my breath before the next call came in. It was from a west coast number that I didn't recognize.

"Davidovich."

"Mr. Davidovich?" Female voice, polite but insistent.

"Yes."

"Jay Davidovich?"

"Yes." I hissed the word. "For the third time, this is Jay Davidovich. What do you want?"

"Please hold for Mr. Levitt."

I came *that* close to throwing my phone across the room.

"Hello. This is Davidovich, right?"

"Yes. What's on your mind?"

"Davidovich, I'm going to ask you a question. I want a yes or no answer, and I want the truth. Did Jeff Wells allow cocaine to be planted in Trowbridge's suite in Omaha?"

"No."

"Are you sure about that?"

"Absolutely positive. Guy named Stan Chaladian tried to, and convinced the cops it was there, but his plan for getting the bait in the water didn't work. "

"What plan?"

"One of the maids, probably. Wouldn't cost much to get one to play along."

"Is Stan Chaladian that two-bit *gonif* punk who tried to put the squeeze on Kent over *Venus Infers*?"

"I'm guessing yes. Lost money on your boy's last flick and hasn't gotten over it. And just so we're crystal clear on this, he didn't get cocaine into the suite but he did get Omaha cops into it. So this 'absolutely did not happen' stuff Wells wants me to peddle if any scribblers call is amateur-hour bullshit."

"Oh, I see. On top of your rent-a-thug duties, you handle PR on the side."

"This isn't PR, it's walking-around-without-your-head-up-your-ass common sense. The cops got a warrant, they came to the suite, and they searched the suite. There's no way you stonewall that."

"So what's your brilliant suggestion?"

"'The cops got a warrant, they came to the suite, they searched the suite in a thorough and professional manner—and they didn't find anything because there was nothing to find.'"

He hung up. I shrugged. In that entire conversation, I'd only said three words that mattered: "No" and "Absolutely positive."

The question was whether they mattered enough to generate one more phone call.

They did. It came at 4:24 p.m.

"Davidovich."

"Mr. Davidovich, this is Sydney Wellstein. I owe you an apology."

"Accepted."

"My son tells me you stood up for him when that twenty-four carat sonofabitch Levitt, who by the way sometimes makes me ashamed to be a Jew, was about to castrate him."

"I appreciate his saying that."

"You called me last week because there was something you wanted to talk to me about. You have now earned that conversation."

I told him why I'd called then, and why I wanted to talk to him now.

"For reasons that you'll find hard to understand, Mr. Davidovich, this isn't an easy thing for me to say. But we might be able to do business. Unfortunately, I need to have a face-to-face conversation about the details. My mobility is limited, so I'll have to ask you to come to me."

"How about Wednesday afternoon?"

"I'll see you then."

He ended the call. I sat there, looking at my phone as I felt the juice. *YESSS!* I was pumped. Moving pieces around an electronic chessboard with my phone gave me a kind of not-bad rush. And the very best part was telling Chaladian I didn't have his Russian peashooter anymore. Being able to lie like that is a *gift*.

# Chapter Thirty-five

Wednesday afternoon. Two-room unit in a low-rise office strip on the northern edge of the San Diego sprawl. Wellstein had a mop of black and silver hair over a narrow, angular face that tapered in bulldog folds toward his chin. On the paneled wall behind him I saw two pictures, both framed eight-by-tens. The black-and-white photo showed a dark-haired young Wellstein in tennis whites at the peak of a serve: feet just off the ground, leaning forward a little as his old-fashioned wooden racket smashed the ball. The color picture showed a middle-aged Wellstein in a group of maybe a dozen people, some with faces that I vaguely recognized. One of the people was holding an Oscar statuette. Wellstein was the fourth face to her right.

"Financing movies is lousy with dirty money. Drug money, cartel money, Cosa Nostra money, you name it." Sydney Wellstein's Ocean Pacific pullover shirt sagged on his frame. "You got a mass-market flick with A-list talent and a nine-figure budget—fine. You can do conventional financing on that. But if you want to make some crap with unknown talent framing a C-lister—or, even worse, some Serious Cinema vehicle like *Venus Infers*—and you need to raise a couple-million bucks for it, odds are half the money started out as cash stuffed in garbage bags."

"Yeah, Jeff told me a little about how it works."

"So I'm a big boy, I know the score." Wellstein had his hands clasped on the desk in front of him as he spoke to me in a raspy, listen-up-and-you-might-learn-something-kid tone that reminded me of New York City. "But so did the people I raised the money from. No one was kidding anyone. There were no guarantees. Kent Trowbridge or no Kent Trowbridge, everyone knew the movie might tank."

"But Chaladian came after you anyway."

"Came after me in total bastard mode. If he'd tried it with someone like Korvette he'd probably be dead. Or not. Can't be certain. Hard to tell who's mobbed up in town these days. Not like the seventies. Not such a mystery then, believe me. You could do a pretty good reality series on low-talent hustlers who crossed the wrong people and died young from say, 'fifty to 'eighty."

"But you didn't have any muscle behind you."

"Didn't have a studio, didn't have an agency, standing out there stark naked. So I humored Chaladian. Threw him some spare change now and then. Treated it like a cost of doing business. You know, like a trade show in New York, you hafta give some swag to the unions. Same thing."

"He told me he hates to be strung along."

"Like I give a fuck what he hates." A pale, angry white showed under Wellstein's tan. "Small time chisler. But he crossed a line."

"When he went after Jeff."

"That's right. Jeff didn't tell me when Chaladian came to him. I found out after the fact." He paused and looked longingly at a spot on his desk where I guessed an ashtray had rested for many years. "Which is bullshit."

"Right."

"So that's why we can do business."

"Good."

"I know what I sound like. 'You're graciously telling us you'll let us spend a ton of money solving a problem for you and you act like you're doing us a favor.' Like I said, I know the score. Nothin' for nothin'. That's the way the west was won. You guys are gonna want something out of this. Not sure what. Don't care, as long as it doesn't end up with me doing a perp walk. Point is, you're not helping me out as a public service."

"That's true."

"No reason you should be. But it has to be handled my way."

"Shouldn't be a problem."

"No cash. Wire transfers to onshore accounts that check out on Dun and Bradstreet. Receipts. Documentation."

"You got it."

"Details, I know, the details will be a bitch. Don't worry your pretty little head about those. Give your lawyer my phone number. The grown-ups will take care of all that."

"Fine with me."

I guess I should have felt insulted by now, but I just couldn't work myself up to it. Wellstein had peaked four faces from an Oscar. The day was long past when he could talk tough and bully anyone who mattered, so he was tough talking me for old time's sake. Fine. Knock yourself out, Syd.

"There's one more thing." His voice got real, *real* serious.

I braced myself for the touch, the noodge, the nickel-grab. How much would he want? A hundred thousand? Fifty? Probably enough to give Proxy heartburn, which would complicate my life. Oh, well. Might as well get it over with.

"What's the one more thing?"

"A gun. A handgun. Something simple."

Oh, is *that* all? My body temperature went up a degree or two, and the world suddenly seemed very quiet.

"Could be a problem. There's something in the employee manual about aiding and abetting. Trans/Oxana frowns on it."

"Let me explain." He shifted in his chair, closed rheumy brown eyes with sagging lower sockets and rubbed them with both hands, and then fixed his gaze on me. "I have Lou Gehrig's disease."

"I'm very sorry."

"That's okay. I've had a decent run. Now I'm in the end-game. Fine. So be it. I'm not the world's best Jew, but if I need consolation I know where to find Psalm one-forty-nine."

"Where does the gun come in?"

"Best case I've got three halfway-decent years before it gets so bad I have to start looking for an exit strategy. Probably more like two. I *want* those years. Stan Chaladian doesn't get ten percent of them just because he comes down with seller's remorse three months from now."

"I'm not following you."

"Then let me spell it out. That bastard walks through my door looking for another touch—and it's fifty-fifty he will—then I'm putting a bullet in the fucker."

"Seems reasonable."

"I spent two years in the United States armed forces. I know how to use a gun. But I need one to use. One that can't be traced to Jeff. That's why I won't have him buy it for me. He's too weak to handle cops."

"But you figure I can handle cops."

"You're damn right I do. I've checked you out. You helped deliver nineteen-year-old boys to Abu Ghraib. And I expect you got some dope about improvised explosive devices by doing stuff that ain't in the field manual. You've got that extra layer of moral skin."

I shrugged noncommittally. He was half right. Maybe sixty percent right if you want to get technical about it.

"So I need you to do this, Mr. Davidovich. 'No' on this is a deal breaker."

My answer did *not* come from the field manual.

"It just so happens that I have a gun."

# Chapter Thirty-six

"Neat gun." Proxy bent forward a little so that she could peer over my right shoulder without getting in the way.

"It is. The Russians actually make pretty good small arms. Cheap, efficient, and functional."

Curtain-filtered sunlight made its way through the window of my fourth-floor room at the U.S. Grant Hotel in San Diego. Eight-fifteen in the morning, one week after my face-to-face with Wellstein. We'd flown out the afternoon before. I wiped one of the hotel's towels carefully over both sides and the bottom of the clip Thompson had traded to me for the loaded clip from Chaladian's pistol. I'd just pushed six nine-millimeter cartridges into it. I saw Proxy's eyebrows go up when I pulled on skintight plastic sanitary gloves for that chore.

"Do you really think Wellstein is going to shoot Chaladian?"

"No. I'd say the chances of that are almost zero. The idea of the gun is to give him a feeling that he has some way to defend himself, that he's not totally vulnerable. But 'almost zero' ain't zero. If he does put a bullet in someone, I don't want my prints on it."

I snapped the clip cleanly back into the automatic's handle. Gave the entire weapon one final going-over with the towel. Proxy was right: the Russian piece was a neat little gun.

"Was the flight out here the first time you've ever used a company plane?"

"Yep. Thanks for pulling those strings."

"The alternative was to have you chew a three-day hole in my budget driving across the country."

"True. There are legal ways to bring a gun along with you on a commercial flight, but they involve paperwork that I'd just as soon avoid."

After making sure the safety was on, I slipped Chaladian's gun into a Baggie freezer bag. I put the bag into a generic attaché case that I'd used about three times since Trans/Oxana gave it to me shortly after I signed on. Only after I'd snapped the case shut did I pull the gloves off. I put them aside to throw away in a public wastebasket sometime later in the day. My hands felt sweaty now, so I ducked into the bathroom to wipe them off with a different towel than I'd used on the clip and the gun.

"Okay." I stuffed the disposable gloves in my trouser pocket and picked up the attaché case. "I'm meeting Wellstein at his lawyer's office in about twenty minutes to give him the gun. I should be able to get that done and be out of there before the rest of you show up for the closing at nine."

Proxy folded her arms across her chest. She walked a few steps toward the window, and then turned back to face me.

"I want you to stay for the closing."

"Your call. But why?"

"To keep Legal from wetting her pants. That speakerphone chat with Chaladian shook her up. She tried everything short of hysterical pregnancy to avoid this trip."

"Fair enough."

Putting the attaché case down, I crossed to the gym bag sitting on my bed where the rest of the stuff I'd brought was packed. Didn't have to rummage inside because I knew exactly where to find what I was looking for. I hauled it out. Colt Trooper double-action revolver with a four-inch barrel, chambered for either .38 caliber or .357 magnum. All in a slick little hard rubber skeleton holster. Not an automatic, a revolver. Real retro thing, looks like it's out of some 'fifties movie. Designed by Colt specifically for cops. One of my buddies from Iraq gave it to me when

I was accepted into the training program for the Connecticut State Police. His idea of a joke. I bailed on CSP training about two weeks in, on the strong suggestion of a coordinator who said he thought there might be more of a future for me in Loss Prevention at Trans/Oxana. But I kept the gun. Not the kind of gun you'd use for a target shooting competition, but I can plink a silver dollar with it at twenty feet, and it's never jammed on me—which is more than I can say for the first automatic I got from Uncle Sam.

I clipped the thing on my belt at the back of my waist. Checked the mirror to make sure my sport coat tail covered it with some room to spare. Then I retrieved my attaché case and headed out.

Wellstein's lawyer had offices on the sixth floor of a building on A Street in downtown San Diego. Not elegant but functional— sort of like the skeleton holster. I handed Chaladian's gun off to Wellstein without a hitch, then killed time in the reception area while I waited for everyone else to show up. By nine-ten I was sitting in a windowless conference room with Proxy, Galliano ("Legal" in Proxy-speak), Wellstein, Wellstein's lawyer, Chaladian's lawyer—and Chaladian. I got a bellydrop when I saw the SOB. He was smiling and jovial and full of patter, but I could tell the smile was strictly for the record. Made me glad I had that Colt.

The closing seemed off to me. I felt like we should have been passing around shoeboxes full of hundred-dollar bills, maybe in a private room at a strip joint. After all, we were paying off an extortionist. He was going to use our money to do bad stuff to people. Best case, we wouldn't be the people.

But Proxy and company handled it like a straight-up corporate deal, all legal and aboveboard. The lawyers had something called a "closing binder" that they played with in a self-important way. Passed around multiple copies of documents to be signed. Sat there chatting while they waited for electronic confirmation from Wellstein's bank that it had received $450,000 from Trans/ Oxana. Punched some keys on a computer. Passed some more time while we waited for electronic confirmation from a bank for the escrow agent for whatever company Chaladian was using to front for him that *it* had received a wire transfer of $450,000 from Wellstein's company.

Then Wellstein opened his attaché case. I expected to see the gun displayed prominently inside. A little macho swagger. That could get awkward. But he'd stashed the gun somewhere else, or maybe he'd covered it with some legal papers that said BANKRUPTCY COURT on them. Bottom line: no drama.

We were done. Everyone smiled. Everyone shook hands. I checked my watch: 10:12. By 11:15 we were wheels up in one of Trans/Oxana's Gulfstream 450s, headed east at three-quarters of the speed of sound. Galliano pulled her Kindle out and looked over at Proxy.

"ETA Hartford?"

"Pretty close to eight-fifteen local time." Proxy hadn't even glanced at her watch. "Sorry we can't drop you off in D.C. first, Davidovich, but a senior executive V-P has to pop down to help some K Street guys pat fannies on the Hill tomorrow, so he'll be hitching a ride with you."

"No problem. Lobbying Congress helps pay my salary."

"Besides," Galliano said, grinning, "someone has to eat an extra two hours."

"If it weren't for the senior exec, you'd be the one eating them and you'd have them on toast. Davidovich is on my budget and you're not."

*Welcome to the NFL, shysterette.* As far as I could tell, though, Galliano didn't notice Proxy's little jab. She seemed flat out giddy. She was already on the phone, leaving a message for the significant other who'd be meeting her that night.

"Due in about eight-fifteen. When I get home I'll need a martini the size of a swimming pool. And you know those Cohibas we've been saving for a special occasion? This is a special occasion. See you then. Love ya."

"Deal high," Proxy murmured for my benefit, shaking her head. "Anytime you close a transaction, unless you just got hammered, you get a rush out of it."

"You seem kind of up there yourself."

"Life is good. Trowbridge's tour is officially considered a success. As of yesterday New Paradigm Studios still planned to release *Prescott Trail* on schedule. Estimates for the opening weekend gross have been revised downward, but that's not his fault. We don't have to dodge another bullet until his trial."

So I settled back, with nothing in particular to do but think. I thought about Rachel, mostly. Chaladian was out of the picture now. Which killed the rationale for Rachel staying in my apartment any longer. She had to go back to the house until she got whatever her problem with me was out on the table. This woman who freely confessed to me about sleeping with other men, and beat herself up about it but then went on doing it—there was something this woman was *afraid* to tell me. What could it be? What's worse than *I cheated on you while you were at war?*

# Chapter Thirty-seven

The suit who shared the Hartford/D.C. jump with me called himself Chip Fleming. Still had a trace of Dixie in his voice. Said he was a West Pointer. By the time we had ten minutes of air behind us he'd explained that he'd gotten an MBA courtesy of our Army before Gulf War One started, and a career-shortening wound courtesy of the Iraqi Army while it was going on.

"So what were you doin' out in California that justified pulling this toy airplane out of the hangar?"

I thought about how to answer that. Common sense said to just keep my head down, but he struck me as someone with a pretty low bullshit quotient.

"Buying protection."

"I thought our business was selling protection."

"I'm in Loss Prevention." I shrugged.

"Loss Prevention?" The cabin was dark, but I could tell from the way he said the words that he was grinning. "Every now and then I get a memo about Loss Prevention."

"From Legal, I'm guessing."

"Mostly."

"They think we're a bunch of cowboys."

"Hell's bells, son, you *are* a bunch of cowboys." This time he chuckled out loud. "Legal doesn't like it when people color outside the lines."

"I guess you can't please everyone."

"Oh, I wouldn't worry too much about not pleasing Legal. Legal doesn't produce. It consumes. Best case, Legal makes things get worse more slowly than they would without it."

We flew on through the night, over the continuous ribbon of lights that defines the Eastern seaboard. Fleming fired up a laptop and seemed to flip through graphs and tables on the screen. After maybe half-an-hour of that, he glanced back up at me.

"This protection we were buyin' out on the coast. Who were we buying it from?"

"Guy named Chaladian."

"'Guy.' Not a company."

"Oh, he's using a company. But what we were buying with it was Chaladian's promise to be a good boy."

"In other words, you're tellin' me we paid off an extortionist."

"That's about the size of it."

"This have anything to do with that movie star contract?"

"It has everything to do with it."

"Damn. I'd like to get out of that damned business, but we can't. Make too damn much money at it. You mark my words, though. Sooner or later it's gonna bite us in the ass."

"No argument on that from me."

He went back to the laptop. We were getting set to land before he said another word.

"Just remember one thing, son. Suits are like politicians. We talk a good game and use all the right words. But when we're up to our eyebrows in serious shit we don't call Legal. We send for the sonsofbitches."

Good exit line. I figured I'd better give Rachel a call while I walked to my truck to let her know I was on my way. I reached her voice-mail.

"Hey. This is Jay. Calling at, what, after ten-thirty. Should be back to the shack soon. So don't blow me away when you hear the door opening."

Less than ten minutes into my drive my phone buzzed with a text. I broke my rule against texting and driving long enough to sneak a peek at it:

"Bk home. Cn tlk here. Pls. R."

"Cn tlk here." As in *talk?* A little tingle ran through my gut. Could this be it? Fish-or-cut-bait time? And the Pls—*please*—that had to be a good sign. Or not. Was she really going to lay the big problem on me, whatever it was?

I noticed a funny gut tingle, wondered what it was. Not fear. Fear I knew. Then I recognized it. Dam*nation!* Butterflies! I was as nervous as a zit-specked freshman trying to work up the nerve to ask a girl out on a date. And why not? I might be on my way to divorce or back to a real marriage before midnight.

I just had to live with the tingle for the thirty more minutes it took me to reach the house. When I turned onto her street I could see light glowing through the drawn curtains at every window I noticed. Pulled into the driveway, jumped out with my gym bag, hustled to the front door. I stood there for a second, sneaking a couple of deep breaths. Ring or knock? Hell no. This was still *our* house. I opened the door and went in.

"It's me."

I'm not sure I got the second word all the way out. I only felt the blinding pain for a second. Right side of the back of my head. Blackjack, as it turned out, but I wouldn't learn that until later. At the moment I was too busy collapsing unconscious in the entrance hall to speculate about stuff like that.

# Chapter Thirty-eight

I wasn't out all that long. Probably three or four minutes. But that was long enough for Marcus Plankinton to handcuff me and duct-tape my legs together from ankle to midcalf. The first thing I remember when I came to was the smell of shoe polish on his right boot. The next thing I remember was the boot kicking my left temple.

"Sit up, white boy. NOW!"

I rolled onto my rear end and brought my taped legs up in front of me. Quick inventory. Head aching something fierce. Concussion for sure. Hands hurting from the cuffs, but not numb. No ringing in my ears, no feeling of internal bleeding.

I saw Rachel across the living room from me, roped to a straight-back dining room chair. Arms tied behind her back, and four coils of rope running around her torso, lashing her to the back of the chair. Not duct tape with Rachel. Regular rope. Hemp. Yellowish-brown. He'd gagged her with a sock. This was way more effort than needed just to immobilize her. Looked to me like Plankinton had some serious kink going on. I filed that away in case it might come in handy later.

Once he'd made sure I was watching, he walked over to Rachel and backhanded her across the chops. I saw her face contort in pain as the gag stifled her scream.

I might have thought a lot of things at that point. Like how could I have missed the risk of Plankinton grabbing Rachel and using her mobile phone to text me? Or why hadn't I thought it was funny that she'd texted instead of calling? Or how damn *stupid* it was just to walk into the house. But I didn't think any of that stuff. Saved the chewing out for the after-action report. Because right now I was thinking something else: *I can't BELIEVE this dumbass used handcuffs.*

Plankinton whirled around and flung himself in my general direction. He was limping a bit on his right leg. Cold hatred in his eyes chilled my gut.

"I'm not going to kill you." He leaned down over me, his face close enough to mine that I could smell the stale tobacco on his breath. "I'm going to take your *eyes*. Your *eyes*, man! I walk out of here, you never see again."

I kept my face blank. I was wondering how much it was going to hurt my cuffed wrists to force them under my fanny and to the other side. I inched them past the point of first resistance, all the while holding Plankinton's attention with my eyes. Just like that I had my answer. It was going to hurt *a lot*. The metal dug into my wrists. Pain shot up my arms like sheet lightning. I figured I'd better say something to Plankinton so he wouldn't notice my face flushing with agony.

"You understand this is going to cost your buddy Chaladian a lot of money, right? Because I am definitely pissed off about this little stunt."

"Fuck Chaladian!" The back of his balled fist smacked my nose, lips, and right cheekbone. "He left me in that cracker town with my brain bleeding."

Speaking of blood, I had a mouthful of it right now. I spat as much as I could onto my shirt. Meanwhile I pressed my knuckles into the hardwood floor and pushed the handcuff chain forward. Green and scarlet lights went off right behind my eyes. I'd never seen the green kind before.

Plankinton was busy showing me his Special Forces knife— real macho thing with three knuckle-rings built into the side of the hilt. This was apparently supposed to scare me. It did. It scared the *hell* out of me.

"This is what I'm going to take your eyes with. But I'm not going to do it yet. Because first I want you to watch what I'm going to do to *that!*" He snapped his right arm back toward Rachel. "The last thing you will ever see on Earth is me having your woman."

He gave me another clop across the chops, just for luck. It hurt all right, but his heart wasn't really in it. He now seemed pretty focused on his plans for Rachel. He stalked back over to the chair where she was tied, whimpering. I could see her face paling as she pressed against the ladderback.

Plankinton's knife flicked and sawed. After three or four seconds, the top rope in the coil fell away. I noticed a tiny speck of Rachel's blood arc through the air as the knife snapped upward when the rope gave.

Wiggling and twisting my butt, I tugged the handcuff chain forward. Hot, blistering bolts of pain shot through my wrists. I felt the temperature in my head drop. If I didn't actually black out for a second, I came close to it. The kind of splitting pain that comes with stress fractures throbbed in the inside bone of my left arm. But my handcuffed wrists finally slid past my fanny.

Plankinton sliced the second rope. He was taking his sweet time about it, indulging his rope fetish for all it was worth. I brought the handcuff chain up to the top of the duct tape lashing my legs together. He sliced the third coil of rope. There's always a burr or a rough patch somewhere on handcuff metal. The things get abused in normal use, and you've got to make them cheap to start with.

The fourth and last coil of rope dropped away from Rachel's body. Grabbing the top and front of her blouse with his left hand, Plankinton jerked her out of the chair. I got the first, tiny notch cut in the top of the duct tape. Rachel's torso arched backward as Plankinton swung her around about a quarter circle. I tried to find the notch again with the center of the handcuff chain. Missed. Plankinton flung Rachel to the floor. Tried yet again for the notch. Missed it again.

I suddenly caught a quicksilver reflection as the knife slashed down through the air. I caught my breath. The knife sliced through Rachel's skirt, inches from her left thigh, and pinned the skirt to the floor.

The notch! Got it! *Gotcha, you sonofabitch!*

Plankinton squatted. He reached under Rachel's skirt. I heard a long tear as he ripped her panties off.

I sawed with the handcuff chain at the notch. My left wrist and now my left shoulder throbbed. *Pain is weakness leaving the body.* I pushed the metal back and forth, maybe half-an-inch at a time.

Almost manically, Plankinton started pulling down his pants. Just forced them down to knee level.

The duct tape was really going now. The sides tore from each other with a *rippp!* so loud I thought Plankinton had to hear it. He didn't. Or maybe he just didn't care. I sliced through the bottom of the duct tape. Three determined kicks and my legs were free. No hope of getting the cuffs under my feet and up in front of me. Not at six-four with a broken wrist. But all I needed was free legs.

I pulled myself to my feet. Just as I thought I was going to pass out, the black and white dots dancing in front of my eyes cleared.

*Now* Plankinton heard me. His head snapped around. An instant later he had pivoted and leaped with cat-like grace to his feet, grimacing as his right foot hit the floor.

I was already moving by then. Three quick strides, and I launched myself into a horizontal dive, sailing through the air and aiming my head at the hollow spot just below the top of his ribcage.

I nailed it. I paid for it as his fists smashed my temples, but the sound of breath exploding from his body made that pain worthwhile. Knocked off his feet and hobbled by the pants bunched below his knees, Plankinton flew backward. His tail-bone smacked the hardwood a good foot past Rachel's head.

I had to clump over her thighs and belly to follow him. I managed it. Plankinton writhed as I landed on top of him, but my sixty-five pound weight advantage cut his writhing potential way down.

Blood rushed to my brain. A kill thrill that you only know if you've been in combat raced through me. *This ends NOW!*

Except it didn't. His head snapped up from the floor and caught the bridge of my nose. For an instant I felt like I'd gone blind. My freshly-broken nose sent pain geysering through my brain. Blood clouded both eyes from the inside. In the instant it took for the blood to clear, Plankinton had his torso out from under me and was scrambling for the knife.

With the last ounce of strength I had I wrapped my legs around his waist. I squeezed for everything I was worth, but right now that wasn't much. His left hand grabbed the knife hilt. Another loud *ripppp!* as Rachel scrambled away, leaving half her skirt behind.

"Get out!" A desperate savagery contorted my face as I screamed that at her. "Get out, goddammit! Run!"

It was over now. I knew that. In three seconds he'd have that knife buried hilt deep in my top leg. Then he'd twist it. No way I could stand that. With a little *thok* the knife came out of the floor.

Suddenly a blur sailed through the air. A Jewish Ukrainian-American blur. Arms still tied behind her, Rachel leaped at Plankinton like some pissed-off dropout from the *corps de ballet*. She must have gotten a good three feet off the floor. Ten toes pressed together and aiming straight down landed *en pointe* on Plankinton's throat. I don't know whether it was a *demi-plié* or a double axel or something else, but it did the job. I felt a spasm in the flesh pinned between my legs. The knife dropped to the floor. I heard a dry rattle from what was left of Plankinton's throat.

Right after that everything got very chilly and very blurry and then very dark.

# Chapter Thirty-nine

"…not filing charges." Male voice. Sounded far off. "Source told me this morning. Technically under investigation for the rest of the week, but on Friday afternoon they'll formally close the case without charges."

I knew I was lying down. Knew my torso was propped up at maybe a thirty degree angle. As I rolled my head toward the voice, the back of my scalp rubbed on what felt like a thin, plastic-coated pillow. Turning my head didn't hurt but it felt like it should've. Like this bolt of pain was trying its damnedest to get through, but couldn't quite manage it.

My right eye found Rachel. Left eye wasn't finding anything. She was sitting. She looked like hell: skin swollen, yellow and purple bruises around her right eye, upper lip puffy and specked with scabs. Next to her sat an African American guy, smooth skin, short hair, wearing a tan, three-piece suit as sharp as anything I'd seen in a long time. For some reason I particularly noticed his brown wing-tips, polished to a gloss that would have stood inspection in my last outfit for sure. He had an old-fashioned black leather briefcase on his lap.

I figured I might as well say something. I specifically ordered my mouth to open and words to come out, but at first nothing happened. When I finally heard my own voice, it sounded as far away as the guy's had.

"Charges for what?"

"For Marcus Plankinton's murder." He switched his gaze from Rachel to me.

"Murder?" Suddenly my voice didn't sound so far away. "The bastard was going after us! He had a *knife*."

"He did. Only his prints on it, too. That was a helpful fact. Also, he'd wounded the missus with that knife. Plus, he'd conked you with a blackjack. Not to mention the piece he had under his shirt. Sig Sauer nine millimeter. And then there were the details that you were handcuffed and the lady had her hands tied behind her back, and you'd both gotten the crap beaten out of you."

All at once Rachel and the black guy began to rotate clockwise, going round and round in lazy circles. I closed my unbandaged eye.

"So…Murder?"

"Some bright spark in the DA's office had this theory about a bondage-SM scene gone way, way wrong. Black guy dead, two white people alive, no sign of forced entry. You can't be jumping to conclusions in that situation these days, after that thing in Florida. And then, of course, there was the confession."

I re-opened my eye. Rachel and the guy had stopped rotating. Nice of them.

"Whose confession?"

"Mine." Rachel's voice was dull, listless.

"The lady was in deep shock when the cops got there. Just kept saying, 'I *murdered* him, I *murdered* him.'"

"That's ridiculous! They can't—"

"Calm down, tiger. You get yourself worked up, Nurse Ratchet is gonna come in here and slap *me* around. Like it's *my* fault."

"Sorry." I lay back on the pillow.

"The forensics all came out one way, though." He had a way of widening his eyes and O-ing his mouth when he talked, and making this uplift gesture with his right hand. "I don't know how it would've gone down otherwise, but that's a moot point now. Bad news for me. Probably would've been a pretty easy win. I don't get all that many innocent clients. But good news for you and the lady."

"Thanks."

"Anyway, don't tell anyone. Not a soul. Including your priest in confession."

"No danger of that."

"Just keep your heads down and your mouths shut for three more days."

I did some mental math. Friday minus three.

"You mean this is Tuesday?"

"Yep."

"I've been out for four days?"

"You haven't been out, exactly, as I understand it. More like so drugged up you could've passed for a Grateful Dead fan at an Occupy Wall Street rally. You came in here with a concussion, and you've been through two operations."

"Broken wrist and what else?"

"Eyeball socket filled with what looked like the Nile River during the plagues of Egypt. You were a hurtin' puppy for sure."

*Did they save the eye?* I choked that question back. Wouldn't be fair to make him answer it.

"Well, thanks for trucking down here to bring me the news."

"Actually, I trucked down here to bring your lady the news. Ever since they got through with her at the cop shop on Saturday, this has been the only place I could find her. Had no idea you were gonna wake up on us."

He stood up, hefting the briefcase with his left hand and giving the crease in his pants a quick check with his right.

"Later, folks. Gotta date with a guy the Commonwealth Attorney thinks is a drug dealer, for some damn reason. Keep it real."

Rachel half rose to shake his hand. Five seconds later he was gone and we had the room to ourselves. I looked at her, as best I could.

"Thanks for staying with me all this time."

She nodded.

"Also for jumping on the SOB's throat and killing him. I appreciate that."

She nodded and, this time, she smiled a little in an almost embarrassed way, as if I'd complimented her on an old hat or something.

"Do you know if they saved my eye?"

"The doctor thinks they probably did. It was responding to light after the operation. But I guess they won't know for sure until you're awake enough for them to take the bandages off."

I tried to smile at her, but I'm not sure my mouth did what I wanted it to.

"I'm assuming he grabbed you on your way home from work."

"Right. He was waiting in my car in the parking ramp. Hiding on the back seat floor."

"That had to be terrible, Rache. Sorry I brought this on you. This is on me."

She shook her head emphatically.

"No. The only terrible part was that after he tied me up I wet my pants. Awful. I killed him deliberately, you know. I knew exactly what I was doing. It felt so *good* to kill him. So *right*."

"Some kills are like that." I didn't tell her that it might not feel so hot after awhile. She'd learn that without any help from me.

We looked at each other. The obvious question was why she'd been screaming *I murdered him* when the cops got there. The obvious answer was that she'd been in shock. She'd never been beaten up like that before, never had her life in danger before, never killed anyone before.

Then, all at once, I saw tears running down her cheeks and I noticed her body almost imperceptibly shaking, just like in the Houston hotel room what seemed like a lifetime before. She jumped up from her chair, took two urgent steps toward the bed and flung the top of her body across mine, barely avoiding the cast on my left wrist. I felt rather than heard the wracking sobs that throbbed through her body.

"I killed our son, Jay." Rachel choked the words out.

"What are you talking about, Rache?"

She lifted her head to look at me, our faces maybe three inches apart.

"After they sent you to Iraq, I found out I was pregnant. It was our baby. I'd never cheated on you up to then. Please believe that."

"I do."

"I panicked. I was absolutely certain you wouldn't come back. Or if you did you'd have a leg blown off or something. I was furious with you for going."

"I didn't exactly volunteer."

"I know, I know. I just…I don't know, I just blamed you for it. I thought there must be some hustle you could have come up with to get out of it. I felt so *alone*, with this wretched little invader trespassing in my belly. It wasn't that I'd be supporting both of us and getting up at five o'clock in the morning to take a kid to day care and you to some Veterans Hospital for rehab and then working all day and half the night. It wasn't that. I just had to get control of my own life."

"So you got an abortion."

"Yes." She stood up, her face suddenly defiant as if she were daring me to judge her. "It ate at me for your whole tour. I knew I should tell you, but I was terrified about what you'd do."

"So that was what made you crazy?"

"It's obvious, isn't it? Now. But I repressed it. I am *so* good at repression. If they ever make repression an Olympic event, I'll make the American team. "

"Shrink-speak?"

"Self-diagnosis. I told one of them about it. She said I should think of the abortion like getting my navel pierced. Just a personal choice about my own body. Not your business or anybody else's."

"Sounds like a pretty standard view."

"Yes. What everyone says, except she used longer words."

Rachel folded her arms across her chest. Her lower lip was trembling as she struggled to speak.

"I could sell it to anyone but myself. In the depths of my soul I knew it was bullshit. When I looked at you I knew it was bullshit. I dealt with that by pushing you out and fucking other men. Then, in the hotel, I heard about that little girl."

"Luci."

"Yes. You had described her so vividly I could see her, as if she were skipping rope in the driveway or playing in the front lawn. She was so *real*. Which meant she was real when her mother tried to have her aborted. And that meant that the baby I'd killed was just as real. Our baby. Our son. I murdered him."

Three or four pat answers reached my lips. I choked them all back. Good thing. Mostly chicks don't want answers. They don't want to hear your brilliant solution to their problem. They just want you to wallow in the problem with them for awhile, like it's a mud pit. Anyway, I didn't need to say a word. She wasn't anything like through talking yet.

"I suppose when I was having my tawdry little flings and rubbing your nose in them, something in my subconscious was hoping that you'd get mad enough to storm in and slap me around. Punish me. But you punished me far more harshly by accepting it. I wept more bitterly over that than I would have over split lips and black eyes."

That sounded like typical chick shit, and I started to tell her so. *You might want to check with someone who's actually gotten split lips and black eyes from someone she loves.* But I stopped myself. Even with one eye I noticed the bruises and the scabs again in time.

"I guess you've earned the right to say that."

"Yes. Like you, I didn't exactly volunteer. But I don't think that matters. I've been punished now. One hell of an atonement. It wasn't justice. Justice would have been a life for a life. Maybe my life goes on so the atonement can continue."

"Does that mean you want me back?" That just slipped out.

She looked at me for a second like I'd just said something in Swahili. Mouth slightly open, eyes big and round, arms drooping at her side. Then she started giggling. She brought her right hand up to cover her mouth, like an embarrassed schoolgirl, but the giggles turned to laughter. Her cheeks turned scarlet as her body shook with mirth. Borderline hysterical. She finally stumbled toward me, as if she were walking in a dream. Bending over the bed she hugged me, not like a lover but like you hug a little kid who's just said something adorable. Her cheek brushing mine, she whispered something so softly that I had to strain to make it out.

"You are such a goddamned idiot."

# Chapter Forty

"By the way, there's someone waiting to see you." A doctor who'd just told me I still had two eyes threw that out as he headed for the door. "I'll tell the nurse that it's okay for her to come in."

Exit doctor. Enter Proxy. I blinked.

"This is a surprise."

"You have some friends back in Hartford. Quindel didn't want to pay for a lawyer to handle the criminal investigation. Said you were off on some frolic unrelated to the course of your employment and we should distance ourselves from it. The V-P who shared the plane down to D.C. with you called Quindel into his office. The only part I heard was 'we don't leave our soldiers lying on the beach, goddammit.' Basically everyone in Hartford heard that."

"Thanks, but you didn't fly all the way down here to tell me that."

"Right. I thought I should update you on the *Prescott Trail* project. We've hit a bit of a speed bump."

"Test audiences stopped loving the mud-wrestling scene?"

"No, they're eating it up. That's the problem. Little too much t-and-a in the thing, apparently. MPAA wants to bump the rating up to R. That would mean that if anyone under seventeen wanted to see the thing they'd have to bring their mom, which would turn the marketing plan into lunchmeat. So they're negotiating."

"How is Trowbridge handling that?"

Proxy set her computer bag on the floor and leaned forward to rest her forearms on her knees. This was Proxy being Earnest.

"According to Wells, he wants to talk to you."

"Can do." I tried to look gung ho.

"I think he wants to talk you into getting Thompson back to him. His trial isn't all that far off, and jail is looming over him. He's putting up a good front, but Wells says he's hanging on by his fingernails."

"'The difficult we do immediately. The impossible takes a little time.' That was one of Sergeant Rutledge's pet lines. I'll talk to our boy, and I'll do my best."

"There's a final item on my agenda, Davidovich."

"Namely?"

"Two things you can't stand: Guys who beat up your wife, and the people who pay them."

"You're on to something."

"You can't kill Stan Chaladian. I know you want to. I don't blame you. But no matter how many friends you have in Hartford, you can't pull Trans/Oxana into the middle of a murder investigation. Trans/Oxana shows up in the Business section of the *New York Times*, not on the front page. If Trowbridge goes off the deep end, we write a check. But we don't kill the bad guy—or look like we have because one of our cowboys greased him for another reason."

The smart way to answer her would have been to fake amusement or indignation. Unfortunately, as actors go I'm a hell of an engineer. Besides, she'd played straight with me and she had a right to have me play straight with her.

"Okay, Proxy. Word of honor. As long as I'm employed by Trans/Oxana Insurance Company, I won't kill Chaladian."

"Thanks, Davidovich. I know how hard it is for you to make that promise."

"You have no *idea* how hard it is."

# Chapter Forty-one

On Friday at 1:47 p.m. Katrina Thompson accepted my Friend request for her Facebook page. The only other person who'd ever done that was Rachel, because she was the only other person I'd ever asked. The only reason I even *had* a Facebook page was that Rachel had set one up for me.

Okay, what should I write to Thompson? I glanced around Rachel's dining room—now our dining room again—where we'd set up my computer after moving the stuff from my apartment back over here.

"Love to talk. Doable?" I hit POST.

The closest thing I had to a plan was to reach out to Thompson every way I could think of and see if one of them clicked. I'd called the roommate who'd trucked stuff out to Tucson, and asked her to get word to Thompson that I'd like to talk. She'd said something about seeing what she could do, but she'd sounded like your basic brick wall. A sweet, polite brick wall, but a brick wall. I'd tried a tweet and an email to the addresses I had for Thompson, and they'd both come back undeliverable. A snarky little robot informed me that Thompson's mobile phone number was "no longer in service." All I could do was keep trying.

Rachel got home that afternoon a little after five. She had two plastic grocery bags with her.

"You're early. Pleasant surprise."

"I left the office at four so I could pick up our stuff from the police. The Commonwealth Attorney officially closed the file today. No charges."

"Good for us."

"Good for me, mostly." Rachel emptied the sacks on the dining room table. "I was the one they were thinking about indicting. *I murdered him* was my line."

I pawed through the stuff on the table and retrieved the only thing I really cared about: my mobile phone.

"If they weren't thinking about charging me, why did they take my phone?"

"Because they found it on Plankinton's body. It was one of the first things he glommed onto after he conked you and got you cuffed."

"What?" I snapped my head around. "Plankinton didn't bother with either my wallet or my keys, but he took the time to steal my phone?"

"Yep." Rachel met my gaze without backing up. "So what?"

"This wasn't just a revenge thing, to get back at me for giving him a couple of owies and a permanent limp. The revenge was window dressing. Something he threw in to make it look like he was acting alone. Chaladian is still after Thompson. He wanted to put me out of the game for sure, but he also wanted anything I had that might give him a lead on her."

"So he's still a danger to us."

"Yep."

"Does that mean you have to kill him?" Rachel asked this question without a hint of drama. Just your everyday conversation around the dining room table. *My husband is a trained killer, and I like to show an interest in his work.*

"Not an easy call."

"You're right, of course. Stupid question."

I had a funny little disoriented feeling. The youngest prisoner I ever turned over to Iraqi soldiers was sixteen. He was Sunni, they were Shi'a, he was looking at an eleven mile drive in the back of a paneled truck, and it wasn't going to be a good trip.

Sometimes hard things have to be done. But doing them should be *hard*. Not routine. Turning that kid over had been routine for me. Item four to check off that day's to-do list.

Three nights later I'd gotten my first nightmare about the kid. My first vision of him with his eyes gouged out and his bloody face grotesquely swollen and his balls jammed in his mouth. No idea if any of that stuff happened to him, but that's what my subconscious dredged up to flog me with. I cherished that nightmare. Clung to it. It meant I hadn't lost—yet.

I looked pointedly at Rachel. I wanted to be sure she'd understand exactly what I meant when I spoke.

"It wasn't a stupid question."

# Chapter Forty-two

On the thirty-eighth rotation, just as the hammer was starting to feel heavy in my left hand, I heard the mailman stuffing mostly useless crap into our box. I was sitting at our kitchen table just after noon, not quite a week after I told Rachel her question wasn't stupid. They'd taken the cast off twenty-four hours before. Turning the hammer to the left until it was parallel with the table and then back to the right was rehab.

I hurried compulsively through the last dozen rotations before I went to get the mail. Usual stuff. Bills. Flyers about big sales and bargain prices. A magazine for people who are into ballet. And—*Hello.* A battered, white business envelope. Dirty, dimpled, wrinkled, and torn a little at one corner. Mexican stamp. Postmarked the previous Friday. Addressed in droopy, loopy penmanship to Tall Dude.

My fingers shook a little as I opened the thing up. Inside I found a folded sheet of yellow paper:

> Oasis Project. TALK it up to your friends.
> Check One More Chance in El Paso.
> Good time to TALK: 6/29 1715/courthouse.

June 29th was three days from now. I memorized the words and numbers, struck a kitchen match, and burned the slip of paper and the envelope over the sink.

Googling "Oasis Project" turned up nothing relevant. Putting "One More Chance" in the same box as "El Paso," on the other hand, produced plenty of hits. They included references to a program for teenagers who, reading between the lines, were known to local law enforcement.

Could be a trap, of course. But 1715 made me think it wasn't. To a grunt or a jarhead, 1715 is quarter after five. Chaladian would probably know that. But would he realize that Thompson would use military notation in writing to me? Couldn't see it. Anyway, what difference did it make? I was going regardless.

I ambled back over to the butcher-block table. Another letter in a white business envelope lay there. Addressed to Proxy, that letter had my signature on it. My formal resignation. Effective, as far as I was concerned, the moment I dropped the envelope in a mailbox. I'd promised Proxy that I wouldn't kill Chaladian as long as I was employed by Trans/Oxana. Instead of mailing it right away, I decided to take it to El Paso with me. Just in case.

I had the sense to bring a hat to El Paso. In high summer, a Stetson with a broad brim isn't just a fashion statement in southwestern Texas. Especially if you're standing outside the courthouse instead of inside. Given the Colt Trooper in my attaché case, inside the courthouse was out of the question.

I'd gotten to El Paso the night before. The two restaurants and one café where I'd eaten so far took pesos as well as dollars. Every professional sign I passed had two names, one Anglo and one Spanish: Frederick & Alvarez, Attorneys at Law; Hinojosa & Barnstable, CPAs. I'd checked the place out as thoroughly as I could, without noticing any sign of Chaladian. Now, at exactly 5:15, I stood on the courthouse steps, scanning the baking streets for some hint that Thompson might be in the vicinity. I felt reasonably safe. I figured that even Chaladian wasn't crazy enough to try a drive-by shooting under the noses of people with badges and guns.

"Are you Tall Dude?"

The question came from a couple of steps above me, in a voice that was gentle and skeptical at the same time. Turning toward it, I saw an Anglo woman in her early fifties. Her curly hair clocked in at maybe one or two shades grayer than the scarf that covered it. The smile she showed me was guarded and probationary, the kind you get at the beginning of a new school year from a teacher who's heard that you were a royal pain in the butt the year before.

"Yes, I'm Jay Davidovich. Also known as Tall Dude."

"I'm Amber Hilliard with One More Chance. Katrina asked me to meet you here." She held out her hand and I shook it.

"Great. Can you take me to her?"

"That remains to be seen. My Jeep is this way."

The Jeep was a big rugged thing, fifteen years old if it was a day. Clean but battered. Had a little sticker on the windshield that showed a palm tree rising out of cool, blue water surrounded by sand. She'd parked it two blocks away, in an asphalt lot surrounded by an eight-foot chain link fence topped by razor wire. She had to flash a card at a black box to click the service gate open. I stashed my gym bag in the cargo bay. I had to pick up a small Bible to make room for myself on the front seat.

"Are you, like, a sister?"

"Not a nun, which is what I think you mean. I belong to the Society of Friends. Quakers. We call each other 'sister' and 'brother,' but it's not the same thing."

She started the thing and headed toward the exit. It rode like a tank in a bad mood. I've had smoother going in armored personnel carriers.

"Why do you want to see Katrina?"

"So I can try to talk her into going back to LA for a few weeks. There's someone out there who wants to see her."

"The actor?"

I nodded. We were bumping down a street lined with working class shops now, stores with big sale signs on most of their windows: PEPSI .89; KIDS SHOES 6.99.

"Katrina left Los Angeles for a reason."

"Yes she did. And I'm not kidding anyone. That reason is still around. He's been paid off, but that doesn't mean he's been neutralized.'"

I had a funny feeling that lying to Hilliard would be point-less. We turned a corner. Same kind of street, except the shops were smaller and darker inside.

"Given that, would you go back if you were she?"

I blinked. *If you were SHE?* That's the kind of thing Proxy would say.

"I don't know, to tell you the truth. She's done her bit, that's for sure. On the other hand, the guy needs her. Then there's the whole no-such-thing-as-an-ex-Marine thing."

"I hope she's gotten bravely over that by now."

"Maybe."

As we neared the corner, she suddenly wrenched the Jeep into a tire-squealing turn that brought us across the street. She double-parked T-style next to an ancient Omni that half shielded eight or nine adolescents hanging out in a smoky group in front of a bodega. Hilliard was instantly out and striding up to the group. A girl who was *maybe* sixteen watched with a deer-in-the-headlights face as Hilliard approached. She dropped her right hand straight down to her side, as if that would keep anyone from noticing the can of Coors she was holding.

Hilliard walked up to within eight inches of the girl and, without a word, held out her hand. Looking like she didn't know whether to cuss or cry, the girl handed her beer to Hilliard, who turned the can upside down and emptied the beer into the street. Slumping, the girl studied the soles of her shoes. Hilliard handed the empty can back to the girl.

"Throw this away, Maria."

The girl shuffled a few yards to the head of an alley running beside the store. She dropped the can in a rusty, fifty-five gallon oil drum. Then she glanced back at Hilliard, as if hoping she could stay right there for awhile.

"Come back here."

Head bowed, the girl came back over. On the way, she murmured something that I couldn't hear. Judging from what I could see of her expression, my guess would be, "I'm sorry."

"Get your phone out."

The girl's head snapped up and her dark brown eyes widened. Her mouth formed a "no" without saying it, but she fished into the left pocket of her pink shorts and worried a phone out.

"Now call your mother and tell her what you did. Right now."

"No! Please! She'll beat me! She'll slap me silly!"

"I'll pray that she won't." Hilliard's voice softened, to the same gentle-but-skeptical tone I'd heard in her first words to me. "But you have to report yourself, Maria. While I'm standing here. It won't get any easier. Do it now."

Close to tears, the girl hit a single key on the phone as she lifted it toward her ear and mouth. She said something in Spanish, paused, looked like she wanted to throw up, said something else, listened in obvious discomfort for a few more seconds, then lowered the phone.

"She said to come home right now."

"Then that's what you'd better do."

Maria worked her way to the other end of the group. As soon as she was clear, she started running. A couple of the others giggled at her haste. Hilliard gave them your basic paradeground stare, and the giggles stopped. She turned, came back to the Jeep at a stately pace, and got in. Six seconds later we were back on our way.

"Sorry about that. Maria is one of my girls."

"I'd say she's in good hands."

"She has a marijuana bust on her sheet from a pot party last year, and her dad is an unauthorized entrant. Deferred prosecution, so no-harm/no-foul on the happy hay if she keeps her nose clean. A couple of months back, though, our local sheriff went on one of his periodic zero-tolerance binges. If Maria gets run in for underage drinking, that prosecution won't be deferred, the pot thing will come back to life, and she'll have something a lot worse than a slap or two to worry about."

"'Unauthorized entrant' is the politically correct term for 'illegal alien' these days?"

"It's my term. Conduct is illegal; people aren't."

"The U.S. Attorney down here must be seriously under-worked if he's got time to worry about juvenile pot smoking."

"Maria is a state case. I do both state and federal."

"How does that work? Most places, the feds and the state boys barely even talk to each other."

"I'm privately funded. Grant from the One More Chance Foundation and some help now and then from my fellow Quakers." She held up her right hand as I started to respond. "Give me just a minute. I want to say the prayer I promised Maria before I forget."

I shut my mouth. Hilliard's lips moved silently. It must've been one hell of a prayer. It took a good minute-and-a-half. As the seconds ticked by, I thought of this woman—this smart, together lady—having a little chat with God about getting Maria through her latest delinquency without a beating. I rolled the idea around in my head. I wasn't sure what to do with it.

"Okay," Hilliard said when she'd wrapped up her God-talk. "Here's the deal. You ready?"

"Ready."

"You're who you say you are and I think you're playing straight with me. At least if I were lying I'd come up with a better line than you did. I'm going to drop you at your hotel. I need to think over what you told me, and pray about it a bit. And talk to Katrina."

"Then what?"

"Then I'll give you a call. Write down your mobile phone number for me."

I wrote the number on the back of a Trans/Oxana business card. I reached up to stick the card in the visor, but there wasn't any visor on my side. I opened her Bible at random and stuck the card somewhere near the end of Psalms.

"Which hotel are you staying at?"

"Radisson. But maybe you should drop me at the Hyatt instead and I'll take a cab from there to the Radisson. That way if someone has my hotel staked out they won't associate me with your Jeep."

She shot me an intrigued look as she found a major street and turned left.

"Katrina said you were careful."

I was still holding the Bible where I'd stuck my card. Wells' dad had said something about seeking consolation in Psalm one-forty-nine. I don't know the Psalms the way a good Jew should. Twenty-third, of course, which everybody knows, and the twenty-second, because Uncle Morty gave me five dollars to memorize it when I was eight. That's about it.

On a pure whim I opened the Bible up to where my card was, and then paged a few leaves over to Psalm one-forty-nine. The first few verses seemed like pretty conventional stuff, but then it reached out and grabbed me:

Let the praise of God be on their lips
and a two-edged sword in their hand,
to deal out vengeance to the nations
and punishment on all the peoples;
to bind their kings in chains
and their nobles in fetters of iron;
to carry out the sentence pre-ordained.

Hmmm. I didn't realize it at the time, but that's when I really started putting it together. Looking back on it, I already knew basically what I was going to do and how I was going to do it—and that's the way it would have gone down except for a piece or two of bad luck.

# Chapter Forty-three

An alarm bell went off in my head a little after six the next morning when I got a look at the cargo bay in Hilliard's Jeep. A tarp was covering a load of something or other, and whatever it was there was a lot of it. That wasn't what set the bell off. Anchoring the four corners of the tarp were two five-gallon jugs of water and two five-gallon gas cans secured with cargo netting. That told me the Jeep was headed for someplace lonely and desolate. I did *not* pat my right rear hip to check for the Colt Trooper. I knew it was there.

Hilliard had called me a little after 9:30 the night before. She'd given me an address and asked if I could be there around six. My answer was yes and here I was, at a storefront on a street near downtown where you could tell people in suits didn't go except by accident. Someone had given the place's outside walls and trim a fresh coat of paint in the last six months or so, but aside from that it had the old-fashioned, slapped-together-in-a-hurry look of something in a sepia-toned photograph. Lettering on the front window read SOF COMMUNITY MISSION.

"So," Hilliard said, "you up for a ride?"

"As long as Thompson is at the other end of it."

"Here's hoping. No guarantees."

A boy—young man, I guess, eighteen or nineteen—came out the front door, carrying a Stanley stainless steel thermos and two one-liter plastic bottles of water.

"Tom, this is Jay. Jay, Tom." Hilliard took the load from Tom and stashed the stuff in the Jeep's front seat while Tom and I shook hands. He looked more like a Tommy than a Tom to me. Said he was glad to meet me in a polite voice with a mid-Atlantic accent. I decided he must be a Quaker doing a mission stint out here between high school and college.

"I should be back before dark. Hold the fort. Don't try to reach me. If something big comes up, call Ben in San Antonio."

"Okay, Amber."

"All right, then." Hilliard circled the Jeep and climbed into the driver's seat. "We're off."

Six hours of driving took us from an interstate freeway to a state highway—a New Mexico state highway—to a county road and then off-road. The thermos held tea. Hilliard had two cups in the first couple of hours, before the temperature got too high, and talked me into trying one. She said something about how Pony Express riders used to carry tea in their canteens instead of water because it was more bracing.

I tried not to be too obvious about checking behind us now and then once we left the county road, but Hilliard noticed me.

"Don't worry too much. I know the country, and checking to see if I-C-E wants to play hide-and-seek is second nature by now. If something is back there that's out of place, I'll spot it."

"Would you care to elaborate?"

"Are you sure you want to know?"

That was actually a fairly good question. I thought about it for a few seconds before I answered.

"I don't need all the gory details. Just a rough idea of how many years I'll be looking at if we find a welcoming committee when we get wherever we're going."

"I'm no lawyer, but I'd say you're reasonably clear."

"That's very comforting." I shut up then. She didn't have to draw me a picture.

An hour or so later she slowed down and started to survey the landscape carefully, as if trying to make sure of her bearings. I'm not sure what the technical definition of "desert" is, but if what we were driving through didn't qualify someone should revise it. Nothing but scorched earth and rock. Not even a cactus, as far as I could tell.

Hilliard nosed the Jeep toward an outcropping of rock that climbed thirty feet into the air. She stopped the Jeep in the shade that the rock provided. Even before I got out I saw signs that people had been here recently: bits of footprints, a few cigarette butts.

The first thing Hilliard did after hopping out was take the gas cans and water bottles out and line them up on the shady side of our vehicle. I gave her a hand with it. Then she pulled the tarp back to expose a dozen well-filled camelbacks and a bunch of MREs still in their Pentagon-approved pouches. A "camelback" is a large water pouch designed to be carried comfortably on your back if you're hiking or mountain climbing. According to the Defense Department, "MRE" stands for "Meals Ready to Eat;" according to every GI I've ever heard express an opinion about it, "MRE" stands for "Meals Rejected by Ethiopians." Not exactly fun food, in other words, but they'll keep you alive.

"Can you give me a hand with the tarp?"

"Sure."

We laid the thing out on the ground and folded it over one time. Then we carried the folded edge to the base of the rock, where Hilliard worried it into a crevice as best she could. I held the open end up for her while she carefully arrayed the food and water pouches on the tarp's ground surface. She did this methodically and without wasted effort. Once she had all the stuff stashed, we pulled the tarp's top flap over them. We pounded tent pegs through the grommets to secure the tarp— and *that* was *work*; I didn't think ground could be that hard. We sealed the deal by scrounging some more or less flat rocks and piling them along the tarp's edges, between the grommets. I don't think our efforts would have defeated a real determined coyote, but any coyote that got into this Godforsaken country would probably be trying to commit suicide anyway.

"Okay," Hilliard said cheerfully, "time for lunch."

"When will it be time for Katrina Thompson?"

"That's up to her, but I told her I absolutely had to leave here by two. I really want to get back to El Paso before it's too dark, like I promised Tom."

Lunch was turkey and lettuce on hard rolls. I'm not sure the rolls were hard when they left the bakery, but they'd gotten that way by now.

"So." I let the syllable just lie there while I meditatively chewed turkey and rabbit food. "This would be, like, an artificial oasis for illegal aliens—excuse me, *unauthorized entrants*—sneaking in from Mexico."

"Yep. I-C-E would like to know where the oases are, but that's more a nuisance than a real threat. There could be twenty or thirty people here tonight. Or tomorrow night, or some night this week."

"So you don't have any problem with them coming into the country illegally?"

"I have a huge problem with people dying of thirst in the desert, regardless of how they got there."

"You understand that if some U.S. Attorney decided to be a total jerk about it, you could go to prison for doing this, right?"

"I've been to prison." She said this placidly, the way people say they used to smoke or went to Europe once. "One-hundred-ninety-seven days actual time served for trying to break into a nuclear facility as part of a protest. Second offense, post-nine-eleven. The government was not amused. Same prison in West Virginia where Martha Stewart served her sentence."

"I'm sorry to hear that."

"I actually found it a very fruitful time. I had a chance to read and pray and think, and manual labor can be very satisfying. Plus, it gives me some credibility with girls like Maria. It's amazing how bracing it is for them to see the picture of me in my orange jumpsuit. I realized when I saw women serving five and six and eight years for low-level drug running that my real vocation was with girls like her. With time to think things through and prayerfully reflect, I got it through my skull that the nuclear break-in stunt was grandstanding. Searching for martyrdom without really moving the ball. I figured the bad parts about prison—the indignity, the strip searches, using the toilet in front of other people, the lousy food, the zero privacy—was a way to atone for my self-importance. "

"Well what you're doing now sure isn't grandstanding."

"I'd feel very blessed if I went to prison for doing this. That would be true witness."

A few seconds after Hilliard's last sentence I heard an engine that, as it turned out, was still almost a mile away from us. I heard it because there just wasn't anything else to hear. Popping up to sidle to the edge of the rock, and then peering cautiously south toward the sound, I saw a plume of dust.

"That would be Katrina, unless I miss my guess," Hilliard said.

It was. It took her a good two minutes to reach us, but she eventually parked a Ford pickup truck that looked like the younger brother of the one her dad had driven. It had a little palm-tree-and-water sticker in the upper right-hand corner of the windshield, just like the one on Hilliard's Jeep. She and Hilliard gave each other a quick hug and a broad smile, but they didn't spend all afternoon at it. Thompson got right down to business.

"Can you spare one of those gas cans? Dad hasn't gotten this crate into the shop in a while and it drinks more than it should."

"Sure. I got gas just before we left the interstate, and one can will be more than enough to get me back to that station. I brought the water for you, too, except what I need to refill my bottle."

"That's wonderful. Thank you."

"It's really good to see you again, Katrina. I've been praying for you, and I ask all my girls to pray for you."

"Well I just *love* the way Mexican girls pray, and I need every *Ave Maria* I can get. So thank you for that."

I went to help Thompson transfer the spare gas and water. I wanted to make sure we were on the same page.

"I'm guessing you didn't drive all the way out here to tell me to go to hell."

"Nope. I'm goin' back to LA, and you're welcome to ride along. 'Course, if you'd rather ride back to El Paso with Amber and fly out from there, I wouldn't blame you."

"No, I'll take you up on your offer. Somewhere along the way, in fact, I'd like to trade you for that Russian pistol clip I gave you in Tucson."

"As long as it's a trade, I'm fine with that. But I need a loaded clip in return."

"I understand. In LA, you might run into Chaladian again."

"Yes, I just might." She turned and looked directly into my eyes, her unblinking gaze fierce but not angry. "And if I do I'm gonna take that sonofabitch out."

# Chapter Forty-four

It took us the rest of that day, all the next day, and part of the following morning to get to LA. Until we finally reached southern California, we didn't drive a mile of the trip on interstate highways. The roads we drove show up on maps as narrow red or blue strips.

For the first two hours I don't think we said a word to each other, except for my offering to share the driving and her saying she'd let me know if she needed me. I didn't tell her that if she did get within striking distance of Chaladian, the odds were about twenty-five-to-one that she was the one who'd end up dead. I may be dumb, but I'm not crazy.

Somewhere after that two-hour mark she glanced in my direction and spoke over the tinny hum of Tex/Mex music from the radio.

"You're back with your lady, aren't you?"

"Yeah, I am."

"I could tell, somehow. Don't know how. I just could. Anyway, I'm real happy for the two of you."

"Thanks." I waited about five beats, then continued speaking. "I wouldn't have guessed the Oasis Project was something your dad would support."

"He's a funny old buzzard. Says the illegals are just like pioneers in the old west. 'You wanna stop 'em, then git the Army out there an' goddamn seal the goddamn border. But don't let the desert stop 'em for ya.' That's pink water bullshit, that's what that is. I don't hold with that."

"That's a pretty good imitation of him."

"I've had lots of time to work on it."

That covered us until it was time for her to ask whether I wanted burgers or chicken for dinner.

This being the American west, I didn't have any trouble finding a gun-and-ammo store the next day. In a dusty Arizona town called Les Calles I stepped into Desert Empire Fishing, Hunting and Sporting Goods while Thompson pumped gas into the pickup's tank and then into the reserve cans. I'm not sure about the 'Empire' part, but everything else on the sign was dead accurate.

The crusty old gent who ran the place knew a mark when he saw one. For a spare nine-millimeter clip he charged me roughly a quarter of what the whole gun would have cost. He sold me the box of cartridges at the sticker price, so thank God for small favors. While he was ringing me up, I asked him how the town got to be called Les Calles instead of Los Calles.

"Founded by Lester Calles." He pronounced the last name *Cawls*, and grinned at me under his white, soup-strainer moustache. "Went by Les."

I loaded the clip and traded it to Thompson for the one from Chaladian's gun. I held my breath when she slipped it in. No guarantee, after all, that American and Russian clips are interchangeable. But it clicked into place with that neat precision that makes firearms so beautiful. I wrapped Chaladian's clip in a handkerchief and stuck it in my lower right pants pocket.

I offered to drive, again, and Thompson again said no, she'd just as soon stay behind the wheel. Fine. I leaned back as best I could and put the Stetson over my face.

I dreamed about the Iraqi teenager.

# Chapter Forty-five

I delivered Thompson to Trowbridge in an elegant suite at the Beverly Hills Hilton that Trowbridge was paying for, so screw Trans/Oxana's cap on hotel rates. The Beverly Hills Hilton caters to exactly the kind of people you'd think it does, so it has security that makes Fort Knox look like a main street bank in Hooterville. Go through the last ten years of *People* sometime and see if you can find a single *paparazzi* shot taken inside the BHH. That's why we were there.

The Thompson/Trowbridge hug seemed real, and so did Thompson's squeal and the radiant glow on Trowbridge's face. Who knew how long it was good for, but at least it wasn't fake. Plus, while they were locking lips I had a chance to filch the valet parking ticket for Thompson's truck from her purse. I called Proxy to give her the good news: Thompson and Trowbridge hooked up, Trowbridge mellow (for him), and no uptick in the body count (yet). I didn't say *yet* out loud.

"So far so good, then. Listen, as long as you're out there running up charges against my budget anyway, I need you to do something. See if you can squeeze a word out of Wells or someone about how the MPAA negotiations over the rating are going. I've been drilling dry holes on that for a week, and I'm getting nervous."

"Will do."

I had some other things to do, but I figured I could fit that in. On the way down to the lobby I called Wells, got a voice mail prompt, and left a message asking him to call me back. As I re-holstered my phone, I pulled the valet tag from my side pocket and stowed it in my wallet. I wanted to keep it safe. I couldn't control the timing of what I had in mind. What I could control was the preparation, so I wanted to get that right.

I stepped from the lobby onto the sidewalk bordering the vast drive-through area in front of the hotel. Surveyed the street and the sidewalk across from it. Chaladian had to have someone watching the main entrance. Judging by the *paparazzi* congregated as close to hotel property as they could legally get, everyone in LA knew that Trowbridge was up to something at the BHH. I was looking for someone sitting in a parked car or lolling in a doorway or walking up and down the sidewalk across the street. Probably someone with binoculars, because all they'd have is a physical description of Thompson or at best a grainy, third-generation copy of a digital photograph.

But *nada*. This hypothetical spotter was eluding my attention. Then, just in case I wasn't bummed enough, I had a *paparazzi* surge to contend with. The eight or nine pathetic souls started trotting after a brown Infiniti that pulled into the driveway. Some of them were shouting, "*Car-rie! Car-rie!* " Two Hilton security guys moved in to make sure they didn't get too close. The Infiniti pulled to a stop about ten feet past where I was standing. A lovely young woman who looked vaguely like Carrie Deshane but wasn't Carrie Deshane got out.

The surge stopped. The collective letdown was palpable.

"It's no one!" a camera-jockey yelled. He said it as if it were the woman's fault they'd mistaken her for a star. Then they all turned and headed back toward their original gathering place near the street.

All except one. A woman who looked nineteen or twenty, with two cameras slung around her neck, hadn't moved. You don't need binoculars if you have telephoto lenses. You don't need to sit or wander with suspicious aimlessness if you're ostensibly there to snap candid pictures of famous people. I'd just spotted the spotter. But I needed to confirm that theory.

Step one: check the Asset. I took a look at my watch. 3:10. I dialed Thompson's mobile phone number. Got her on the third ring.

"What's up?"

"Is Kent within arm's reach? I need to talk to him about something."

"No, he's in the fitness center while I'm gettin' gone over in the spa. Not the regular fitness center. The Presidential Fitness Center."

"Okay. Thanks."

It took me ten minutes to find the damn thing. The key to my plebian, $400-a-night room didn't open the door. Trowbridge noticed me through the glass, though, and sent one of his handlers over to let me in. I found him doing curls with twenty-five pound weights, and he didn't miss a rep when he started talking to me.

"Hey, my man Jay." Big grin, delighted expression. "What's on your mind?"

"First, my brass are panting for an MPAA update. I left a message for Wells and he hasn't called me back yet."

"Good luck with Wells. His dad said something to Saul that got the kid sent on some boondoggle to China for two weeks."

"Nuts."

"I know. Sucks to be you." He put the weight down, mopped his face and neck with a towel, then glanced up with another grin. "Fortunately, I can help you. I don't work for Saul so I'm not as important as Jeff, but I happen to know what's going on with MPAA."

"That'd be a big help."

"They'll get the deal done. The last hang-up is a little ass-slapping that Carrie couldn't restrain herself from. We'll snip the actual bodily contact, leave in the sound, and let imagination do the rest. That should pull us off the R."

"Thanks."

Trowbridge grabbed one of his handler's wrists and glanced at the guy's watch. Then he shooed the crew away and gestured toward the weight bench opposite him, inviting me to sit there.

"Katrina has a good hour left in the spa. If you've got a few minutes, there's something I'd like to talk to you about."

"Namely, Katrina."

"Namely Katrina. Seems like the pitch is going okay, but I don't feel like I'm closing the deal. You know what I mean?"

"Yep."

"So. Help! Please."

I took a deep breath. Coming to me for advice about chicks is like asking George W. Bush to help you with your particle physics homework. But Trowbridge didn't need to hear that, so I tried to come up with something else.

"In the time I've been working on this project, I've run into a lot of people. Some good people, some lousy people, one total bastard, but mostly people who are just doing their best to make it through the day without hurting anyone else."

"Out of curiosity, which category am I in?"

"I'd say you're sharing space with me in the make-it-through-the-day crowd. Nothing close to saints, but better than Levitt or Korvette."

"Talk about low bars. I'm not sure a C-plus will cut it with Katrina. What can I do for extra credit?"

I'd been leading up to something when I was talking about all those people I'd met. The only two that I really admired were Thompson and Hilliard—two women who had absolutely nothing in common except that neither one of them wanted Mexicans to die of thirst in the desert, and they'd both been behind bars for something that mattered more to them than themselves. But spelling that out to the Asset could lead to awkward questions the next time I was in Hartford. So I fell back on something else.

"The basketball coach I had in high school believed that any idea that really mattered could be expressed in three words: 'It's called pride.' 'Pick and roll.' 'It's called honor.' 'Pass the ball.' 'It's called guts.' 'Take the charge.' 'It's about teamwork.' 'Be a man.' One of the English teachers would make fun of him, and I used to laugh at it myself. But you know what? When I was overseas, I never saw anybody risk his life for *Stopping by the Woods on a Snowy Evening.*"

"So you think maybe your coach was onto something."

"Doesn't matter what I think, does it? What matters to you is what Katrina thinks. And I'll give you eight to one on a fast track that she'd say my coach was the smartest guy who ever lived, except Jesus."

"Okay." He nodded pensively.

"I'm sorry. I mean, I know that isn't much help. I wish I could script it for you. But this is real life."

"No, I hear what you're saying."

I swallowed. Calculated risk coming up.

"Listen. I think Chaladian has someone staking out the hotel. I think I've nailed the schlub he has doing it. And I've got a plan."

"Whatever it is, I'm in."

"What I need you to do is keep Thompson out of sight from now until I call you."

"When will that be?"

"Hard to say. I'll lead him as far away from here as I can. When I'm absolutely sure he's too far out of range to double back easily, I'll call you."

"And what do I do?"

"Move Thompson to some other decadent luxury hotel. When Chaladian gets tired of chasing me, he can come back here and start over from square one."

"You understand you could be driving halfway to San Diego?"

"If I can string him along that far, I will."

"I love this plan! Now, the lady has a mind of her own, as you well know. But I'll see what I can do."

# Chapter Forty-six

Next step: Find a decoy. That figured to be a snap.

The Beverly Hills Hilton has at least three bars. There may be a couple more that I missed. I went to the one on the floor below the lobby, where you're not going to be seen by everyone who casually strolls into the hotel. The two willowy blondes in little black dresses that I spotted—one at the bar and one in the booth farthest from the door—told me I'd made the right choice. I caught the eye of the one in the booth, nodded, went to the bar, and ordered a vodka neat.

It took her a full eighty seconds to join me. That didn't absolutely prove she was a party girl, of course. She could have been a librarian or a choir director. Sure she could. Judging from her opening question, she made me for an out-of-towner from the get-go.

"What brings you to LA?"

"*Star Trek* convention. Plus, I thought as long as I was here I might try out for the Clippers."

"Almost tall enough, but the wrong color."

"I get that a lot."

She sipped something clear. My guess would be Seven-Up, but that's just a guess. She gave me a half smile, but made sure I understood she wasn't exactly blown away by my idea of snappy patter. Then came the pitch.

"You interested in anything in particular?"

"A trip to San Diego."

"I never heard of that before. Is that anything like Around the World?"

"Just what it sounds like. We drive out, we come back. Maybe all the way to San Diego, but probably not. Guaranteed that you're back in time for Leno."

"That counts as all night. Five hundred."

"You take plastic?"

"Jesus Christ!" She looked away in disgust and started to slide off her stool.

"Just kidding." I showed her the money so she'd know I really had it. "Go up to the lobby and wait for me."

"Where will you be?"

"Getting my wheels."

I waited for a minute after she walked out of the bar before I paid my tab and left. Up to the lobby, handed Thompson's valet tag to the concierge, got it back from him after he'd phoned for the truck, then walked over to Party-girl.

"Can we wait outside? I could use a smoke."

"Nope. Sorry. Suck it up for about ten more minutes."

Four of those minutes had passed before I saw Thompson's truck roll up to the hotel's massive revolving door. I took Party-girl's right arm.

"Show time, babe."

I led her to the left, to a smaller, standard door near the concierge's desk. I had her go through before I did, so that she was between me and the street as we walked the dozen feet or so to the truck. No way anyone who was paying attention could possibly miss her. Someone watching through a telephoto lens would see a tall blonde striding up to Thompson's truck and then along the bed until she disappeared through the passenger-side door.

Around the truck for me, five dollars of Trans/Oxana's money to the valet, collect the key, slip behind the wheel and—*AWAY ALL BOATS!* I had that puppy making tracks on Wilshire before you could say, "San Fernando Valley." I did a little lane-to-lane weaving around Priuses and other crap that LA calls cars to make it look like I was trying to get somewhere in a hurry. Then I headed for I-5 south.

"The smoking lamp is now on, if you really can't do without it."

"No, that's okay. I only smoke when I'm bored."

I figured Chaladian couldn't be too far away. It's not like he was the CIA who could put seven people on this stakeout. He had to be waiting within a few blocks, close to a car he could jump into as soon as he got a call from his lookout. He could cut himself a little slack, because no way anyone was going fast for long in LA afternoon traffic, and Thompson's truck figured to stand out. But he couldn't plan on driving all the way across town or letting any grass grow under his feet either.

I spotted him just before we hit the freeway. Not quite a block behind us. He'd hidden his head and face with a biker helmet that looked like a prop from *Iron Man*, but his general shape and the way he moved his body as he maneuvered the hog he was riding struck very familiar chords in my memory.

I pulled onto I-5 and settled into the traffic flow. It wasn't freeway speed, but it wasn't bumper-to-bumper either. There's a ton of traffic on LA freeways, almost twenty-four-hours a day, but most of the time it *moves*. I kept to the far outside lane, in case he was tempted to cruise past on the right for a good look at my blond passenger. He didn't try it. Never got closer than four or five car lengths.

Forty minutes of this was plenty for my purposes. Mission accomplished. I pulled out my phone and punched in Trowbridge's number.

"Yo."

"This is Davidovich. The coast should be clear. I'll keep him on this wild goose chase for as long as he'll play along, so you can make your move."

"Um, actually, we're uh, kind of already moving. Sort of."

"What's that supposed to mean?"

"I got a text from Wellstein. He has a project he thinks would be a perfect vehicle for Katrina. We're headed down to see him."

"YOU'RE WHAT?"

"Yeah, I figured you'd be pissed. Sorry. My bad. But, you know, the lady has a dream. We're in a Mercedes and I'm driving, so even with your head start there's a chance we'll get there before you." He hung up.

*Shit.* The text to Trowbridge was Wellstein yelling, "Play ball!" Setting the wheels in motion for his own personal star turn. His spectacular final scene. He was thinking just like I was. He figured Chaladian would see Trowbridge and Thompson leaving and follow them. The three of them would end up somewhere in the neighborhood of his office. Then he'd blow Chaladian away in front of an A-list audience. Or go down in a blaze of glory trying to.

I'd seen this coming. I'd figured out what Wellstein had in mind when I stumbled over Psalm one-forty-nine. And I had decided days ago, somewhere in the desert, that I wasn't going to let it happen. I'm not sure what it was. Maybe Hilliard and her riff on prison, maybe the Iraqi teenager, maybe Thompson—probably some combination. This old Jewish man with a horrible disease was not going to end his life as a murderer—or, much more likely, as a grotesquely failed attempted murderer, writhing on the ground in agony with a couple of Chaladian's bullets in his gut. It would solve a lot of my problems if he actually managed to waste the guy, and if anyone ever needed killing Chaladian did. Saddam Hussein needed killing too. That doesn't mean you forget about the collateral damage.

That was the big reason to get Trowbridge and Thompson stashed someplace where Chaladian wouldn't know where to look for them. I couldn't control Wellstein's timing, but once I got those two out of the way I wouldn't have to. I could just make my way down there, pour out my soul to him, tell him my plans for Chaladian and, if that didn't work, muscle the gun away from him. But Wellstein hadn't politely waited around while I got my ducks in a row. And now he'd dealt Trowbridge and Thompson into the game. Caught me flat-footed on that one.

Okay, fine. No battle plan survives contact with the enemy. One piece of good luck, though. I had Chaladian following me instead of Trowbridge and Thompson. I could lead the SOB all the way to La Jolla. *If* I could just keep him on my tail, he wouldn't come anywhere close to Wellstein tonight.

But that was a big IF. Suppose Chaladian still had someone watching the Beverly Hills Hilton? Suppose that someone had seen Trowbridge and Thompson leave and was getting word to him? Reflexively, I patted the back of my right hip where the Colt Trooper nestled in its skeleton holster under my shirt tail. Angela—turned out that was Party-girl's name—caught my gesture. She put it together with my half of the phone conversation, and suddenly I was getting a you're-the-hottest-stud-in-LA vibe from her. I shook my head. Chicks love bad boys, and then they wonder why guys won't put the toilet seat down.

Angela's case of the hots, though, wasn't at the top of my list of things to worry about right now. My gut was tingling. I checked the rear-view mirror for the Harley. *Not* four car lengths behind me anymore. Closing fast in the lane inside mine, looking for a chance to squeeze past. No way I'd still be ahead of him in two minutes. I looked over at Angela.

"Bad news, bright-eyes. Looks like we're going all the way to San Diego after all."

She'd gotten a cigarette out and had been playing with it, tapping one end against her cigarette case and that kind of jazz. Now she opened the case, put the cigarette back inside, and laid her head complacently against the seat cushion.

"I wouldn't necessarily call that *bad* news."

# Chapter Forty-seven

They didn't beat me to the suburban office strip where Wellstein did business, but they came too damn close for my liking. Angela and her Marlboro Lights had been pouting next to the truck for less than twenty minutes when Trowbridge's midnight blue Mercedes sports coupe cruised into the parking lot around 7:45. He must have driven like a maniac. No sign of Chaladian or his Harley anywhere.

I let loose with a very relieved sigh when a brown Chrysler Imperial turned ponderously into the parking lot from its other entrance. Channeling my inner Proxy, I'd called for the thing when I'd hit the first San Diego exit. Angela was busy telling me her one hundred favorite rom-com lines at the time, so she hadn't quite grasped what I was doing.

"There's your ride home, Angie. Back in plenty of time for Leno, just like I promised. Unless you'd rather pull the late shift at BHH."

"WHAT?" She whirled to face me while Trowbridge and Thompson climbed out of the Mercedes. "This is IT? A drive to San Diego?"

"For five hundred bucks, and you earned every penny." I raised my voice to cover the thirty feet separating us from the Mercedes. "Hey, Trow."

"What? Who's 'Trow'?" Angela reversed her about-face and caught sight of Trowbridge. The vision reduced her voice to a breathless and reverent whisper. "Holy shit. Holy fucking shit. Who's that with him?"

Trowbridge had gathered Thompson into a major squeeze with his left arm and was giving me a huge, grinning wave with his right.

"Her name is Katrina Thompson. They get along real well."

"I don't see what the big deal is." Angela's petulance was almost touching. "I'm prettier than she is. I'm blonder than she is. I'm more stacked than she is. What's so special about her?"

"She doesn't smoke."

"Really? Do you think that's it?" Angela got rid of her cigarette. "The least you could do is introduce me."

I shrugged as Trowbridge and Thompson approached us. Didn't seem like much to ask.

"Angela, Kent and Katrina. Kent and Katrina, Angela."

She air kissed both of them, offered a little sigh, and then began sauntering toward the Chrysler. Three fetching, booty-swinging steps into the trek she turned back in my direction.

"Could you just turn your head about three inches to your right?"

I did. She lashed out suddenly and slapped my cheek—a good, sharp, no-kidding smack. I saw it coming and could have stopped it, but I figured everything would go faster if she just got it off her chest. While the *crack!* was still echoing in my ear, she wagged her right index finger in my face.

"That was for teasing."

Then she finally simpered off to the Chrysler.

"Spirited little minx."

This from Trowbridge. For a blinding, red-eyed second I had the urge to grab his shirt the way I had Wells' in Omaha and explain that this was real life and real serious, not some damn summer blockbuster from New Paradigm Studios. But I got past that. What was the point? He was trying to impress a girl. Guys have started wars to do that. I wasn't going to reverse humpty-million years of evolution with a little heart-to-heart.

"Okay." I cleared my throat, trying to be low-key. "Not the play I called, but we're where we are and we'll try to make it work somehow. Let's go see what's on Sydney Wellstein's mind."

# Chapter Forty-eight

His office was the only one of the eight in the strip that still had lights on. I hustled in front of Trowbridge as we approached the door. He was the Asset and I wasn't. If we were walking into a trap, I was supposed to take the punch or the bullet. The outside door wasn't locked. I cautiously opened it. No one in the reception area, but the door to the office behind it was half open, and Wellstein's raspy, sarcastic voice came through clearly.

"You don't know what the novelization will cost? Well, it must be a matter of no importance then. We won't worry about it. We'll just wait for the bill to come in and pay it."

Trowbridge and I looked at each other. Trowbridge shrugged. I couldn't improve on that. While we loitered in indecision in the outside doorway, Wellstein went right on with his rant.

"T-L squared, Mandy. Too little, too late. I want this project to work and I see a way forward, but we've gotta get past finger-fucking. Call me back tomorrow and be ready to say something."

We heard the receiver slam into the cradle. I stepped all the way into the reception area and started toward the door to Wellstein's office. Trowbridge, following, tapped me gingerly on the shoulder. I looked around at him.

"Maybe I should go first? Because he technically invited me? And you're not strictly speaking on the list?"

I was about to explain who was the Asset and who wasn't when we heard the shot. It boomed out at us, minimally muffled by the thin walls. Someone who's only heard large-caliber gunfire from sound effects machines has no idea what it's like. It doesn't just blast your ears, it shocks your whole body. Rocks you backward, as if you'd been shoved. Trowbridge screamed something blasphemous. Thompson, the Marine veteran, contented herself with yelping, "Shit!"

I drew the Colt with my right hand and slammed the outside door shut with my left. Cocking the Colt, I fixed my eyes on the office doorway, while talking over my shoulder to the other two.

"Make sure that front door is locked."

I barked that order without yelling it. Thompson hopped to that chore. I deliberately kept my voice at normal volume but with a now-hear-this tone that Thompson, at least, would recognize. People in a situation like this want orders, not suggestions, but not from someone who sounds like he's panicking.

"You two stay right here. I'm going into the office. If you hear anything that sounds like a shot or a struggle, run like hell and call nine-one-one on the way."

Four measured paces brought me to the office doorway. I stopped and showed my handsome profile. Arm raised and Colt pointed toward the ceiling, I gave the hollow-core wooden door a nudge kick that sent it all the way open. Waited for shots or sounds or something. Nothing. Bright, fluorescent light spilled through the opening. Danger, if there was any, figured to come from my right as I entered. I took a couple of deep breaths. *Here goes nothin'.*

I plunged through the doorway, pivoting immediately to my right and leveling the Colt. I didn't dive or roll or turn my gun sideways or anything, like Trowbridge undoubtedly would have if this were a scene in a retro-*noir* flick. I just kept moving until I was all the way past the far end of the desk. No danger lurked in the office. The only other creature there was Wellstein, and he wouldn't be shooting anybody. I put two fingers on his neck to check for a pulse, just to be sure. Zilch. I didn't need a coroner to know Sydney Wellstein was dead.

He sprawled against the back of his desk chair. A massive purple stain spoiled the part of his white Ocean Pacific pullover in the area of his heart. The Russian automatic that I'd taken from Chaladian and transferred to Wellstein lay on the desk in front of his body. Some papers lay under the gun. I could read **BANKRUPTCY** in oversized, boldfaced type on the top one. A window in the back wall, behind and to the left of the desk, was open and the screen was brutally punched through. I could read the setup like a book.

*An old man looking at a terrible death decided to kill himself, make it look like murder, and frame Chaladian for the crime. He got his son out of the country. Put on a big, showy act for us and for someone named Mandy to make it look like he had a big project going and was focused on the future. Shot himself through the heart instead of eating the gun because that would look more like murder. Meticulously drew up bankruptcy papers to document a motive that would only work for Chaladian. Opened the back window and smashed the screen to make it look the murderer escaped that way. And then shot himself.*

Not bad, but I could improve on it. Holstering the Colt, I wrapped the clip that originally came from Chaladian's gun in my handkerchief and pulled it from the lower pocket of my cargo pants. I'd gotten that clip back from Thompson because I figured I could do something mischievous with it someday. I'd never get a better opportunity. Pushed the release on the butt of the gun in front of Wellstein. Pulled the clip that was in there out. Inserted Chaladian's clip. Wiping clean and then hankie-wrapping the clip I'd removed, I hustled behind the desk, cracked open a drawer on the right side, and dropped that clip into it.

Back to the reception area as I took out my phone. Trowbridge and Thompson were exactly where I'd told them to stay. I made a sweeping MOVE! motion with my right hand while I punched nine-one-one with my left.

"Out to the truck," I told them. "Don't touch anything in here. Go."

"Nine-one-one. What is your emergency?"

"A man has been shot at Wellstein Properties LLC. Looks like he's dead." I gave her the address.

"Are you with the body?"

"Negative. Afraid of who might still be in the area."

"Where are you now?"

"In the parking lot outside the building."

"Have you seen anyone armed or dangerous in the vicinity?"

"Negative."

"All right. Stay there. We don't want you looking around for anyone or doing any cops-and-robbers stuff, okay?"

"Got it."

"Dispatching. Stay on the line."

After a few seconds doing whatever operators do to dispatch cops, she came back on and asked for my name. I gave it. Then she had me repeat some stuff. By the time she was through with me, we could hear sirens.

I herded our cozy little group over to Thompson's truck. I unclipped the Trooper's holster from my belt and stowed it inside the cargo netting under the tarp in the pickup's cargo bay. Then I pulled on the best attention-to-orders face I could manage and turned to Trowbridge and Thompson.

"We're going to be here awhile. The police will want to talk to us separately. Tell them exactly what you heard and saw—not what you think or guess or imagine. Don't leave anything out, don't make anything up, don't make any smart-ass cracks, don't give them any shit. If they ask for your consent to search you or the car or the truck, the answer is yes. We will *not* insist that they get a warrant. We're good citizens and we have nothing to hide. Clear?"

"Yo," from Thompson.

"This is so not like the movies," Trowbridge said.

A squad car boiled into the parking lot, lights flashing and siren wailing.

# Chapter Forty-nine

The cops actually got it done pretty fast, considering. Just over ninety minutes all told. The uniform sized the situation up in a hurry, called for detectives and crime-scene folks and dead body folks, and secured the scene. He took short statements from each of us. When the detective got there, the uniform gave him the gist of our story. Then the detective took longer statements from each of us. Somehow the Colt didn't come up, which saved me a lot of palaver about whether walking around with the thing was, strictly speaking, legal.

Without making a production out of it, I tried to get a handle on what the evidence techies were taking out of Wellstein's office. Paper, lots of paper. Good. Computer. Good. They weren't treating this like a cut-and-dried, close-the-file-and-slam-the-drawer suicide.

The detective—Detective-Sergeant Jalil Kinjaro, according to his card—saved me for last. He taped his chat with me, but made notes along the way. After we'd gotten through it he looked at the notes pensively, rubbed his chin with dark brown fingers, and glanced up at me.

"Former MP, huh?"

"Yep."

"Ever do any CID stuff?"

"Nope. Strictly operational." 'CID' is Criminal Investigation Division—basically, detectives in army uniforms.

"All this see-a-way-forward jazz you overheard Wellstein spouting about—are you sure about that?"

"Yep."

"Sure doesn't sound like suicide, does it?"

"Well, I'm an amateur, but I see your point."

"How long did you say it took you to get into the office after the shot?"

"Hard to say, but I sure wasn't in any hurry. As much as a minute, I guess."

"Hear anything that sounded like someone crashing through a window?"

"Nope. All I heard until I was actually in the office was that gunshot ringing in my ear."

"Yeah, I can see that. Anything else you think I should know?"

*Yeah, you should know he'd been diagnosed with Lou Gehrig's disease. But you're going to have to dig that up on your own. Good luck.*

"Nope."

He thanked me, made sure he had my card, and headed for the squad car that had driven him out here. The evidence techs and the crime-scene guys and the first squad car had long since left. Another twenty seconds and we had the parking lot to ourselves again. I joined Trowbridge and Thompson back at the truck and fished my holstered Colt out of the cargo bay as I offered a comment.

"Eventful night."

"Yeah." Trowbridge seemed a little letdown, now that the excitement was over. "I talked to Saul. He thinks he can spin it into a huge positive. 'Deeply saddened by the tragic death of Hollywood legend Sydney Brandeis Wellstein whose body Kent Trowbridge discovered when he came to speak to him about a major project.' He'll try to make it sound like Wellstein died in my arms without actually saying it. You know? But I won't let him go that far."

"Whatever."

"You know. I mean, he wants to preempt anyone who's tempted to take the other angle. The 'isn't it funny that Trowbridge just happened to be there?' angle."

"We wouldn't want that."

We had made our way back over to the Mercedes by now. Trowbridge wasn't through talking, though.

"So, what, get back to LA and pull an all-nighter talking about next steps?"

"There's something we'd better take care of first." I got the Colt out, cocked it, and held it casually beside my leg. "Come on out, Stan. We need to chat."

I didn't have to ask twice. The far door clicked open. Chaladian dove to the pavement on the other side of the car and rolled to his feet. He turned to face us, grinning like a PFC whose claptest just came back negative. I let him see the Colt, in case he had any fast-draw stuff in mind. He didn't.

"Put your forearms on top of the car, palms up."

"Careful." He complied, but with an expression suggesting it was his idea. "If you piss me off I won't tell you how to get Trowbridge off."

"Stan, you need to listen and not talk. You're in a very delicate situation."

"Why don't we just kill him?" This question came from Thompson, and I could tell she was serious. "Right here? Self-defense. He's gotta be carrying."

"Too much paperwork." I put the Colt back down next to my leg again. "Now everyone please shut up. The tall guy has the floor."

I paused and glanced around to make sure they'd gotten the message. Then I looked directly at Chaladian.

"You remember that big payment that Wellstein's company made to one of your companies not long ago?"

"Payment in full." Chaladian nodded vigorously. "Wellstein was a good man to do business with. It was a shock to see him wheeled into a meat wagon tonight."

"Well, while I was checking for a pulse, I noticed bankruptcy papers on his desk. Looks like he was going to file for chapter eleven before long—specifically, less than ninety days after that payment in full he made."

"So what? I've been paid. What do I care if he stiffs his other creditors?"

"Well, Stan, my wife the lawyer tells me that if Wellstein had filed in the next couple of months, a federal bankruptcy trustee could come knocking on your door and take all that money back. That's probably why Wellstein insisted on paying an on-shore company that the trustee could serve process on without complications. It's a motive Stan. A motive just for you. Doesn't fit anyone else. By killing him before he filed, you'd get to keep all that money."

The grin disappeared. I wasn't going to miss it.

"I know nothing about this lawyer shit."

"'Just a coincidence.' Try that one on the jury and see if it works. After all, O.J. Simpson and Robert Blake walked. Maybe you will too."

"What are you saying? That the police will accuse me of murdering a man who obviously committed suicide?"

"Suicide? Not so sure. No note. Shot through the heart at close range but not point-blank. You would have had time to get out through the window before I entered the office after the shot. And you were found hiding in Kent's car afterward, which you have to admit is pretty suspicious."

"Fairy tales. The police will see through it like that." He snapped his fingers.

"You're probably right. Nothing for you to worry about. After all, apart from everything else, there's the forensics. There won't be any of your prints on the gun—*unless* Wellstein somehow managed to get his hands on your old gun. And how in the world would he do that?"

"Are you telling me you gave him the pistol you stole from me?"

"Of course not. That would be illegal. Besides, if I *had* done that I would have had to wipe the gun clean of all prints, including yours, because otherwise my prints and Thompson's would turn up on it. Same thing with the clip."

"You have a point. I'm feeling better."

"On the other hand, there are the cartridges that you originally loaded into the clip. Those would have your prints and no one else's on them, wouldn't they? If it was suicide, that might be hard to explain."

His face lost some of its color. He gave me a long, nasty stare. "All right. What's your price?"

"I'm incorruptible. Can't be bought. So if I were you, what I'd do is, I'd keep my sorry ass as far away from Katrina Thompson as I possibly could. The farther you are from the United States, and the healthier Katrina is, the less chance you'll find yourself in a San Diego courtroom facing a first degree murder charge over the death of beloved Hollywood legend Sydney Wellstein."

He stood there, almost expressionless, for a good twenty seconds. It was almost fun imagining the calculations going on in his head. Then the grin came back, but more subdued than usual this time.

"Very well. I promise to be a good boy. From this moment I would not know Katrina Thompson if I saw her in *People* magazine. So. I can go now?"

"You can go on the condition that you ride that Harley of yours into Mexico as the first step on a one-way trip to Whatthefuckistan so that you can spend the rest of your miserable life hustling Central Asians."

He started walking away, toward the dark-shrouded far edge of the parking lot. I braced myself. I didn't have to wait long for Thompson to lay into me.

"Seriously? You're just going to let him go? Give me that goddamn gun." She reached across my body and started tugging at my right arm while I raised the Colt well out of her reach.

"Careful, Hurricane. It's been a while since I slugged a Marine, but the last one I hit still remembers it."

Chaladian had by now disappeared into blackness. He was presumably making his way down the steep hill beyond the parking lot that was supposed to add visual relief to the development's layout.

"But we can't just take his word for it that he's going to leave us alone!"

"Of course we can't. As soon as we hear that Harley roar off, we're going to call the San Diego police and tell them that we flushed a suspicious character who was hiding in Trow's Mercedes, and the last we saw he was hellbent for Mexico on a motorcycle. We'll have a first-rate description of him and, incredibly enough, something pretty close to the Harley's license number. If he doesn't get himself killed trying to escape which, frankly, is my bet, he'll be hauled back here in irons and held without bail."

If I'd gotten a picture of Thompson's face I could have sold it on eBay. I watched the waves of astonishment roll across her features one after another as her brain processed what I'd just said, one layer at a time. She finally dissolved into an amazed smile, like you might give a five-year-old who'd learned to tie his shoes.

"Well aren't you just the cleverest boy in southern California?"

I was about to decline this compliment with my customary modesty when we heard the Harley's trademark roar. A few seconds later we briefly glimpsed it in a sliver of moonlight, laboring up the far side of the hill toward the street. The next thing I heard was Trowbridge's voice.

"Sorry, bro."

Then he cold-cocked me. I didn't hear anything else for about seventeen seconds.

# Chapter Fifty

Trowbridge was already burning rubber out of the parking lot when Thompson's ungentle pats on my cheek brought me around. She sort of came into focus after I blinked a couple of times.

"He's gone after Chaladian, hasn't he?"

"Sure has."

"Where's my gun?"

"He took it."

"Oh shit."

My head gave me an argument every inch of the way, but I made it to my feet. Thompson kept a concerned hand on my right arm and two worried eyes on my face.

"I'm gonna call an ambulance for you, and then I'm gonna have to leave you on your own. I've got to go after that boy."

"We're going together."

I wasn't in the mood for a debate, so I just started striding toward the truck. She had to run to catch up with me. When she did she still had enough breath left for further conversation.

"All right, then, but I'm driving. It's my truck and my boyfriend. Gimme the keys."

Seemed reasonable to me, to I turned them over and climbed into the passenger seat. After all, now that I thought about it, the whole thing was pretty academic. Trowbridge in a Mercedes wasn't going to catch Chaladian on a Harley, and in a lumbering pickup truck we weren't going to catch Trowbridge. All we had to do was be somewhere in the same time zone when Trowbridge got stopped for going ninety-five miles an hour or wiped out or just gave up the chase.

The Mercedes was nowhere in sight by the time we cleared the lot, so Thompson headed for I-5. I reached Detective-Sergeant Kinjaro's voice mail and left the Chaladian-on-the-run message. Next job was to call Trowbridge and try to talk some sense into him. If he'd already lost sight of Chaladian—and odds were that he had—then he might come in off the ledge without a lot of aggravation.

I dialed his number and hit SEND. Three seconds later I heard an insistent BEEP! from the vicinity of Thompson's thighs. She glanced over and rolled her eyes at me.

"That's Kent's phone. He had me fussing with the GPS app on the way down to help him find Wellstein's place."

"The shortest route to the freeway is Gardenia Street and you just passed it."

"Screw the freeway, I'm following Kent." Thompson said this in a normal tone of voice, as if it weren't a clinically insane remark.

"What do you mean you're following Kent?" I peered intensely through the windshield, wondering if I was somehow missing something. "Are you telling me you can see his Mercedes out there."

"No, of course not." She tapped the phone's glowing screen. "I can see him on here. His Mercedes has a gizmo that sends out signals about where it is, in case it gets stolen. He has an app on his phone that picks those signals up. So I don't know where he's going, but wherever it is, we're going to the same place."

"Perfect."

"That didn't sound sarcastic." Thompson shared a puzzled glance with me. "It's not like you not to sound sarcastic when you use a word like 'perfect.'"

"Life is good again." This was true. Even my headache eased up a bit. "He'll never get close to Chaladian. We'll find him, wherever he ends up. With any luck, San Diego cops or the California Highway Patrol will already have Chaladian in handcuffs by then."

"Maybe."

She sounded dubious. I didn't see any point in pursuing it. We were within smelling distance of the Pacific Ocean by now, driving on dimly-lit commercial streets. I'd say we were at that for another ten minutes before Thompson spoke again.

"I wouldn't blame you if you kicked my butt once we got back. You can start chewing me out right now if you want to. This is all my fault."

"I'm no shrink, Hurricane, but if I were you I'd get out of the habit of thinking it's your fault when a guy you've hooked up with does something stupid. Strikes me as a low-percentage play."

"I hear you, but that's not it." She shook her head. "I was jawing at him about Chaladian all the way down here. About how I had to take him out and be done with it, 'cause he just wouldn't ever give up if I came out on top after turning my back on him. 'Nobody fucks with Mr. Ten Percent.' That's his motto. And I said I couldn't leave it to the cops, 'cause like you said about OJ and that other guy, you couldn't trust a California jury to convict Adolph Hitler."

All this time she was twisting and turning and curving along the route beeped to her by Trowbridge's phone—and I was getting a gut tingle. It didn't look to me like a random course, as if Trowbridge were just driving around hoping that he'd stumble over Chaladian by blind luck. He had to think he was actually following the guy. But the only conceivable way he could be following him was if Chaladian wanted him to. And if Chaladian was leading Trowbridge on, then that was bad news cubed.

The steady, polite beep on the phone suddenly turned shrill and insistent: BEEPBEEPBEEPBEEPBEEPBEEP! A red dot started flashing on the street map displayed on the screen. We were in some kind of warehouse district that looked like it hadn't had much to warehouse for a while. The pale moonlight showed two- and three-story buildings, featureless rectangles looming over an asphalt moonscape.

"Okay, let me out here. I'll take a look around."

Thompson pulled over. As I climbed out, I thought of a question that I knew the answer to, but what the hell.

"You don't by any chance have that Russian pistol of yours, do you?"

"Nope. Back at the hotel. Oughta get my butt kicked for that, too, I guess."

"All right. Just cruise around with the doors locked and your lights off. I'll call you as soon as I have anything."

I found the Mercedes without any problem. It was around the next corner, up on the sidewalk, parked on a slant in an effort to hem a Harley in next to a corrugated steel wall. I stopped and pressed myself against the wall. Listened. Heard nothing special. Worked my way around the car and the cycle, then scooted back against the wall. I inched my way along feeling for a door and straining my ears to pick up a sound.

I had covered maybe forty feet in this way, and saw a huge black space coming up, presumably where the wall ended. That's when I finally heard something: a punch and a grunt, then another punch and a panicky little yelp. It came from the black space, well above ground level. I must be coming up on a loading dock. I heard Chaladian's voice then, calm and menacing.

"You are going to call Katrina and ask her to wait for you at the Rest Area off Exit 3. Tell her you will be there no later than two. You are all right, but you are exhausted and need her to drive you back to LA."

Trowbridge's answer sounded a lot like, "Fuck you." Whatever it was, Chaladian didn't like it. The punch-grunt sequence came again.

I had Thompson's number punched in by the time I got my phone to my ear. I made my voice nice and loud.

"Okay, Hurricane, we got him. Send the cops right around the corner and halfway up the block, to the loading dock."

That figured to get Chaladian's attention, but I didn't see any percentage in standing around waiting for him. I glimpsed him hustling to the edge of the dock as I sprinted past, running all the way to the far end. I half vaulted and half sprawled onto the dock. I rolled three turns along the surface. A shot split the darkness, followed by the fierce whine of lead ricocheting off concrete four inches from me. I prayed that it came from my own gun. For someone used to shooting semiautomatic pistols, shooting a double-action revolver can be a challenge. Unless you cock the hammer first yourself, the trigger pull cocks the hammer and then releases it—and that can throw your aim off if you're not used to it.

I scrambled to my feet, pumped as I could be. This wasn't Hollywood or an upscale hotel. This was a warehouse loading dock where people worked with their hands and their backs and made stuff happen. I finally felt at home. I did a shoulder roll as I ran along the back of the dock, looking for the control panel. It hurt like hell, but it made Chaladian's second shot miss.

All at once, black on yellow on a three-foot square touch-pad in the dock's back wall, I saw the magic words: LOAD LEVELER. I ran right past it, then ducked, turned around, and headed back for it. Chaladian had figured out that shooting with a double-action revolver at a moving target in the dark was a chancy proposition. He turned the Colt toward Trowbridge, crumpled into a gasping ball four feet from him.

"Stop, or I'll kill him!"

Yeah, like *that's* gonna happen.

The thing about loading docks is that trucks come in different heights. So they have load-levelers. I hit the top right button on the pad. Chaladian, at the front edge of the dock, suddenly found himself being lifted up and tilting toward the back of the dock. Taken by surprise, he threw both arms up in the air. The Colt in his right hand barked with shot number three. I made my charge, figuring I had a fifty-fifty chance of getting to him before he could recover his bearings and aim the gun properly.

I probably could have, but I didn't have to. Trowbridge got him for me. Beaten to a pulp by a guy who knew how to make it hurt, Trow somewhere found the guts to spring to his feet and launch himself at Chaladian. He tackled the guy, falling heavily with him onto the dock.

I should have gone for Chaladian's throat but out of instinct I went for the gun instead. Chaladian got his feet under Trowbridge and thrust him away with a double kick. I used my left hand to grab Chaladian's right arm and start wrestling with him for the gun. He used his left hand to grab my testicles and squeeze with everything he had.

Bright light suddenly flooded the dock. Thompson had brought her truck around and was driving straight at us with her brights on. Raising his head and shoulders from the dock, Chaladian twisted his arm against my grip and squeezed off a shot. A supernova star spider-webbed across the windshield. Thompson's reaction—"You sonofabitch!"—came after the shot, so at least she was still alive.

Thinking I had to be close to passing out from the excruciating pain between my legs, I remembered Trowbridge getting up to make his tackle. I lifted Chaladian's right arm in the air and slammed it against the concrete. A high-pitched squeal escaped from him. Then I did it again. The Colt fell from his hand. I managed to push it six feet away. *Gotcha now you bastard.* I balled my left fist and raised it to smash his face. A Mexican-accented voice from the back of the dock stopped me.

"Enough!"

I rolled off of Chaladian as we all looked toward the darkness just beyond the arc of light created by the truck's headlights. A guy in dark jeans and a wife beater stood there holding a major league automatic pistol that he wanted us to see. I could sense other people spilling tentatively out of the service door in the corner where he'd come onto the dock. Things suddenly seemed pretty simple. If drug runners were using the warehouse, we were all about to die. If something else was going on, I had just about one minute to figure out what it was. The guy in the wife beater took one step forward and squatted, resting the hand with the automatic on his right knee. He looked contemptuously at the Colt, then brought his gaze back to Chaladian.

"This is private property."

"They attacked me," Chaladian said. "You saw it."

"I saw you shooting up the neighborhood with a piece-of-shit gun that no self-respecting man would use except to beat whores with. Gunfire attracts attention."

"Ah." Back came the patented Chaladian grin, as he decided to bet on drug dealing. "I apologize. An operational necessity. They had me outnumbered. You know Carlos Manueleza?"

The guy in wife beater bristled at that. I wasn't sure the theory I'd come up with was right, but I decided to go with it—not that I had a hell of a lot of options. I turned a scornful expression toward Chaladian.

"Of course he doesn't know Carlos Manueleza, you dumbass. Didn't they teach you not to ask clumsy questions in baby-narc school? If this gentleman knew Carlos M, that would imply that he was involved in the illegal transport of narcotics, when he is obviously a lawabiding citizen."

The guy in the wife beater kept a poker face, but I caught a couple of snickers from the invisible crowd in the rear. Time to double down.

"You insult him with fairy tales about ambushes when you couldn't pull off a simple bust over a stinking little nineteen-month immigration law sentence."

"This is bullshit!" Chaladian sputtered—all the more entertaining because his indignation was completely genuine. "Total bullshit! Me, a narc! What idiocy!"

"Right. You're an international outlaw living by your wits—the only desperado in the world who uses a U.S. police standard issue Colt revolver—which even most American cops don't use anymore."

I paused for a breath. Then, just as Chaladian was about to speak, I started talking again.

"No, this gentleman doesn't know Carlos M. But if he did know Carlos M., I'll tell you something Carlos M. would have told him. He would have said, 'As long as Anglos want heroin and cocaine and marijuana, the Drug Enforcement Administration and the FBI and the entire Mexican Army cannot stop us. The harder and costlier they make it, the more our profits go up. But there is one thing that can stop us. And that is if we turn the people against us.'" I lowered my voice and made it edgier and angrier as I pointed toward the windshield. "'*Which will happen, my friend, if we do something incredibly STUPID, like helping American cops interfere with Project Oasis.*'"

Chaladian sputtered some more, but I didn't pay much attention. The guy in the wife beater got up, ambled over the edge of the dock, and peered at the windshield where the Project Oasis decal was still visible behind the spider-web cracks produced by Chaladian's bullet. If the guy was a coyote, one of the vultures who sweat pesos out of Mexicans to bring them across the border, I had a chance. If he was a drug dealer I had maybe ten seconds to live.

Still in no hurry, with his automatic ready and a wary eye on Chaladian and me, the guy walked over to the Colt. Pulling a stiletto from a sheath in the middle of his left calf, he thrust the blade down the barrel and picked the gun up. He gave Chaladian a wide berth as he circled around toward me.

"NO!" Chaladian yelled. "This is lunacy! If I were a narc and you killed me, they would never stop looking for you! And you'd have to kill all three of the witnesses, because when they do get busted they'll give you up in a second!"

I understood. I kind of felt sorry for Chaladian, so I thought I'd explain it to him.

"We can't give him up if you're killed with a gun that has our prints on it—and that he keeps."

The guy reached me and held the Colt out to me, butt first. So much for my word of honor. I reached up to take it.

"BULLLLLSHIT!" Thompson yelled that as she pulled herself on to the dock. "*I'm* the one who's gonna take that fucker out!"

For a critical second, just as my fingers brushed the Colt, Thompson's antics distracted me. Chaladian came to his knees and started a feral leap in my direction. I felt my hand smacked aside and sensed the Colt being grabbed away. I braced myself for Chaladian's bone-crunching assault.

The two shots seemed to come almost simultaneously. The second was beside the point, because the first splattered Chaladian's brains over half the dock.

I looked over my right shoulder. Trowbridge stood there, holding the smoking Colt. He hadn't missed. From a range of three feet, aiming isn't a big problem.

The guy calmly held out the stiletto. Trowbridge slipped the Colt's barrel back over it. The guy looked carefully at the cylinder, to be sure all six shots had been fired. Then he held the gun out to Thompson.

She understood. She gripped the handle, contributing her prints to it. She let go. The guy swung the gun to me. I did the same thing Thompson had. Then I pulled back a little knurled knob between the grip and the cylinder and swung the cylinder out. I caught the guy's eyes.

"Souvenirs."

He thought about it for a second and nodded. I pushed a rod in front of the cylinder. Six shell casings popped into my left palm. They would have only my prints. I let go of the gun. The guy pulled it away.

"Get rid of the body."

We did. Pretty creepy stuff. The three of us hopped down from the dock, pulling Chaladian's body along with us. We humped the thing down to the Harley. I climbed on, and they mounted Chaladian's body behind me. Stuck the helmet on him just for luck. Thompson scrounged a couple of bungee cords from the pickup and lashed Chaladian's torso to mine. She used a third to tie his ankles to the Harley frame so his feet wouldn't slip off. With that taken care of, I sent them back to LA. I reminded Thompson to break the glass out of the windshield so that the bullet hole wouldn't be staring in the face of any cop who happened to look.

Two-and-a-half hours later I dumped Chaladian's remains in the Baja desert. A lot things could have gone wrong. Someone could have spotted me. If a cop had gotten within fifty feet, he would have known instantly, even in the dark, that I was riding with a dead body behind me. I could have run off the road or crashed into something in the desert out of sheer fatigue.

A lot of things could have gone wrong, but none of them did. After I dumped Chaladian's body, I cruised into Tijuana on the Harley. No sweat at the border; my papers were in order. I parked the thing just before dawn across the street from a whorehouse six blocks from the bus station. The next bus for LA would leave at eight. Odds were the Harley would already be in a chop shop by then. Someone would find Chaladian's body before too long. Maybe the report and the ID would reach Detective Kinjaro and he'd close the Wellstein case. Just as likely, some bored cop would check the paperwork over, grunt, and throw the report in a file with N-H-I scribbled on it: No Humans Involved.

# Chapter Fifty-one

Rachel and I watched the first and, as it turned out, the last trial day of *California v. Trowbridge* live on TRU TV. Every once in awhile, the camera would show Thompson on the bench right behind the bar, supporting Trowbridge with a resolute, stand-by-your-man demeanor while Luci sat beside her.

The climax came with some poor clerk on the witness stand. Erin of Aaron & Erin stood at a podium, giving him a very hard time.

"And so we have twenty-six hours when the whereabouts of this sample is unaccounted for, is that correct?"

"Well, we know it was either in the evidence locker or the lab. We know it wasn't just lying around somewhere."

"Twenty-six hours when we don't know the temperature at which it was being stored, right?"

"Well, a refrigerator is a refrigerator."

"Twenty-six hours when we can't be sure which people had access to it, right?"

"Look, it was the police evidence control people or the lab staff. It was one or the other. It wasn't just Joe Blow. Someone made a mistake on one of the transfer logs. Got off one day on the date, because it was after midnight, maybe. That's all it was."

"Move to strike."

"Granted." The judge looked like he was mad enough to spit.

"What's the judge so pissed off about?" I asked Rachel.

"He might have to kick the evidence. Which means the case is gone."

Trowbridge's next move caught everyone by surprise. He was already on his feet and talking when the camera found him.

"Your honor, I'd like to make a statement."

"You don't get to make statements. That's why you have lawyers here."

"I want to change my plea."

"What?"

And we were off to the races. I'll skip the legal palaver and cut to the chase. Aaron and Erin started whispering urgently to Trowbridge. Deliberately, I think, he answered them loudly enough to be picked up by the microphone.

"Look, skip it, okay? You're fired." He squared his shoulders and faced the judge. "Your honor, I can't see letting this decent guy get beaten up because someone screwed up some red tape. I'm guilty. I was driving drunk that night. What I did was wrong. It was stupid. I put innocent people's lives in danger. I could've killed someone that night, and I couldn't live with myself if that had happened. I broke the law. So it's on me. My bad. I'll accept whatever sentence you think is appropriate."

It wasn't that simple, of course. In a movie it would have been, but in the real world the judge had to spend what seemed like an hour questioning Trowbridge and explaining this and that to him and asking him if he understood and mentioning "consequences" about forty-seven times and so forth and so on. End of the day, though, Trowbridge made it stick.

"Acceptance of responsibility for an offense is a major factor in penal assessment," the judge said when he got around to sentencing, "especially when it's genuine rather than tactical. By standing up and owning what you did, well before you had to, you have saved yourself about four months in jail. I'm going to sentence you to one-hundred-twenty days in the county house of correction. With good behavior, you'll be out for the World Series instead of the Super Bowl."

"So," Rachel said. "Cool move. This will make him a hero."

"You're right. The twenty-six A-List stars in Hollywood who didn't drive drunk and endanger innocent people in the first place aren't heroes, but he's a hero"

"In a perfect world he wouldn't be. But we don't live in a perfect world."

"No, I guess we don't."

Trowbridge started his sentence the day after *Prescott Trail* opened. Right on the verge of getting sprung on some slick lawyer's technicality, he'd stood up like a man and taken responsibility for what he'd done. *Prescott Trail* topped the grosses for its opening weekend, and it stayed in the top five until Trowbridge waltzed triumphantly out of jail, in a new blaze of publicity that bought the movie a couple of extra weeks in that heady company.

I'd long since moved on to preventing losses in factories and shipyards and truck depots, but Proxy and Rachel independently updated me on the totals. Rachel seemed weirdly fascinated by it and ashamed of herself for the fascination. As if it were a guilty pleasure, like enjoying boy bands. I tried to shrug it off.

"Who would have thought that doing time could be a career move?"

"I think he was doing time long before he went to jail." She looked like she was thinking about having a cigarette and decided not to. "He wasn't trapped by money or job limitations or any of the stuff that traps ninety-nine percent of the people on Earth, but he was imprisoned by his own doubts and insecurities. If he hadn't refused to give up Thompson when Chaladian beat him, he'd never have known he had guts. He might have lived his entire life without knowing that he was a real man."

I realized there wasn't going to be a clean getaway from this conversation. No choice but to engage.

"You realize that what you're saying is that everyone is in prison."

"I suppose so. We make our own prisons. Most of us, anyway. *I* made *my* own prison. I forged the bars and built the walls all by myself. But it turned out that I had a good jail coach."

She kissed me. Cute little peck on my right eyelid. Guess where *this* was going.

The next morning, as I got up to make coffee, she planted her left elbow on her pillows and propped herself up.

"Before you go to the kitchen, I have a question."

"Shoot."

"What's the over/under on Thompson's marriage to Trowbridge?"

"Eighteen months."

"What did you take?"

"Over. I'm an optimist."

To receive a free catalog of Poisoned Pen Press titles, please contact us in one of the following ways:

Phone: 1-800-421-3976
Facsimile: 1-480-949-1707
Email: info@poisonedpenpress.com
Website: www.poisonedpenpress.com

Poisoned Pen Press
6962 E. First Ave. Ste 103
Scottsdale, AZ 85251